D1528416

Giving

Up

Grace

Christina

Edgar Olds

This book is a work of fiction. Names, characters, organizations, places, and events are either the product of the author's imagination or are used fictitiously to benefit the storyline. No part of this book may be used in any form without the permission of the author.

Copyright © 2022 Christina Edgar Olds

All rights reserved.

ISBN (e-book): 9798790879166

ISBN (paperback): 9798794287158

christinaedgarolds.com

Book Jacket Design: Lauren Nelson / Emily Rollins

Author Photo: Bob Nemmers

Printed in the United States of America

For my mom . . .
if only you were still here to read this.

Chapter One

December 2014

It was almost Christmas, and the cloudless sky covered Southern California in robin's egg blue. I sat in the window seat at the back of the house looking out over the large yard and pool area. A soft breeze turned the ceiling fan above the outdoor kitchen reminding me of better times, but empty chairs arranged among brightly colored flowerpots only accentuated my loneliness.

The morning air was cool as it leaked in from the small opening of the bay window. My skin prickled from the cold, and tiny goosebumps appeared on my forearms. I shivered and took another sip of herbal tea before leaning in to crank the window closed. I'd become a Californian; chilly now when the temperature outside reached anything below 70 degrees. How could I have forgotten the Iowa winters of my childhood when it dipped to twenty below zero on some January nights?

I removed the tie from my small ponytail and tousled my new shorter and darker hair. Mom would be happy to see me looking more like my old self again. Graham was the one who thought I looked good with shoulder-length blond hair that never seemed to fit my personality, but his opinion didn't matter anymore.

His voice echoed in my head, *"This isn't what you think..."* and the familiar feeling of betrayal washed over me.

I should've said, *"Oh really, Graham? What is it then?"* and hung around to hear his response as he attempted to explain. Instead, I closed the door to our walk-in closet and went back to the guests at his surprise birthday party hoping another glass of wine would make it all go away.

I remember the first time I questioned whether Graham was the one for me. It was about a month before our wedding, and we were standing in front of our favorite Thai restaurant waiting for the valet driver to bring the car around.

"I don't want to take an unfulfilling job," I'd said. "The position at the hospital would pay more, but private practice is where I can make the greatest difference in my patients' lives," I'd argued, hoping he would recognize my need to do something meaningful with my new medical degree.

"If you already know what you're going to do, why ask my opinion? We've got more than $200,000 in school loans to pay off so it seems pretty obvious to me which job you should take."

"I want to know you'll support my decision on this, no matter which one I choose," I'd answered, searching his eyes for common ground.

"It's not my job to make you feel secure. That's on you." His voice was flat and uncaring.

Those few words had taken my breath away and made me feel small. Through that simple exchange I realized we had different expectations of a relationship.

I believed marriage was about taking care of each other. Not in a way diminishing either's ability to be an independent person but in a mutual way making that bond different than all the others in your life. I guess it wasn't a value we shared.

At that moment, I felt alone in our relationship for the first time. I should have trusted my gut, calling my mom to tell her she'd been right. We *didn't* know each other well enough to make a lifetime commitment.

I pushed the feelings aside, not allowing myself to comprehend he'd just told me he'd never love me in the way I needed to be loved. I married him anyway, giving myself to a man who didn't begin to deserve me.

Our marriage had been a difficult one; two people joined in matrimony and not much else, and the birthday party incident had hammered the final nail into our marital coffin.

Ever since I'd opened the door to the master bedroom closet and discovered Graham and Becca together, I'd been on a downward spiral. The sting of rejection was humiliating, even if the outcome was a blessing.

Suddenly, I could see everything that was wrong with our relationship. We didn't have the same political views or taste in music. I'd never taken his last name or joined our checking accounts and wasn't completely sure of his favorite color. Maybe we'd been doomed from the beginning, as if we'd settled for a roommate instead of putting in the work to find a soulmate.

After I filed for divorce, I couldn't eat or sleep and felt like I'd lost control of everything. Eight years of a bad marriage had sucked the life out of me, and it took every ounce of strength I had to hold it all together.

Preoccupied and short with my colleagues, I'd even had an

outburst with a patient. I'd let my personal life affect my medical practice, and a formal grievance had been filed against me.

Apparently, my emotional eruption hadn't been the only thing reported to my boss. Staff members had complained of my moodiness and neglect of duties like forgetting to give prescriptions and lab orders to the nurses.

Even a stellar record wasn't going to keep me from answering for my actions. Dr. Peele didn't hold back, giving me a six-week suspension. I'd always felt like one of his favorites, but there was no doubt in my mind that he'd never look at me in the same way again.

I thought my time off work would drag on, but it had flown by faster than expected. I'd spent a month trying to get my focus in place again with yoga and days at the beach giving me the respite I needed, but now it was almost time to get back to work and begin the difficult job of reclaiming my career.

I'd worked up the courage to make a trip back to Iowa for the last two weeks of my employment hiatus. I wanted to eat some home cooked food and sleep in a bed that didn't remind me of Graham. Although hesitant about my return, I was excited to see my mom and get one of her big hugs that made everything better.

Our mother-daughter relationship had taken a beating when I left without much of an explanation the summer after my senior year of high school. Although we'd slowly made our way to being close again, I'd only been back home a handful of times since graduation.

I preferred living the life I'd created for myself on the West Coast, and Mom enjoyed trips out to see me a couple of times per year to take in the sights and enjoy the California weather.

There were too many memories in Elmwood, and shame always accompanied me home like an invisible companion I couldn't shake.

Mom knew I'd be alone for Christmas, and she insisted I fly back for a few days. I'd tried to convince her to visit me instead, bribing her with a first-class ticket, but she wouldn't hear of leaving home during the holidays. She was thrilled when I agreed to come and never imagined my time away from work wasn't exactly voluntary.

***

The cab dropped me off with less than two hours to spare. At LAX you needed as much time as possible to make a flight, and I'd be cutting it close.

"Excuse me," I repeated, racing through the throngs of people, always the well-mannered Midwesterner at heart. A part of me hoped a missed departure would give me an excuse to cancel the entire trip, but delaying the inevitable wasn't going to change anything.

Security was a nightmare, and I had to wait in line for nearly a half-hour while people fought with TSA agents about everything from taking a jacket off to why they couldn't bring a large pocketknife on the flight. I finally made my way to the gate where they were already beginning to board the plane.

I found my seat next to an elderly woman and silently thanked God she seemed normal. I struggled to get past her in the aisle seat taking my place next to the window, hoping to put my earbuds in and take a nap during the long flight. After learning she was on her way home from visiting her grandchildren in Pasadena, the brief chat eventually turned to my profession.

"I'm a doctor," I shared, feeling apprehensive about my current status.

How would I reclaim my reputation after doing something so unprofessional?

"That must be rewarding . . . I'm sure you're able to help many people with your expertise," she remarked, clueless to how her words hurt considering my recent suspension.

"Yes, I feel privileged to have the opportunity to serve so many in the community," I replied. I was optimistic I'd have many more years to treat patients and families, but going home seemed like an even bigger challenge to overcome.

***

"We've begun our descent into Des Moines, please place your belongings in the overhead bins or under your seat and prepare for landing," the flight attendant said cheerfully. I began to feel pressure in my ears and the anxiety of returning home in the rest of my body.

I looked out the small airplane window to see farmland below highlighted by red barns and fields of dark fertile soil partially covered in snow. Country roads and meandering streams looked like a beautiful piece of artwork from the sky and reminded me I wasn't in California anymore.

I'd been sleeping for a couple of hours, so I pulled my purse out from under the seat in front of me and retrieved my cosmetic bag to freshen up. I reached for a navy jacket tied around the strap to put on after I removed my seatbelt.

It had been eighty degrees when I left Los Angeles, but I'd

be lucky if the temperature topped thirty once we landed. A shudder went through my body, and it was more than the weather outside giving me a chill.

I closed my eyes and breathed deeply as the aircraft picked up speed, propelling me toward the secrets of my past.

Chapter Two
December 1995

I could hardly believe my senior year of high school was half over. I'd already been accepted into the pre-med program at The University of Iowa and had finished filling out my housing preferences for the fall.

I'd visited the freshman dorms in my junior year and stayed in Burge Hall, deciding that night I wouldn't live anywhere with parties all weekend and vomit in the stairwells fermenting until the cleaning staff came in on Monday morning. My good grades would allow me to live on an honors floor where a quieter atmosphere would be more my speed.

Ben had decided to go to Elmwood Community College so he could keep working at his dad's auto repair shop. He was sweet and thoughtful and loved me more than anyone could ever love me, and I knew we'd get married someday.

He'd run his dad's business, and I'd be a doctor at the hospital. We'd have plenty of money and at least a couple of kids running around. He wanted me to follow my dreams as long as they brought me back to Elmwood someday, and I felt pretty sure they would.

I pulled my 1980 Ford Fiesta in front of the Sinclair's house so that my recurring oil leak wouldn't stain their pristine cement. Ben had fixed it over the weekend, but I didn't want to risk it. Plus, there was already an extra car in the driveway because Dr. Sinclair's brother and his wife were visiting from California for the holidays.

Christmas lights twinkled around the big houses along Primrose Avenue. Lincoln Estates was the newest development in Elmwood, and most of the houses were nestled in wooded areas butting up to the grounds of the Elmwood Country Club. During the holidays, every house looked like a magazine cover.

Ben and I had been a couple ever since we'd shared an unexpected New Year's Eve kiss at Angie Stanford's party a year earlier. Angie's dad was the pastor of Elmwood's largest church, but she didn't let that stop her from trying to corrupt many of her high school classmates whenever she got the chance.

Angie was born well after her parents thought they were done raising kids, and they treated her more like an overindulged grandchild than a teenager needing guidance. Lots of kids were more than happy to spend Saturday nights watching MTV and mixing drinks with stolen shots from Pastor Stanford's "special" cupboard hidden in the back of the storage room.

Her parents occasionally checked on their house guests from the top of the stairs, but Angie's friends still used the finished rec room for unsupervised fun, which was not possible at homes with parents who had more rules.

When the clock struck midnight, everyone else seemed to be paired up, and Ben looked at me and smiled before pulling me toward him for a kiss.

At that moment, I realized Ben O'Brien might be the cutest boy I'd ever seen. It was funny how one kiss could change everything between two people who'd known each other since kindergarten.

"Hello, Cass! Happy New Year!" Jess opened the door wide, and I could smell the fragrant Christmas tree still standing tall in the picture window of the formal living room. Having a room set aside for important conversations and Christmas morning seemed like a waste. Even so, I wanted to have one someday after I became a successful doctor.

Christmas was an especially festive time of year at the Sinclairs with red and green decorations everywhere. I loved spending time in their home because they were so warm and welcoming to me. Even though I worked for them, they treated me like a trusted member of their family.

"Hi! Where is everyone?" I asked. The house was quiet even though four other people were staying with them. A fire crackled in the massive stone fireplace in the family room, and something delicious was cooking in the oven filling the house with the smell of garlic and tomatoes.

"They're in the backyard sledding, I called them in because our movie starts in about an hour, and the guys are going to want to shower before we go."

Of course, they were sledding. Isn't that what the perfect family does on New Year's Eve afternoon?

Turner was about two when I became their regular babysitter. Jess paid me well and made sure I got first pick when she had clothes and shoes ready to go to Goodwill. Mom couldn't afford to buy me the kind of trendy clothes I got for free from Jess, and it was a perk I was grateful for.

Mom did the best she could on her salary as a pre-school teacher and the social security we got after my dad died. She had savings from a small inheritance received from my grandparents but not enough to allow us to live much more than paycheck to paycheck. My babysitting money helped with the extras like prom dresses and new cheerleading shoes when I needed them.

After the Sinclairs found out I wanted to be a doctor, they helped me figure out what classes to take so I'd have what was needed to get into Iowa. In addition to babysitting for Turner, I also worked at Dr. Sinclair's office a couple of afternoons per week to get some experience in a medical clinic. With their guidance and my 4.0 GPA, I easily got a scholarship, so I didn't mind giving them my time on New Year's Eve.

The door flew open at the back of the house, and I could hear boots on the hardwood floor. "Stay on the rugs!" Jess hollered as she grabbed towels and began to mop up the melted snow.

She and her sister-in-law formed a human laundry chain as they piled wet clothes in the mudroom. The kids were laughing and squealing in mock horror as they stepped in the cold water with their bare feet. Their big smiles and red cheeks confirmed the fun they'd had on the enormous hill behind the Sinclair's house.

Mark and Leslie Sinclair and their three-year-old twin daughters visited Iowa once a year. Mark worked as a professor at the University of California at Berkeley, and Leslie was a partner in a West Coast law firm. I imagined a similar ideal existence for the California Sinclairs as the one enjoyed by Elmwood's most envied family.

It didn't take long for the two couples to get ready and out the door for their night on the town. In the meantime, I removed lasagna from the oven and pulled a veggie tray out of the refrigerator for the kids and me.

Once we were seated at the kitchen island, Turner asked me, "What time's Ben going to be here?" Turner thought Ben was a super star because he played quarterback for the Elmwood High School Eagles. In a small town, that coveted role has clout with young and old alike.

"He's having dinner with his family first," I replied, feeling excited to spend the evening with my boyfriend. Ben was terrible at keeping secrets, and he'd already told me he had an anniversary gift for me.

The Sinclairs were going to see "Forrest Gump" at the Capitol Theatre and then head over to the country club for a New Year's Eve celebration. We'd have several hours alone together, and I was eager to see what Ben had gotten for me and even more anxious to give him the scrapbook I'd made of memories from our first year together.

The large clock above the fireplace read 8:00 p.m., so I had plenty of time to get the kitchen cleaned up and the kids settled in before Ben's arrival. There was a tray of homemade Christmas cookies on the counter, and I broke off a piece of a decorated snowman and popped it into my mouth.

The flavorful frosting and light sugar cookie melted on my tongue and reminded me of special times with my mom. She always made sure I had wonderful memories. Every Christmas we'd make goodies and deliver plates adorned with colorful ribbons and a thoughtful card to everyone in our neighborhood.

It was such a nice gesture, and even the crankiest lady on our block would soften when she opened the door to a platter full of sweets. Mom looked out for other people, even if it meant we had to endure the bitter cold so we could shovel a path to our neighbor's mailbox. I had bigger aspirations for my life than my mom had ever had, but I hoped I'd always have her tender heart.

Jess had asked me if Mom would care if Ben helped me babysit, as he'd never come with me before. I told her I'd ask but had conveniently forgotten that part of our agreement. A twinge of conscience found its place in the pit of my stomach at the thought of my mom finding out Ben had joined me at the Sinclairs, which I knew would not make her happy.

What could it hurt?

With the last glass in the dishwasher and the counter tops cleaned, I started upstairs to check on the kids. Halfway up, the doorbell rang, and I headed back downstairs to the entryway to see Ben's smiling face in the glass insert next to the front door. I opened the door and was scooped up in the arms of the most amazing boy I'd ever known. He pulled his gloves off, dropping them as he put his cold hands on either side of my face and kissed me.

"Happy anniversary!" he said excitedly.

We heard running from upstairs and charging footsteps as the three kids barreled down the stairway. "You're here!" Turner bolted across the room and into Ben's arms, knocking him to the ground as he was retrieving his gloves.

"Whoa, Turner . . . you're about as tough as the linebacker from Cedar Point! Glad the season is over 'cause you may have put me out of commission for a while!" Ben faked catching his breath as he beat on his chest, and Turner looked on with satisfaction.

Turner was thrilled to have another boy in the house and didn't waste any time leading Ben to his room to show him the new toys and games he'd received for Christmas. I loved how Ben acted around kids; someday he would be a great dad to our children, and it was one of the things I cherished most about him.

With UNO games played and toys put away for the night, it was time to get the kids to bed. The Sinclairs said they could fall asleep on the floor of the game room watching Dick Clark's Rockin' New Year's Eve. Turner was determined to stay awake until midnight, but the girls were out as soon as their heads hit the pillow.

Just before 11 p.m., Ben and I quietly headed up the stairs to check on the kids. When we reached the top step, we could see all three sleeping soundly in their makeshift beds. The carpet was covered in random pillows and blankets from around the house. Emma's arm rested on Turner's leg and her head was leaning on one of the cushions from the upstairs sofa. Libby had made her bed underneath the ping pong table, and I could see the kids had tried to make a fort out of two knitted afghans made by Jess' great-grandma Turner.

As the ball began to drop, signifying the beginning of 1996 on the East Coast, we tiptoed back down the stairs. The sounds of 5...4...3...2...1 rang out as shouts of *"Happy New Year"* mixed with the melody of "Auld Lang Syne" came from the TV. On the bottom step, Ben pulled me toward him and kissed me. His touch made me feel like I was on a roller coaster, and I wanted to kiss him for hours.

"I love you, Cass. Happy New Year...."

"I love you too. But it's not the new year yet in Iowa."

"So, we get to kiss again at midnight?" he asked hopefully.

"We need to keep kissing for the entire hour as a New Year's tradition we start this year and continue the rest of our lives!" Ben was my first boyfriend, making me feel flirtatious in a way I'd never experienced before.

Ben took my hand as we continued into the kitchen. He walked over to his coat hanging on the railing of the stairs and retrieved a tiny box wrapped in silver paper and tied with a delicate white ribbon.

I went over to my purse and pulled the gift for Ben from behind it. I'd tied a white tulle bow around the center of the book, but you could still see a photo of the two of us from the Sadie Hawkins dance in a frame on the front of the scrapbook.

"You go first," he said excitedly.

"No, *you* go first!" I said, hoping it would be me who would go first.

"Cassidy Garrett, I love you, and I want to spend the rest of my life with you. We've got a lot ahead of us before that's going to happen, but anytime we're apart, I want you to have something to remind you of us." Ben was beaming from ear to ear as he placed the gift in my hands and held it there for a moment, making me feel protected and loved.

I tore at the package and opened the green box from Carlson's Jewelry. It was an Elmwood staple, and every woman in town knew it stood for quality and excellence. At least that's what their commercial said. It also meant the gift had been expensive for the budget of a senior in high school.

"You shouldn't have spent so much money on me...."

Ben stopped me mid-sentence. "I've been saving for six

months to buy this for you and even worked extra shifts at the shop. I want you to have it, but it isn't as nice as the engagement ring I'm going to buy for you someday."

He wanted to buy me an engagement ring?

The box revealed the prettiest heart shaped locket I'd ever seen. "Oh my gosh, this is gorgeous!" I exclaimed.

I took the necklace from the velvet insert and unclasped it for Ben to place around my neck. The locket sat perfectly below the indentation of my neck bones, and a tiny diamond on the front sparkled in the reflection of the mirror hanging in the Sinclair's entryway.

"Do you like it?" Ben asked excitedly.

"I adore it!" I said, wrapping my arms around his neck and kissing him all over his face until he pulled me toward him in a big hug.

"You're everything to me, and I don't want to lose you."

"Why would you lose me? I'm right here," I said emphatically.

"You're leaving for college in a few months, and I don't want anything to change between us."

"The only thing changing is my address. And it's not like I'm going too far away, plus you promised you'd come and visit. We're going to be fine." I had to admit I was worried about a long-distance relationship too.

We went back in the kitchen, and Ben untied the bow on the scrapbook I'd made for him. We looked at the photos and notes he'd given me from the past year as we fondly recalled each memory. We'd done so many special things together, and it made me excited for our future.

Our trip down memory lane was interrupted by the ring of the telephone. I grabbed the wall extension near where we were standing and answered as Jess confirmed their plans for the rest of the evening. After I assured her I didn't need to be home by any certain time, she asked if it would be okay if they went to another party with friends before coming home.

With the confirmation we had at least a couple of hours before the Sinclairs would return, we settled into the den to celebrate the New Year again in Central Standard Time by watching the festivities televised from Chicago. After we kissed each other at midnight, just as we'd done one year earlier, something began to change between us.

Ben seemed more intent and quickly moved to the place where we'd stopped ourselves in the past. His hands explored my body as he pulled my t-shirt off and moved me to the floor. His kisses became more passionate, and I knew what was happening but didn't tell him to stop.

I looked over my shoulder toward the steps, worried a sleepy child might make their way downstairs needing a drink or to be tucked in after a bad dream.

What if the Sinclairs had a change in plans and got home early? Adrenaline surged through my body as we awkwardly crossed the line we'd never crossed before.

I briefly thought of birth control, but I could tell Ben was already too far into it to have a rational conversation, and I wanted to hurry up and get it over with.

Our first time together wasn't what I'd imagined. I hadn't intended to lose my virginity on the floor of the Sinclair's den. It had been a spur of the moment decision that would change our lives forever and was exactly why my mom would have been against Ben helping me babysit. I felt guilty for lying to her by omission and not expecting more of myself.

"You okay?" Ben asked as he pulled his sweatshirt over his head. The look on his face told me he wasn't nearly as terrified as me.

"Yeah," I answered flatly.

"We love each other, it's okay. We've been together for a year now."

"We didn't use a condom. What if I'm pregnant?" Terror gripped me as I thought about the possible consequences of our spontaneous actions.

"There's no way you're pregnant. I don't think you can even get pregnant your first time," he said, not at all concerned about the possibility.

Some of my friends were having sex with their boyfriends, and none of them had gotten pregnant.

"Where'd you hear that? It isn't true, is it?" I asked, knowing the answer but wishing there was something I'd never heard of before to give me hope to hang on to in the coming weeks.

"I think Tommy told me. His mom's a nurse." I wasn't calmed by getting our reproductive information from a guy who'd eaten forty chicken nuggets on a dare in the lunchroom the week before. Tommy Meyers wasn't qualified to be an expert on anything, let alone whether or not a girl could get pregnant the first time she had sex.

"Well, then maybe it's true," I said, faking sincerity. "It's okay. We'll be fine, but we can't do it again without protection. You better go. I'll be really nervous if you're here when the Sinclairs get home."

"Okay . . . relax. We didn't do anything wrong. This is between me and you and nobody else." Ben pulled me into his arms telling me again how much he loved me.

I was freaking out for no reason.

I'd go to Planned Parenthood the following week and get on the pill like some of the other girls at my high school had done. They provided services without telling your parents, and I was already eighteen so could make the decision on my own.

We'd be prepared the next time…if there was a next time. I wasn't sure it was something I wanted to do again because it hurt, and I felt smothered with Ben on top of me doing something he didn't seem to know how to do.

"Call me tomorrow after you get up. Mom and Dad want you and your mom to come over and watch the Rose Bowl with us. Mom's making a bunch of food, and we can watch Northwestern beat USC." Ben loved football, and even though he wasn't going to be an Iowa Hawkeye with me, he never missed the opportunity to watch the Big Ten teams.

"Yeah, sure," I agreed as we hugged goodbye. I hated football but loved spending time with Ben's family, and Mom would appreciate being included too.

Snow had begun to fall again, and I turned on the outside light so Ben could see as he made his way out to his car. He opened the door and went back to my vehicle kneeling beside it as he turned a flashlight to the underside checking for oil spots. He gave me a quick wave goodbye as he yelled back toward the house, "It's all good!"

I didn't know at the time an oil leak was the least of my worries.

Chapter Three
December 2014

It was Christmas Eve morning, and I awoke to the smell of coffee and homemade cinnamon rolls wafting into the guest room. I put my bathrobe on and made my way out to the kitchen where Mom was busy preparing the feast for our dinner guests.

Although my dad had been gone for years, his relatives still celebrated holidays with us and regarded my mom as an integral part of their family. I was happy for her since I lived so far away, and she had no other family of her own still living. We'd be joined later in the day by two of my dad's sisters and their families, and I looked forward to connecting with my cousins again.

Mom still had some of the furniture and trinkets from my childhood when she enjoyed shopping at thrift stores and garage sales. She'd always said her decorating style was more about reclaiming treasures from people who didn't know what they had, not settling for what others discarded.

The familiar surroundings comforted me, although she'd bought several new pieces of furniture along with more contemporary decor to fit with the style of 2014 now that she was comfortably settled in a new condo.

"Well, look at you," Mom said as if she was surprised to see me up. "I figured you'd sleep later with the time change and all."

"I didn't want to miss any of the cookie baking!" I said happily. She handed me a cup of coffee, and the first sip reminded me she liked it strong.

"Oh, Lord! How can you drink this crap?"

"It gets me going—don't be such a prima donna," she joked. "There's some cream and sugar on the counter if you choose to ruin a perfect pot of coffee! And eat some breakfast, you're way too skinny." Mom was the same fireball she'd always been.

There was something special about the two of us enjoying coffee in front of the fireplace. Even when we were across the country from each other, we usually had coffee together on the weekends by phone. It was my favorite part of the week, and to be able to do it in person made me happy.

Being at home reminded me of the wonderful Midwestern upbringing I'd had despite the death of my father, Max, when I was ten. Mom made sure I knew this was not an excuse for failure. She taught me that everyone had something to deal with in life, and the key to success was to accept what God handed you and move on the best you could. As a little girl with a bedroom right next to hers, I wondered why she hadn't reminded herself of that fact on the nights when I could hear her crying herself to sleep.

Widowed at thirty, Mom never considered finding someone else to share her life with. "Why would I spend time with someone who wouldn't be as good as your dad?" she'd ask me whenever the topic came up. In twenty-six years, she'd never removed her wedding ring. I wanted that kind of love in my life.

"How's the divorce coming along?" she asked, getting right to the point.

"I'm hoping it'll be over soon. We have no debts; we have no kids. Besides figuring out who gets what in the house and putting it up for sale, it's nearly over—except for deciding on spousal support. That's the biggest issue right now." I didn't want her to worry about me, so I left out some of the more unpleasant details.

"Well, honey… you don't need spousal support. You have a good job and can take care of yourself!"

"I'm talking about paying support to Graham, not him paying me!"

"What? He cheats on you, and you have to pay *him* spousal support? That makes no sense," she said disgustedly.

"I make a lot more money than Graham, and I'm going to owe him something. I don't know how much or for how long, but California law doesn't care who's at fault in a divorce."

My attorney said Graham had plenty of earning capacity and the judge would take that into consideration and not make me pay more than he deserved. Even though he didn't always stick with a job, I was hoping Graham's career *potential* was enough to keep me from being financially gutted.

The fact I'd earned more than Graham hadn't mattered to me when we both benefited from the life we had together. The thought of giving him money he'd probably squander on his new girlfriend was a point of contention for me but a necessary part of separating our lives.

I was starting to think it wasn't such a bad thing to be getting rid of Graham. He'd done what I didn't have the guts to do. Through his infidelity, he'd ended a marriage that had already run its course.

I'd found myself feeling grateful the night of his birthday party had been chilly. The need to go upstairs and get a jacket out of the closet had given me the perfect excuse for a justified exit from a marriage that should never have happened in the first place.

"I knew the first time I met him he'd bring you nothing but unhappiness," Mom said.

"Well, you were right . . . don't worry about it. The attorneys are handling it, and I'll be fine."

Graham was educated and extremely smart. He loved academia, but colleagues never measured up to his expectations. My salary had given him the luxury of quitting any position not meeting his sometimes-unattainable standards. In the time we'd been together, he'd had five different jobs.

I'd mistakenly thought since Graham had been unfaithful, that the divorce would be quick and easy. I figured he'd feel so bad about what he'd done, he'd back away from our marriage and move on with his new life. It had been a mistake to think a selfish person like Graham would suddenly have my best interest at heart.

The divorce turned ugly when Graham decided his new ambition was to be a full-time author, supported by ungodly amounts of spousal support demanded of me by his cut-throat attorney. I wondered if there were matters brewing behind the scenes pushing him to consider leaving his current job, with me bankrolling his newest enterprise.

His stance was that his ability to earn an income had been greatly damaged when we moved to Ventura to further my medical career. He'd forgotten the part where he couldn't get along with the other professors at UCLA, and he'd left just short of being fired by the department head due to his constant complaining and demands for things he wasn't entitled to.

I *had* encouraged him to find a job closer to Ventura, hoping to keep things from exploding and affecting future employment opportunities. I'd stroked his ego making him believe he was right, instead of telling him how I really felt. I'd known better than to tell him to suck it up and teach the extra class he'd been assigned, risking the silent treatment for days.

"Well, I don't think it's fair. You've worked so hard, and you shouldn't have to pay him when he's the one who ended the marriage through his selfish actions. There's something I never told you about Graham because I didn't want you to think I didn't like him. One of his friends said something to me I've never forgotten."

"What was it?" I asked, wondering what she'd harbored for all these years. I wasn't the only Garrett woman who could keep a secret.

"At your wedding rehearsal dinner, one of his groomsmen made an offhanded remark that stuck with me. He said he hoped Graham had finally found the woman who would be able to keep him in check. And he kind of laughed like he didn't think it could ever happen. Now it all makes sense to me. My gut was right all along."

I loved my mom but was annoyed at her revelation of the obvious. I'd chosen poorly in the husband department, and now I'd have to pay for it in a variety of ways.

I'd met Graham Martin through one of my colleagues at work. He was a little younger than me but was tall and handsome with the most piercing blue eyes I'd ever seen.

Good looks aside, his confidence and charm drew me to him.

I fell for him quickly, and we were married in less than a year. We seemed to have so much in common when we'd met. He even liked yoga, which we did together most Saturday mornings unless I was on call. He felt like an ideal match, and we agreed on one very important thing. Neither of us wanted kids.

Although we had different reasons for remaining childless, it definitely made him more attractive to me. I never told him I didn't think I deserved children, and he didn't care about the particulars. I let other issues slide because he agreed with me on this lifestyle choice, and I'd already found it incredibly hard to find a partner who didn't want to have a family someday.

When relationships got serious during those years, I'd end them after the first sign of commitment. It was devastating to give up on love with men who may have wanted to be with me anyway. I couldn't bear the thought of taking the opportunity to be a father away from someone, and in my twenties, I never imagined I'd change my mind about motherhood.

When Graham came into the picture, it seemed like he was the one I'd been waiting for. Things fell into place without much time for second thoughts.

I didn't factor in Graham's love of Graham, allowing him a level of selfishness never reciprocated to me in our relationship. His fondness for himself was more than I was ever able to give him. I was surprised he even noticed when my affections began to wane, but apparently, he did, considering what happened.

I came to realize the real reason he didn't want to become a parent was because he couldn't stop thinking of himself long enough to figure out what anyone else wanted or needed, and ultimately that made for a terrible life partner.

I'd experienced the kind of loneliness that only comes from being in a marriage with someone who isn't your other half. Graham never filled the void in my soul despite the life we'd had from the world's view. I couldn't blame him completely; he had no idea of the hole inside my heart that had never healed.

I'd pulled away from him on so many occasions that it wasn't hard to see how he could have found comfort in the arms of someone else. I hadn't been the best partner either, with emotional baggage I'd never unpacked in what was supposed to be the comforting security of marriage.

Graham never really knew the woman he was spending his life with. I'd never gone beyond the surface of his feelings either to protect myself from revealing my own truths. I'd felt our lack of connection for a long time, but I didn't know he felt the same way. My anger and hurt came from the way he'd left our marriage, not in the leaving itself.

"I'm thinking I might quit my job and move up to wine country…people need doctors in Napa Valley too!" A clean slate was what I needed, and starting over in a new location offering the utopia of being one of the nation's most beautiful areas was very appealing.

"Why don't you move back to Iowa? They're always looking for physicians at the clinic. I'm sure you could get on with your credentials. Maybe Dr. Sinclair could put in a good word for you. You know he's now the Medical Director at Elmwood Regional Medical Center, don't you?"

I wasn't aware of Dr. Steven Sinclair's medical promotions.

"And you've probably heard Ben and Angie O'Brien got divorced," she added. How clever of her to drop that little bit of information into the conversation. I *didn't* know Ben and Angie had divorced. I couldn't believe they'd ever gotten married.

When I was home for my grandmother's funeral in the summer of 2002, I'd run into Ben at the grocery store. That day as we stood next to the lettuce and tomatoes in the produce aisle we shared a few awkward moments before Angie Stanford came around the corner and interrupted us.

The smile on her face quickly vanished when she saw me, looking at Ben in a way that made *me* feel like the outsider. He and Angie had gotten married a few weeks earlier, but her pregnant belly told me the marriage may have been an afterthought.

My mind wandered to the Stanford's basement where Ben and I had our first kiss. I childishly wondered if the baby had been conceived there with Angie's dad reading the newspaper and her mom knitting a scarf in the living room upstairs; still oblivious to what was taking place in the lower level of their home.

I'd expected Ben to move on, but he'd never even liked Angie when we were in high school. Maybe his limited choices for dating in Elmwood had led him to settle for someone like I'd done when I found out there weren't many guys out there who didn't want to have kids.

Could he have shared our secret with someone he loved more than me?

After Mom and I had our coffee, we decided to take a walk before finishing the holiday cooking. It was an unseasonably warm 50 degrees, and the air was fresh and still. The sidewalk glistened from melting snow, and a bird sang at the top of an oak tree in the neighbor's yard. It reminded me of spring, and a feeling of excitement filled me as I realized the possibility of rebirth for myself at this difficult time in my life.

I'd been seeing a counselor ever since I'd been assigned to take my unexpected vacation from work, and she'd told me to look for signs making me feel optimistic and happy. This homework wasn't easy, but I felt a flood of joyfulness I hadn't expected from spending time with my mom and being out in the fresh air.

We'd woken up to a beautiful frost, which covered the naked trees with festive white crystals of ice. It had been so long since I'd been home at Christmas, and the gorgeous sight outdoors made me feel nostalgic about the holidays of my childhood.

"Hey, slow down a little." Mom was out of breath and looked exhausted.

"What's wrong? Don't you want to work off some calories before Christmas dinner?" I joked, picking up my pace. Exercise was a way of life for me in California, and I never did anything halfway.

"No, I've been having this bothersome pain in my side," she said indifferently.

"What does it feel like?" The physician in me kicked into high gear. "How long have you had it?"

"It's nothing…I'm out of shape. My pants have been so tight lately, although I'm not gaining weight. I hate to admit that my body is changing as I'm getting older, and I've been doing some exercises, so maybe I've pulled a muscle or something. I have a doctor's appointment on Friday; don't worry yourself about it any longer. On this trip you're in the role of visiting daughter—not on call as a doctor, and I want you to enjoy yourself!"

My mother was like a stick of dynamite—small, compact, and full of fire. She only stood five feet tall but had taken good care of herself. She had dark eyes with thick lashes and a short dark haircut thanks to regular visits to Aunt Barb's salon in downtown Elmwood. My mom's grandfather had come to the United States from Italy, and Josephine Giraldo Garrett favored her Italian relatives. I'd been lucky enough to get good genes from both of my parents giving me the olive skin and darker hair of my mother's family and blue eyes from the Midwestern roots on my dad's side. I had the good fortune to have a few inches on my mom's height due to my dad's 6' 4" frame and was happy to have years of dying my hair lighter to adhere to the standards of California beauty behind me and embrace my natural look again.

I knew Mom's symptoms probably weren't anything to worry about, but I didn't like knowing she wasn't feeling well. Especially when she was cooking a holiday meal for twenty people.

"I'm going to help you with the rest of the dinner preparations, and you're going to take a nap before everyone arrives."

"Yes, Dr. Garrett," Mom replied as she rolled her eyes.

***

The doorbell rang at 5 p.m., and the first of our Christmas Eve guests began to arrive. The house was lit up with multi-colored LED lights, and holiday music played on a seasonal channel tuned in on the big TV above the fireplace.

Hot cider on the stove was clearly marked "spiked" and

"not spiked", so no one would get the wrong one by mistake. I happened to be looking through to the kitchen when I saw one of my cousin's daughters pour herself a cup of spiked cider. As she lifted the cup to her lips, she gave me a smile letting me know it hadn't been a mistake.

How old was little Kerri? She had to be at least sixteen, but the years passed so quickly I couldn't be sure. Regardless, I doubted her mom would want her drinking on Christmas Eve. Teenagers grew up too fast, and it made me think about all the trouble a young girl could get into if they weren't careful.

We ate hors d'oeuvres and soups brought by various family members, and the younger kids all decorated sugar cookies with colorful frosting and sprinkles.

Once the party was in full swing, we exchanged gifts with the person whose name we'd drawn and watched as the kids emptied their stockings from Santa. We recalled memories from the past and toasted those who were no longer with us before everyone packed up the things they'd hauled into the house a few hours earlier and headed for home.

It was after 10:00 p.m. when our last guest left, and I began picking up wine glasses in every corner of the house as Mom put dishes into the dishwasher.

"Hey, Cass? Would you mind if I laid down for a few minutes before we head out to midnight Mass?"

"Are you okay?" She always acted more like the energizer bunny than your average middle-aged woman. Maybe the time spent away had lured me into a false sense of security that my mother would never age.

"It's been a long day. I want to take a power nap, and I'll be good to go," she said. "Let's not worry about cleaning up now. We can finish tomorrow."

Mom headed to her room, and I continued with the cleanup. The last thing I wanted to do on Christmas Day was scrape food off plates from the night before. The festive music made the job seem easy, and everything was back in its place within the hour.

I got ready for church, pairing black pants with a gray cowl neck sweater. I applied lipstick and a little blush and added a pair of rhinestone earrings to complete the look. Standing in front of the mirror, my reflection showed the woman I'd hoped to become. What the outside world couldn't see was the teenage girl living inside me, stunted emotionally by a choice she hadn't been prepared to hide for a lifetime.

With a final glance in the mirror, I flipped the bathroom light off, and my insecurities disappeared into the darkness.

I knocked lightly on Mom's bedroom door. "We probably need to get going. You know how the church fills up on Christmas Eve."

"I don't think I'm going to be able to go," she said from the darkness inside. I opened the door wider and stepped into her room and took a seat on the edge of the bed.

"What do you mean? You never miss midnight Mass." She was starting to worry me; missing church on Christmas Eve didn't even seem like a consideration.

"I'm not feeling well at all. Maybe it's the flu. You go without me, and I'll feel better in the morning. We need to be at Barb's by 10:00 a.m. to watch the kids open presents."

"I don't need to go to Mass either," I was relieved at the possibility of bypassing a public event bringing me face to face with people I'd rather avoid.

"No, you go on without me. You can't miss church on Christmas Eve. I'll be fine." There was no getting out of it, so

I kissed Mom on the cheek and grabbed her keys off the kitchen island.

As the car eased out of the garage, snow crunched under the tires. I shifted into drive and started down the street toward church. The car hesitated and jerked into gear as I put my foot on the gas pedal to get it going, and I worried it would stall completely. Even Mom's Honda Accord knew this was a bad idea, but it kept going toward St. Cecilia's Catholic Church anyway, as if it didn't want to rock the boat on Christmas Eve either.

The clear sky was illuminated by a white moon and bright stars. Passing through neighborhoods on my way to church, I could see cars parked in long lines in front of houses where families were still celebrating. Picture windows framed the lives of loved ones spending time together, and I could almost hear the laughter from inside. I'd missed this place, even though it was hard to come back home.

The bell tower of St. Cecilia's came into view, and cars were pulling into the parking lot. I made a pass by the front of the church and saw parishioners streaming in to celebrate Christmas Eve Mass. The sight of all the people brought on the familiar feeling of panic, and I couldn't park the car and walk into the church and kneel. God would understand, even if Mom wouldn't.

I stopped at a twenty-four-hour Casey's General Store and bought a hot chocolate to sip on while spending the next hour driving around Elmwood, passing the time until I could return to Mom's condo without suspicion.

I went past the high school and through some of the old neighborhoods where my friends had lived, not knowing if their families still resided there as I hadn't kept in contact with anyone after moving to California.

The small house where I'd grown up was illuminated by lights and had been painted tan. I wondered if the home was filled with as much love as it had been when we occupied it. There was a tire swing tied to the big oak tree in the front yard, and I thought about our chocolate lab, Butch, who loved to chase squirrels around the tree. Dad had loved that dog, and when Butchie died a year after him, it felt like another insurmountable loss for Mom and me.

O'Brien's Auto Repair was dark except for a clock lit on the back wall of the front office. Sometimes Ben's dad would work until midnight, but on Christmas Eve, he'd be celebrating with his family and sitting at St. Cecelia's with the rest of Elmwood's good Catholics.

I drained the last of the hot chocolate as Frank Sinatra sang "I'll Be Home for Christmas" on the radio. It was 12:45 a.m., and church would be letting out in fifteen minutes.

Turning on Porter Street, I made a right into Lincoln Estates. Most of the homes were dark except for Christmas lights and a few porch lights. Dr. Sinclair and Jess' house on Primrose Avenue still had a light on in the kitchen. There were two cars parked in the driveway. I wondered if the California Sinclairs were visiting or if Turner was home for the holidays. I counted the years in my head and figured Turner to be about twenty-seven and wondered how his life had turned out. He'd been such a sweet little boy, and I'd hated to lose touch with him.

I slowly drove down the street, noting the new houses built where there used to be only woods. The people of Elmwood seemed to be doing well for themselves if you looked at the large homes springing up in Lincoln Estates.

Looking at the stately white brick house at 127 Primrose, I remembered watching Turner while his parents planted small saplings in the front yard. Those trees were now fully grown, and although their leaves were gone in the winter, I could imagine the protection they gave in the summer.

Jess was right to have Dr. Sinclair take exactly ten big steps between each planting to space them perfectly, making sure their yard would be beautiful in the years to come.

**

"Cassie?" I heard my mom's voice as soon as I came in the back door.

"Yeah, Mom . . . are you okay?" I asked. I went to her doorway, which was still open from earlier.

"I'm feeling much better, I should have gotten up and gone with you."

I felt bad about playing hooky from church like a disobedient teenager.

"Are you going right to bed?" she asked.

"Yes, unless you need something."

"I was thinking maybe I'd get up and make us some hot chocolate. No one can sleep after midnight Mass. I'd love to hear what Father Burk had to say in his Christmas homily."

"Sure, Mom. That would be nice." My voice was dripping with guilt.

I enjoyed my second hot chocolate of the night while making up what I thought the priest would have said in his holiday message about peace, love, and the joy of family.

Nestled under a red fleece blanket, I felt the warm embrace of my mother's love. It was a perfect Christmas Eve.

Chapter Four
February 1996

My alarm went off at 6:00 a.m., and I jumped out of bed and into the shower as quickly as possible. It was a big day, and I needed to be at school early to work on the decorations for the Valentine's Day dance.

The entire committee would meet after school to finish up, but as the chairperson, it was my job to organize everything ahead of time. With a Friday night basketball game to work around, all the plans for the dance had to be set early.

Jess volunteered to do my hair and makeup for the dance, which worked out great since I was borrowing a dress and shoes from her. She and Dr. Sinclair had attended the hospital's Heart Ball, and she wore a gorgeous red sheath with a rhinestone neckline. We were nearly the same size, and it fit me like a glove. She had matching red pumps to go with it and was willing to loan both to me.

I wanted to be excited about the dance but had something more distressing on my mind. I was late.

My periods were sometimes sporadic, and once I'd gone three months without one. But, I'd never had sex before so hadn't worried about it.

Besides preparing for the big dance on Saturday, Ben and I had another date, which couldn't be put off any longer. We planned to drive to Cedar Point to buy a pregnancy test.

It was only thirty minutes away but would allow us to purchase the test at a pharmacy without being recognized. In Elmwood, there was always someone's parent or neighbor to run into, and we didn't want to take that risk.

I loved Ben for coming up with the idea to make the trip out of town to prove everything was okay. Maybe I'd get my period before we left, and our Friday night could be spent going to a movie or out for pizza.

The bell rang at 3:20, and I joined the rest of the dance committee in the art room and began making work assignments.

"Hey, don't forget to leave a hole in the top of those hearts for the fishing line," I directed to several girls working at a table together.

"Cassie, do you want some pink hearts or just red and white?"

"What do all of you think? Should we add pink?" I asked the room full of students, and they all agreed pink hearts would add the right touch to the decorations.

My mind wandered. Nervous and worried about taking the pregnancy test; the color of the hearts on the wall couldn't take my mind off my predicament. I hadn't kept track of when my last period came because I didn't think I had to. It had been before Christmas, but I wasn't sure of the exact date. If I *was* pregnant, wouldn't I be throwing up from morning sickness? I was sure things were fine. They had to be fine. Ben felt the same way, and he *promised* me I wasn't pregnant. I so wanted to believe him, but we were both scared.

–

We finished the work on the decorations and took what we could into the storage area of the gym just as the Varsity Cheerleaders were setting up for the basketball game.

"Hey, Cassie, we miss you on the squad this season," the coach said as I walked by.

I'd cheered for football in the fall, but I had to get straight A's my last semester to secure my college scholarships. I'd dropped most of my school activities to concentrate on my homework. Chairing the Valentine's Day dance was my last big commitment.

Ben was waiting for me by the gym doors, and he pulled his car up giving me a big smile. "Hey, need a ride?" Ben said as he rolled down the passenger side window.

"Let's get this over with," I said, throwing my bag in the backseat. There was no time for flirting until we knew everything was all right.

"Yes, I agree. Come on...." he said. He patted the leather seat next to him, encouraging me to get in. He didn't seem like he was worried at all.

Ben always drove an awesome car. When your dad owned an auto repair shop, it was easy to have a sweet ride. His dad had several cars, and Ben would take turns driving them to school. On any other day I would have enjoyed taking a drive outside of town with Ben in a rebuilt black Mustang.

"You know Cass, no matter what... I'm going to be by your side. Even if you *are* pregnant, we'll be fine."

"How are we going to be fine if I'm pregnant?" Ben's confidence couldn't fix our problem.

We pulled into the parking lot of Tyler Drug Store on the

south side of Cedar Point. Ben handed me a twenty-dollar bill, and I went inside by myself, walking to the back of the store where they sold creams for yeast infections and condoms and considered my choices for pregnancy tests.

I had no idea they were so expensive but decided on the single package instead of the twin tests. I certainly didn't plan on having another occasion to have to take a pregnancy test.

I headed to the front of the store only stopping to grab a Diet Coke and a candy bar. I couldn't *just* buy the test, and the other items would make it look like I was casually shopping for snacks when it dawned on me that I should find out if I was pregnant.

There were two lines open, and one had an older gentleman working the check-out. The other checker was a girl about twenty, but there were several people in her line. I chose the longer line and averted my gaze from the other one. I felt more comfortable buying a pregnancy test from someone closer to my own age.

The person checking out in front of me was having an issue with their credit card, which quickly extended the time they should have been standing there. It wasn't long until the other line was free of customers, while mine remained at three.

"Miss? I can take you over here."

I could hear the other checker trying to get my attention. Hoping someone else would move to his line, I continued to look at the magazine cover beside me and pretended not to hear him.

Finally, the person ahead of me moved over to that line, putting me directly behind the credit card lady.

"Okay, now it's going through," the clerk said as she pulled the receipt from the cash register and stuck it in the woman's shopping bag. She began checking me out as soon as the transaction was completed.

"Hello, how are you tonight?" she asked.

"Fine thanks," I replied.

As fine as anyone can be buying a pregnancy test on a Friday night.

"$16.24, please." She didn't seem at all interested in what I was buying. "Would you like a bag?"

"Yes, that would be great." I wasn't going to walk out of Tyler Drug without a sack to hide my confidential purchase.

I was one step closer to knowing the truth. I tore open the package in the car and read the instructions.

"It says the best time to do this is in the morning . . . I don't want to wait until morning!" The thought of waiting twelve more hours to get the information that could change my entire life was too daunting.

"Let me see," Ben said. "It says it's *best* to take it in the morning, especially if it's early. If you were pregnant, it wouldn't be all that early. We had sex on New Year's Eve. That's almost six weeks ago. I think you can take it now, and we'll know for sure. If you were six weeks pregnant you would be sick or something. Everything's going to be fine."

I wished I felt as certain as Ben.

We drove to the Cedar Point McDonalds, and I went into the bathroom while Ben waited in the car. The handicapped stall gave me a little more room and its own trash can and sink to take care of things when I was finished. I'd wrap the test in toilet paper and put it in my purse but wouldn't look at it until I got back in the car with Ben.

When I finished going to the bathroom, I couldn't help but glance at the window where the results would be displayed in just a few minutes. There was a very light plus sign, and a feeling of terror gripped my insides.

With shaking fingers, I quickly put the wrapped test in my bag as it said the results wouldn't be visible for three minutes. Maybe they all started out positive and then changed to negative during that time frame if someone wasn't pregnant.

I couldn't be pregnant…

I left the restaurant and slipped back into Ben's car.

"You okay?" Ben asked.

"No. Let's sit here for a couple of minutes while it records the results, and we'll look together."

"Okay, it says 6:57 on the dash clock. We'll wait until 7:00 to give it enough time," Ben said as he took my hand in his.

I could tell he was nervous, too, as our futures hung in the balance in the parking lot of the golden arches. As soon as the digital clock in Ben's car turned to 7:00 p.m., I took the pregnancy test out of my purse and gave the stick to Ben.

"You look," I said, covering my eyes with my hands.

I could hear him fumbling with the toilet paper, and then the stick dropped on the middle console as Ben sucked in a breath.

"It's positive."

***

I'm not sure how long we sat in the McDonalds parking lot, but it was after 10:00 p.m. when I walked through the front door of my house.

We'd made a return trip to Tyler Drug to buy another pregnancy test to take the following morning as the test had originally instructed. Maybe we'd screwed up the results by going ahead and doing it at night. We both figured it was a long shot, but it gave us a few more hours of hope.

The familiar smell of my mom's perfume made me want to crawl into her lap and cry. The house was dark except for the light above the stove. A note on the counter said Mom had met my aunts for dinner and cards, so I could go to bed without having to face her. She always knew when something was wrong, and I couldn't hold it together if she started asking questions.

I brushed my teeth and got into bed. A picture frame on my nightstand showed Butch and me on the front steps at my ninth birthday party. We were both wearing birthday hats, even though Butch's was falling over his eyes.

I wished he was still alive so he could jump on my bed and let me hold on to him as he licked my face. Things were so much better when Dad and Butch were still with us.

Holding the rosary I'd received for confirmation under my pillow, I began to pray harder than I'd ever prayed before.

Please . . . dear God, don't let me be pregnant.

***

I'd been up since 5:00 a.m. and knew by 5:05 that I was pregnant for sure. I'd waited until 7:00 to call Ben's house and told him the news. The silence on the other end of the phone scared me. We both knew in our hearts what the re-test was going to show, but I'd never seen Ben at a loss for words.

He picked me up at 8:00 a.m. so we could have some time together before we had to be at school to finish getting ready for the dance. We'd made excuses to our parents as to why we had to leave so early, blaming it on the need to buy more supplies at Walmart. I just made it into Ben's car before bursting into tears.

"Drive . . . drive! I don't want my mom to look out the window and see me crying!" I exclaimed.

"Everything will be okay. Don't cry. We'll figure something out."

"Ben, what are we going to figure out? I'm pregnant, my life is over!"

"It's not over. Our baby's life is just beginning. Maybe this is the best thing to ever happen to us. We're both graduating in May, and I can start working full-time for my dad once classes are over. We can get married this summer before the baby is born. You can take some of your classes at Elmwood Community the first couple of years, and we'll move to Iowa City later for you to finish school." He seemed to have it all figured out.

"Ben, you're getting way ahead of yourself. I don't want to go to community college or get married! We're way too young for this. My mom's going to *kill* me! No one is ever going to look at me the same way again!" I cried harder with the realization of my new life.

"What do you want to do? You're not thinking of having an abortion, are you? Cass—you can't do that. It's against everything we believe in. This is our baby...."

"I need time to think, and the last thing I want to worry about is this stupid Valentine's dance!" Ben was a part of what was happening, but I couldn't help feeling alone. He wasn't pregnant, and this didn't affect him nearly as much as it did me. I should have taken the pregnancy test without him knowing, so I could deal with it on my own.

"Let's get everyone started on the decorations, and you can

pretend like you aren't feeling well. That will give us an excuse not to go to the dance tonight. I'll come over, and we can watch a movie or something."

I could hardly think about watching a movie when there was a baby growing inside of me.

"Okay... let me pull myself together." I took several deep breaths and wiped my tears away with a napkin left over from our McDonald's visit. My life was over, and I had to make sure the ideal number of pastel hearts were hung in the gymnasium of my high school before I could sneak away and figure out what to do.

We worked with the dance committee for about an hour. People noticed I wasn't myself, and I complained of being sick and said I had to go home.

Mom was a little more suspicious of the whole thing, asking if I'd had a fight with Ben. I didn't seem sick, and she couldn't figure out why I would miss the dance after I'd been working on it for so long. I didn't have a fever and wasn't throwing up, although I felt like I could puke at any moment.

Once I'd finally convinced her, I went to my room and crawled into bed. Mom called Jess and told her I wouldn't be over to have my hair and makeup done, and before noon, I'd successfully made it through the first set of lies related to my pregnancy.

Mom didn't allow Ben to visit me all weekend. She said if I was sick enough to be in bed, he shouldn't be near me. It gave me time alone to think, and I was glad she'd unknowingly put some distance between us.

She insisted on continuing to take my temperature and gave me Tylenol to help with the body aches I was complaining about. Chicken noodle soup and ginger ale sustained me while

I tried to figure out what to do.

Could I take on motherhood as a teenager? Was my entire future in jeopardy because of one careless night? By the end of the weekend, I'd only made one solid decision. I needed to confide in Jess and ask for her help.

***

Ben wasn't happy about letting Jess in on our secret but agreed we needed *someone's* help. I could tell he thought Jess might be on his side and help him convince me we should keep the baby and get married.

Even if Jess thought marriage was the right thing to do, I wouldn't allow myself to make that mistake. I didn't know what I wanted to do, but I knew what I didn't want to do.

The other thing I was sure of was that my mother could never know about the pregnancy. She'd raised me alone and deserved more from me after losing my dad so young, and I wasn't about to hurt her with the mess I'd created.

On Monday morning after my shower, I looked at my naked profile in the mirror to see if my belly was protruding yet. It looked as flat as a pancake, and I wondered how long it would take before it started to swell.

I couldn't let myself consider an abortion, although it would make everything so much easier. I had to figure out a way to keep the pregnancy a secret and give the baby up for adoption; it was the only answer I could live with.

After school I headed over to the Sinclairs. Jess had aerobics until 4:30, and Dr. Sinclair worked late on Monday nights. I'd meet Turner at home after he got off the school bus and stay with him until his mom got home. We would have some time to talk then as Turner would play his Super Mario 64 game until dinner, and he never hung around to hear our conversations anyway.

At 4:40 p.m., I heard the garage door go up, and Jess came bouncing into the kitchen humming and cheerful as always.

"Hi, Cassie. How are you feeling?"

"What do you mean?" I shot back at her. Did she already know about the pregnancy?

"Well, I was so disappointed for you when your mom called Saturday and said you wouldn't be going to the dance because you were sick. I know how much you were looking forward to it. Are you feeling better now?"

"Oh, yes." In reality, I'd never felt worse.

This was just the right opening to our conversation, but I'd wanted to have a little more time for chit chat before we got into it.

"The thing is, Jess...I need to talk with you about something important," I started.

"Sure, honey. What is it?" There was no way to sugar coat it. I didn't know how to ease into such a difficult topic so decided to come at it from a different angle.

"Well . . . I have this friend who's in trouble, and I don't know how to help her. I was hoping you might know of a place where she could go to get help with a pregnancy. She doesn't want anyone to know about it, and since Dr. Sinclair works at the hospital, maybe you know about some kind of home for unwed mothers?"

Jess had been looking at a pile of mail sitting on the kitchen counter, but when she heard "pregnancy," her head popped up. She stared at me for a moment before speaking.

"That's kind of an archaic way of dealing with a pregnancy.

Most girls have their babies and raise them on their own or with the help of their families now. Even adoptions are handled differently than they used to be, back when those kinds of places were more prevalent. Has your friend talked with her parents?"

"Oh no, she can't tell her mom…I mean her *parents*…about this. That's why she asked for my help."

Jess looked at me suspiciously and asked me to sit down at the counter with her.

"Tell me more about your *friend*. She must trust you very much to be asking for your help with such a private matter. Do you know how far along she is? Does she know who the father is?"

I could tell this wasn't going to go very far. Jess was a smart woman, and she wasn't buying my story. I lowered my head, not able to make eye contact with her, and she took my hand in hers letting me know she understood.

"Cassie, I can't help you if you don't tell me the truth. What's going on?"

"I need your help. I'm pregnant." My eyes filled with tears. I knew if I didn't hold it together, I might never stop crying.

"Oh, Cassie," she said quietly, moving toward me and taking me in her arms. The tightness of the hug showed her grasp of the severity of the situation.

"I don't know what to do. I'm not going to marry Ben and give up on becoming a doctor." Everything came out all at once. "I was hoping you would know what to do. I thought there were still homes where girls could go to have their babies and keep it a secret from everyone else."

"Honey, there are places for homeless girls, and there might be programs I'm not aware of, but I'm just not sure that's the best thing for someone like you. This is a lot of information in a short time. Let me think a minute. You definitely want to have the baby?" Jess looked serious, and I hated that she might think differently of me after knowing the truth.

"I have to."

"No, you don't Cassie. You're an adult, and you have the right to do whatever you want about this pregnancy. Does Ben know?"

"Yes."

"What does he think you should do?" I could see the worry on Jess' face and hoped telling her hadn't been a mistake.

"He wants to get married and have me delay med school for a few years, but that's not what I'm going to do. I'm not ready to be married, and I don't want to abandon my plans to go to college. I still want to be a doctor and have the life I've dreamed of . . . but how do I make it happen now?"

Jess continued to be deep in thought, but I could see she was considering all the options. "Okay, who knows about this?" she asked.

"Only Ben and me. No one else."

"I'll try to support you the best I can, Cassie. I'm going to have to tell Steve about this. He won't tell anyone. But, if we're going to help you, I need to have him involved. Is that okay?"

"I guess. Are you sure he won't tell anyone . . . especially my mom?"

"Like I said, you're an adult, and you have the right to keep this from anyone you want to. No matter what we come up with, I can't see how you can keep your mom from being involved. Are you positive you don't want to tell her?"

"No . . . she can't ever find out."

Jess moved closer to me again and gave me another big

hug, and I knew I could depend on her to help us.

"Give me a few days to see what I can figure out."

Feeling certain Jess would know what to do, a sense of relief finally came over me.

Chapter Five
December 2014

The nurse at Dr. Baylor's office smiled as she called for her next patient in the waiting room, nodding in recognition as Mom started to get up.

"Do you want me to go in with you?" I asked.

"No, this shouldn't take long," she said, squeezing my hand. She continued to be so vibrant in her mid-50's. With only twenty years between us, sometimes it felt like we were sisters.

Doctor's waiting rooms were places where there was nothing to do but look at other people and wonder why they were there. The last thing I needed was to get sick before heading back to California, so I applied hand sanitizer as my mind wandered back to the day that changed my professional life forever.

A girl and her mother had come in to see me. They'd both been patients of mine for a few years, and I'd treated them for a variety of minor issues. Their relationship reminded me of my own with my mother as a teenager, but this appointment stood out from the others when I found out the sixteen-year-old girl was pregnant.

As their primary care physician, I was happy to be pulled into the case and offer information on services the young woman might be eligible for after the baby was born like I'd done for other patients. Things had changed over the years, and it wasn't uncommon for high school girls to get pregnant, the media and society almost glamorizing it.

"Chelsea has decided to give the baby up for adoption, and we'd like for you to refer us to an obstetrician who would be suitable for this type of situation," the mother had said matter of factly.

The statement took me off guard, and in my fragile mental state with all that I was dealing with in my personal life, I went right past the request for a recommendation and on to the adoption issue.

"Is this what you would like to have happen?" I'd directed my words to the young girl, feeling my emotions begin to take over.

"Yeah . . . I don't really care," she'd said quietly.

Chelsea averted her eyes from mine as she fidgeted with the trim on her hoodie. She was barely more than a little girl, with freckles spanning the bridge of her nose. With a long braid hanging down her back and her chipped fingernails painted florescent orange, she looked more like someone's little sister than a woman who was about to become a mother.

"I think you *do* care, and I want to make sure your needs are being addressed as well as those of your baby," I'd said, sympathizing with the difficult choice she faced.

"Dr. Garrett," her mother started, "we've made the decisions necessary and have family members willing to take this baby. We don't need your assistance for anything other than the referral for Chelsea. If you can't provide that information for some reason, we'll find an OBGYN on our own."

I felt my neck and face begin to turn red, and my chin quivered.

"With all due respect, Mrs. Collins, it's important Chelsea makes the right decision. I'm concerned about her emotional well-being *and* her physical health. You see, I know something about giving up a baby."

Once I began to share my own story, I couldn't stop. It felt like road rage taking over a person who'd never even honked at another driver as it came pouring out of me.

"I had a baby at eighteen and gave it up for adoption— not even telling my own mother about it. I've spent my entire life regretting the choice I made and don't want the same thing to happen to your daughter. I'm happy to give a referral, but I'd also like to be assured she knows there are other options." I felt myself lose control as tears began to roll down my cheeks.

"We've made a mistake by coming here today. We're leaving now. Chelsea, grab your backpack," Mrs. Collins said loudly. The girl struggled to get off the exam table and hoisted her bag over one shoulder as she followed her mom out of the room.

After years of keeping my secret buried deep inside, I'd let it come spilling out to strangers who didn't need my opinion on such a private matter. Embarrassed and appalled at my behavior, I knew I'd be called to task for my unprofessional outburst.

Putting the memory out of my mind, I began to think about the new practice I hoped to open someday and how a waiting room could be changed to make it more comfortable for patients. I half-seriously wondered if I *did* move to Napa Valley if state law would allow me to serve wine, making the experience much more relaxing.

There was a lot to make up for in the clinic where I was currently employed, and time off had given me enough clarity to know if I didn't pull myself together, my days in Ventura were numbered.

I grabbed a People magazine and began to read about the newest "Sexiest Man Alive" to take my mind off my problems.

"Cassie?" Someone was calling my name from the patient entry door.

"Yes?" I answered as the nurse looked for me in the sea of sick people.

"Can you come with me, please?" I closed the magazine and grabbed my mother's coat, following her to the exam room.

"Is there something wrong?" I asked the staff member with "Amber" on her nametag.

Why would they tear me away from the Sexiest Man Alive if there wasn't something wrong?

"Your mom asked me to bring you back to talk with the doctor. I'm sure you'll know more once you've visited with them," she said. She had a confidence I didn't know could be trusted considering she didn't look old enough to have graduated from nursing school.

I entered the sterile looking room and saw my mom talking quietly to the doctor.

"Hello, Cassie. It's good to see you again." Dr. Baylor had been our doctor for as long as I could recall. As a little girl, I'd get nervous before going in to see him because he was such a good-looking young man. Now, nearing retirement age, he had gray hair at his temples and a belly sticking out from underneath his white coat.

"What's going on?" I asked, ignoring the pleasantries.

"Well, I hope nothing. However, I'd like your mom to have some tests done. I'm concerned with the pain she's having and the bloating in her abdomen. I'd like to have you take her over to get an ultrasound and a CT scan so we can see what we're dealing with."

"We'll go right over for any scans that need to be done. I'm sure this is nothing, Mom…but it's better to be safe than sorry." The concern on Dr. Baylor's face scared me.

We headed over for the tests Dr. Baylor had ordered and quickly had an answer to why Mom wasn't feeling well.

I'd been so entrenched in my own life's drama that I hadn't used my medical knowledge when Mom complained of specific symptoms. Diagnosing a woman of her age with bloating in her abdomen and stomach pain could have various causes from something minor to a life-threatening diagnosis.

I'd dismissed her health issues as if she was immune to anything bad happening to her because she was my mom, and that had been a mistake. In the span of one afternoon, I'd gone from trying to decide what Mom and I would have for dinner, to having her diagnosed with what appeared to be late-stage ovarian cancer.

It was so serious, we were immediately scheduled to see a gynecological oncologist in Des Moines. We wouldn't know how far the cancer had spread until they did surgery and staged the cancer after assessing the lymph nodes.

I wanted to cry and scream and ask how she could have gone from not having cancer to having cancer in twenty-four hours. I knew the answer to that question because it happened all the time, only this time it was my mom and not a random stranger from the clinic.

A silent killer, ovarian cancer was often found far into the disease progression. There were few symptoms, and once they started to present, it was usually too late. Suddenly, the loss of Graham seemed so inconsequential.

Neither of us said much as we walked to the car. I opened the door for Mom on the passenger side and then took my place behind the wheel, not wanting her to drive after receiving such devastating news.

As we approached a four-way stop sign near the hospital, Mom's car began to sputter. When it was our turn to make the right-hand turn toward the condo, it died all together and wouldn't move.

Like a spoiled child who won't budge when they don't get their way, the car sat immobile in the intersection with cars honking behind us. I wanted to do the same thing as Mom's old Honda, refusing to move in the direction of what lay ahead.

"Oh no," Mom said as she looked at the two cars waiting behind us.

"Go around!" I shouted, waving the vehicles by and putting the emergency blinkers on.

"I forgot to tell you that the car was acting kind of funny on Christmas Eve…like it was skipping or something when the gears shifted."

"It's been a little temperamental lately. I should think about getting a new one. I've got AAA, so they'll send someone out to help us," Mom said, taking her phone out to call a tow truck.

She acted like solving this car problem was our biggest concern. I'd already moved on to how we'd get to her appointment in Des Moines, and how I could keep her alive for the next forty years.

"Hello? Yes . . . we need a tow truck at the Elmwood Regional Medical Center on the corner of First and Pleasant Streets. Yes . . . I have my card and will give the number to the towing company when they arrive. My name is Josephine Garrett . . . thank you so much!"

Mom was polite and cheerful even when she had every reason not to be.

We sat as the late afternoon sky turned pink and evening began to set in. I got out and raised the hood of the car so I could stop waving cars around us. Silence filled the dimly lit space of Mom's broken-down car, and I reached over and took her hand.

She continued to look forward in the passenger seat, her eyes filled with tears. The air was becoming colder as the car sat still and quiet. One tear drop slid down Mom's cheek, and I couldn't hold it together any longer either.

"It'll be okay, please don't cry," she pleaded. "I'll fight this thing! Cancer isn't the death sentence it used to be. I know lots of people who've beaten it."

She had always been the eternal optimist, but Mom was wrong about this one. Ovarian cancer was not one of the cancers easily cured. Although we didn't know the exact staging yet, they thought it to be at least stage three. Not even Mom's good nature could protect her from this reality.

We'd go to Des Moines and figure it all out, but I wouldn't be going back to the clinic in California any time soon. I had to stay in Elmwood to care for my mother who probably wasn't going to survive her diagnosis.

The load on my heart was too great, and I began to sob with

my mom looking on helplessly. The regret from spending too much time away from the woman I loved so much was more than I could take.

"Honey, it'll be all right. We'll figure something out. We've got each other, and that's all that matters now," she said.

She pulled me near her over the center console of the car and planted her brave face close to mine. I was embarrassed that she was trying to comfort me instead of it being the other way around.

Headlights came up behind our car, and I could see the tow truck had arrived. I looked in the rearview mirror and saw the driver switch on his overhead light as he began to write on a clipboard. The words on the front of the truck read O'Brien's Auto Repair.

As the driver glanced up and took our license plate number, I saw the face of the only man I'd ever really loved.

"Mom, it's Ben."

"What do you mean?" she asked as she flipped open the mirror on the passenger side sunshade to get a better look behind us.

"Ben O'Brien is driving the tow truck," I whispered, trying not to make her wonder why this would be so terrible.

"Are you sure? Ben runs the whole show over at his dad's now. I'm sure he's got people to do this kind of thing."

"Well, apparently he doesn't, because he's getting out of the truck right now."

I quickly regained my composure and rolled down the driver's side window as Ben came up to our car. Before I could say anything, Mom started, "Ben, hello! We've had a bit of car trouble here, and I'm hoping you can help us out!"

Ben looked right past me when she started talking, and after greeting her warmly, his glance finally landed on me. I saw his eyes open wide, and he took a surprised step back.

"Hey, Cassie. Gosh, how are you?" I could tell he was shocked to see me as he tried to keep it together to take care of our car.

"Good," I lied. "Thanks for coming out on such a cold night."

"I didn't know you ran the tow truck too. Don't you have people to work for you after hours?" Mom asked as she handed him her AAA card.

"I'm filling in for Tom Meyers. He and his wife just had a baby, so he needed to have some time off with his family. He's better at this than me, but I can get you taken care of, Mrs. Garrett."

So, Tommy Meyers now worked for Ben. I remembered how he'd misinformed his group of high school buddies that a woman couldn't get pregnant the first time she had sex. He must have finally figured out how fertility worked since he had a baby of his own.

I watched Ben as he talked with my mom. He looked like himself but older; nearly twenty years changing his profile to look more like his dad's. A person didn't lose their personality or mannerisms as the years passed, and he was still one of the most attractive men I'd ever known.

He wasn't as muscular as he'd been in high school and had added a few pounds to his frame. He had a hint of gray in his dark hair as well, but he looked as handsome as ever to me. The pull of familiarity I felt toward him was as strong as ever, even after so many years.

He seemed to be avoiding my stare as he tried to be as professional as possible. I could see the pain still existed in his brown eyes. I was ashamed for how I'd treated him all those years earlier. He deserved more, but I hadn't been equipped to handle the situation at such a young age.

Fear and immaturity had caused me to reject an important person in my life. I'd been so cruel, telling him he'd ruined my life. When we'd found out I was pregnant, he'd asked me to marry him without hesitation. He promised we'd make it and live happily ever after. He may have been right, but that option wasn't a consideration for me at the time, and I'd abandoned him without regard to how it might impact *his* life.

I'd begged him not to tell anyone and to agree to our plan. We argued for several months over what to do, and finally he agreed to sign the adoption papers. He wanted to stay together after the baby, but I needed to make a clean break.

"Why don't you ladies hop into my truck while I get this hooked up? Do you want me to take it to my shop for repair or are you taking it to Taylor's?"

Taylor's Standard was the only other place that fixed cars in Elmwood, but I couldn't see hauling it over there and having to figure it all out with someone else.

"We're going to need a loaner car for the duration. Do you have any available?" Mom asked.

"Sure, I'll get you taken care of," Ben replied as he opened his truck door and helped both of us into the cab.

He touched my elbow as I hoisted myself into the truck. I wanted to hug him, apologizing for ending things so terribly, and tell him my mom was sick and I needed him. But, I shut the door after he turned back toward our vehicle without saying a word.

***

The auto repair shop smelled like coffee and popcorn. Ben directed us to sit inside while he went and got a car for us to use. Once Mom had signed all the necessary paperwork, he told us we were good to go, and he would be in contact once he figured out what was wrong with the car.

I moved all our personal belongings from Mom's car to the loaner and made sure she was settled into the passenger seat with the heater warming the inside. I went back into the shop where Ben was already making an order for the car repair.

"Hey," I said sheepishly.

"Hey," he repeated quietly as he continued to look over the paperwork.

"Is it okay if we take the car to Des Moines? Mom needs to see a doctor there, and we didn't want to take it out of town without checking with you first."

He hadn't mentioned any restrictions for driving the car, but I couldn't leave without talking to him again.

"Is everything all right with her?" He still hadn't made eye contact with me.

"No . . . she has cancer," I said quietly.

"Cass—" he said as his head jerked up. "Oh no. Can I do anything?"

"Just let me take this car to Des Moines."

"You can go wherever you need to go . . . *shit,* Cassie. What are you going to do?"

"I'm going to stay here in Elmwood and take care of her," I said, thanking him for helping us out as I headed back to the car where Mom sat waiting.

Glancing back through the window, Ben was looking at us, and I knew we'd both left so much unsaid.

***

I made some soup for dinner, and we put our pajamas on early and watched TV. There wasn't anything we could do until after the appointment with the oncologist, and both of us knew it.

"Mom, I'm not going back to California."

"What? Do you mean you're switching your flight, so you can stay longer? Because . . . you don't have to go changing your entire life for me. Aunt Barb or Aunt Lynn can take me to chemo and bring me anything I need, and you can come back and visit in a couple of months. Everything will be fine. I'm going to beat this thing. Cancer hasn't messed with someone like Josephine Garrett before...."

She had no idea.

"Well, I'm definitely not flying back this week, but we can figure everything out after we know more. I've been thinking about leaving Ventura for a while now, and since you need me here, it makes the decision about where to go pretty easy." Although I'd been struggling with so much over the past months, the decision to stay in Elmwood was the first thing I'd been sure about in weeks.

It gave me purpose and a direction, and I knew I could care for my mom better than anyone else. I'd never been there for her like she needed me to be, and this was a chance to make it up to her.

I kissed my mother goodnight, brushed my teeth, and climbed into the comfy guest room bed. Wide awake in a room full of silence, I heard Mom at the door.

"Cassie, can I come in?"

"Sure," I said quietly, sitting up on one elbow.

She opened the door and slipped into the room where the

hallway light and the darkness of the bedroom came together. She was wearing her light blue nightgown and smelled like the Ivory soap she had used to wash her face every night since my childhood.

She came to my bedside and sat on the edge as she leaned down to kiss me. "I wanted to tuck my girl in and say thank you for being with me today."

Her softness was both physical and spiritual. I'd never spent any time thinking about what it would be like to live in a world without her, and now that I'd had those thoughts, I was terrified to lose her.

"I love you, Cassidy Maxine," she said as she kissed me again.

"I love you too, Mom."

As she left the room and closed the door, I pulled the covers up around my neck. They smelled like a combination of fabric softener and my mom's lingering scent. It made me feel loved in a way I hadn't felt in a long time. I'd spent so many years avoiding home, and now it was the only place I wanted to be.

I knew if things had been different, Mom would know about her only grandchild. I'd be married to Ben, with at least a few kids added to the mix, and would never have left Elmwood, Iowa for a bigger and better life.

Ben would have loved me so much more than any of the men I'd allowed in my life over the years.

Chapter Six
May 1996

Graduation day came faster than I'd imagined it would. I'd begun to wear looser tops and opted for elastic waist shorts instead of the cute cut-offs all my friends were wearing because I was five months pregnant and beginning to show. Mom had joked one day about my face looking fuller and asked if I'd been eating too much ice cream. I'd been sucking my cheeks in ever since.

It had been about three months since Jess had come up with the solution to our problem. When she first told me what she was thinking, I didn't think it could work. I'd almost broken down and told my mom on more than one occasion. Now that it was nearly time to carry out the plan, it seemed like it all might go off without a hitch.

Ben had reluctantly agreed to placing our baby for adoption. He still wanted us to stay together and raise our child, but I wasn't ready to be a mom or a wife. Ben was my first boyfriend, and I couldn't let one reckless night ruin the rest of my life. I tried to eat well and be as healthy as possible, while trying to disconnect from the fact my own child would call someone else "Mommy".

To make sure I had medical care, Dr. Sinclair saw me free of charge for the first months of my pregnancy, and he'd even done the ultrasound telling us we were having a girl. I gave my permission for them to talk with Dr. Sinclair 's brother and sister-in-law in California who arranged things on their end.

It was decided I would apply for a scholarship at Berkeley, where Mark Sinclair was a tenured professor and had some pull for financial awards. I would leave right after graduation for California to help with Mark and Leslie's twin girls all summer as a nanny, and I'd have the baby out there about the same time school started in the fall.

Leslie's law firm would oversee the adoption, and no one would ever have to know. Ben and I could go on with our lives, and our little girl would have a family like she deserved. Convincing my mom to let her only child go to a university thousands of miles away wasn't as easy.

Regardless of why I was heading to Berkeley, it was an amazing opportunity. Mark pulled some strings, but I was able to get the scholarships because of my own efforts as a student—that much wasn't a lie. It was the details surrounding the reason for the change in plans that were less than truthful.

Once my mom knew I had a good summer job and a full-ride scholarship to a prestigious college, she reluctantly accepted my decision to move to California. She wasn't happy about it, but she didn't want to stand in my way either. Mark Sinclair handled all the school matters, so Mom felt comfortable with what she was being told.

My education would be taken care of, but the rest of the plans weren't shared with my mom. Since she didn't know about the baby, it made it much easier for her to think this was the luckiest break a small-town girl like me would ever get. I'd come home at Thanksgiving, giving me the right amount of time to have the baby and get myself together before returning home for the first time. It was a perfect plan, and I only needed to get through a few more days before it could be implemented.

***

The senior class of Elmwood High School filed into the auditorium to the traditional tune of "Pomp and Circumstance" played haphazardly by the marching band. The program started, and I began to get nervous as I waited to be called to the stage.

I took a breath in and let the air out slowly. The speech I was about to give would serve as the bridge between my childhood and everything that would come after. Beads of sweat balanced on my upper lip, and a stream of perspiration ran down the center of my back.

Despite the heat, I was happy to be wearing a graduation gown so I could relax without worry someone would suspect something. In Iowa, you could get any kind of weather in May, and the summer humidity had already settled in like the reality of my desperate situation.

The inflection in Principal Jones' voice began to change, and my name was called. "Please welcome to the stage your 1996 Elmwood High School Class Valedictorian, Cassidy Maxine Garrett."

I stood and began to walk toward the podium, nervous and a bit shaky, applause and whistles encouraging me on my way toward the front. I was proud of my academic accomplishments, but speaking in front of hundreds of people from my hometown was harder than anything I'd done before. Saying goodbye to high school and giving advice about how to be successful in the unknown future seemed ironic considering what I was hiding.

I began my speech, realizing the inspiring words shared with my classmates were the same private pep talks I'd been giving myself for several months. I wouldn't be going to Iowa City as previously planned to attend The University of Iowa like so many of my friends. I wasn't going to be close to home in case I missed my mom in the first semester of college. The decisions had been made, and I couldn't back out now. One night had changed everything for me, and I would pay dearly for my actions. Only a few people knew the real reason things were moving so quickly, and my mom wasn't one of them.

" . . . as we say goodbye to Elmwood High School and go our separate ways, let's remember though time and opportunities may change us, we can always come home." I said the last line with so much conviction, I almost believed it myself.

As my fellow graduates rose to their feet in celebration, I searched for Ben in the crowd. I gave him a little smile, and he returned a half-hearted thumbs up. I could see the sadness in his eyes and wondered if anyone else noticed something was off between us. I loved him so much, but not enough to throw away my entire future.

Walking back to my seat, I felt the first real kick from the baby inside of me and was glad I didn't have to hide my pregnancy much longer.

Looking out over the crowd of familiar faces, I felt jealousy toward my friends. All I wanted was to go back and do things differently. Could I take a detour and still get back on the path I'd dreamed of in a few months? I was giving up so much to keep my pregnancy hidden from everyone in my life and hoped it was worth the sacrifices I would have to make.

***

Mom threw me a lovely graduation party. She hadn't had time to get used to the fact I was going to be so far away, and I knew she was probably wondering what she would do with herself once I was gone.

I'd told her I couldn't pass up this once in a lifetime chance to go to a school that would help me achieve my dreams in a way that could never be done in Iowa. Mom wasn't so sure, but when I suggested she was thinking more about how the decision would change her life instead of mine, she backed off. I hated to hurt her feelings but needed to leave as soon as possible before everything blew up in my face.

She'd worked hard on the party, and I was aware it wouldn't be so festive if she'd known what was going on. Ben's party wouldn't be until the following week, but I'd already be gone.

We planned to stay together for the time being, but it would never work. I wanted him in my life until the baby was born. I needed his phone calls and support even though he wouldn't be with me physically.

He wanted to be there for the birth, but the baby was due only weeks after he would start at Elmwood Community College, and a trip out to see me then would draw too much suspicion.

Mom had chosen a "California Dreamin'" theme for my party, complete with surfboards and palm tree decorations, turning our double garage into a party hall. There were bright pink and yellow napkins with beach balls on the front. She served little sandwiches and potato salad and had ordered a big cake with the words "Good Luck, Cassie" across the front in blue icing.

My aunts and uncles and most of my cousins were in attendance, along with all my friends from school. The Sinclairs were there, too, and gave me a gift card to a department store near where Mark and Leslie lived in California. I'd save it for after the baby's birth when I might need some new clothes. I didn't deserve a party and had to fake appreciation for all the hoopla when I just wanted to stay in my room with the door closed until it was time to leave.

I was going to miss Jess, Dr. Sinclair, and Turner almost as much as my mom. They'd been like a second family to me, and the thought of not having them in my life was terrifying.

It was uncomfortable having them at our home now that there was this secret between us. I couldn't think of a reason why any of us would blurt out the plan for the next few months, but it made me nervous to have them there anyway.

I owed them so much for helping me figure out what to do about my pregnancy and for arranging the help from their family in California. They'd made it possible for us to put the baby up for adoption without anyone in Elmwood finding out about it.

Ben toasted me with his punch cup and motioned for us to slip into the house to talk. Once inside, he took me in his arms. "Are you sure about all of this, Cass?"

"There isn't any other choice, we can't be parents to this child. Our baby needs a family who can give her more than we can right now—it's the right decision."

I couldn't allow myself to consider any other options. We needed to hold it together for a little longer, and then it would be safe to relax and wait for the baby to be born far away from everyone in our hometown.

"It seems like we're selling our baby in exchange for your college education. It just doesn't feel right."

"You can't *sell* a baby, that's illegal. They're just making it easier for me to achieve my goals. They get what they want, and I get what I want. It's like we're making the best of a bad situation...."

"And what do *I* get out of all of this?" he asked sadly. "Doesn't it matter what I want?"

"You get to do whatever you want to do. You don't have to support a baby when you're eighteen years old. They said they'd pay for your college too. You're the one who refused them."

"Well, how was I going to explain that to my parents?"

"We could have figured it out, Elmwood Community College has scholarships."

"Not for mediocre students like me," he answered back quietly.

"There's no time for this. We can't turn back now. I'm the one who's carrying this baby, I should get to make the final decision. You said so yourself."

We'd talked for hours about our decision. He never wavered in wanting to keep the baby. He would have been surprised to know how close I'd come to giving in, but when he finally told me I could decide—it made it easy to do what I wanted to do in the first place.

"Okay, okay. It just doesn't seem right." I knew how Ben felt. It didn't seem right to me either, but how was it supposed to feel to give up your baby? I was lying every time I turned around. It would be stranger if we didn't feel bad about everything happening in our lives. We just had to get through the coming weeks and months.

The door from the garage opened, and Mom walked through with an empty sandwich tray. "Do you need help with that, Mrs. Garrett?" Ben asked.

"That would be great. There's another tray of sandwiches in the refrigerator if you wouldn't mind reloading this while I fill the punch bowl again," she said, giving Ben a little squeeze as she snuck through the small space between us in our less than gourmet kitchen.

Trays and punch refilled, I mingled with the guests at my party and assured them I'd keep in touch between classes and making new friends. I didn't mention how busy I'd be having a baby.

The hardest goodbye came at the end of the night. Ben stayed after the guests left and helped to tear down all the tables and chairs borrowed from St. Cecilia's community room. My uncle would load them into his truck the following day and return them to the church as a favor to my mom.

The garbage was bagged and sitting by the trash can, and Ben swept as I sat in the dark on the patio. Mom had gone to bed early, giving Ben and me some time alone.

I heard the garage door close, and Ben joined me on the patio. Several candles were still burning on the wicker side tables and illuminated the evening with a soft glow. I looked at Ben sadly.

"Thank you."

"Oh, it was nothing. I loved helping out."

"I don't mean for helping with the party . . . thank you for being so good to me. I'm never going to find another person as wonderful as you in my entire life." Tears came quickly, and when I looked at Ben, he was crying too.

I hated to leave so soon after graduation. We'd moved my departure date up by two weeks saying Mark and Leslie needed me sooner than expected when I began showing more every day.

"Cassie, I love you so much. I'm sorry this happened. This whole thing has tainted all the things we've shared over the past year and a half we've been together. It's a terrible way to have to say goodbye. You've never needed me more, and I'm not going to be able to be there for you because you'll be so far away."

"We'll talk on the phone, and we can write letters. I'll have most nights free, and I got some calling cards for graduation. It'll be okay." It was strange for me to be reassuring him instead of it being the other way around.

"If you change your mind about the baby, I'll fly out and get both of you and bring you home. Or if you want to stay in California and go to college, I'll get a job out there, and we'll stay until you graduate. We could make it work," he said in a last-ditch effort to get me to change my mind.

"You better go. I've got to be up early tomorrow. I'll call you in a few days." I didn't want to rehash it again. My bags were packed, and the decisions were made. I needed to get out of Elmwood as soon as possible.

We kissed and hugged each other, holding on longer than we'd ever done before. I was losing someone precious in Ben O'Brien, and I knew it.

What kind of terrible person would give away their own flesh and blood? Maybe he deserved someone better than me too.

Chapter Seven
December 2014

We were fortunate to see the specialist the Monday after Mom's cancer had been discovered. She'd been classified as an emergency, so the doctor made room in her schedule right away.

Dr. Elizabeth Bryn was a leading gynecological oncologist in the Midwest, and luckily, she was in Des Moines. As part of the Heartland Cancer Center, we'd be offered a variety of choices for Mom's treatment if her prognosis gave her enough time to take advantage of them.

Dr. Bryn was a no-nonsense clinician with lots of credentials behind her name, and she was better than most doctors when it came to bedside manner. Her nurse, Jessica, filled in any gaps and made us feel comfortable.

"It appears we're looking at late-stage ovarian cancer," Dr. Bryn started.

"We're going to need an initial surgery to get as much of the cancer out as possible, and we'll determine how to move forward from there. If it looks like you can benefit from chemotherapy, we'll do it. If we conclude after surgery and looking at the lymph nodes that nothing can be done, I'll refer you to hospice, and we'll make sure you are well cared for."

Mom sat looking forward with no emotion.

"Dr. Bryn, I'm a physician myself. Surely there are options for us regardless of what you find in surgery. Perhaps clinical trials she could be involved in or drug regimens to be considered?" I needed to be reassured we would fight this thing no matter what was discovered in the operating room.

As a family practice doctor, when one of my patients had cancer, they were referred to an expert like Dr. Bryn. I only stayed involved as the treating physician for things like high blood pressure or neuropathy brought on by the extreme treatments. Out of my element when it came to the actual therapies for cancer, I wished I'd been better informed to treat my patients more effectively, not to mention my own mother.

Dr. Bryn continued, "We'll look at everything available, but you need to know this is serious. Since you're a doctor she'll have the best home care, which could make a tremendous difference for her level of comfort during this illness. There are trials and drugs to be considered, but sometimes their use is for research purposes more than healing objectives. I have an opening tomorrow in my schedule, so I'll see you back here in the morning so we can get in there to see how much damage has been done. We'll have a good idea what we need to do then. You're in the right place, Mrs. Garrett. I'll do whatever I can to help you."

She left us with nurse Jessica to finalize the specifics for surgery, which included some last-minute pre-op testing to clear her for the procedure. Mom hadn't said a single word since we'd arrived, except to answer any health questions she was asked.

I put my arm around her as she sat on the hard exam table

and gave her a squeeze. "We're going to get you the best care and do anything needed, Mom." Jessica glanced up from her clipboard of instructions and gave me a sympathetic look.

"Josephine, you're a pretty lucky lady to have a doctor in the family. Where do you practice?" she asked me.

"She's my pride and joy," Mom said proudly, fighting back tears.

"I work in Ventura, California. However, I'll be staying here to take care of Mom for the foreseeable future." The words came without hesitation. I looked at Mom and could see a sense of relief come over her, although she immediately began to protest.

"It's decided, Mom."

By the end of the day, two things were confirmed for us. Mom had the fight of her life ahead of her, and I was staying in Elmwood. I'd never forget how it felt to get that kind of diagnosis. It would make me a better doctor, but it didn't help the daughter I was to face the death of my mom.

The only good news we received was that the car was ready to be picked up. I was happy we'd have our own transportation when we returned to Des Moines the following day, since we didn't know how long we'd be there.

Once we were back in Elmwood and Mom was settled, I headed for O'Brien's Auto Repair to switch out the cars and pay for the repairs. A young girl waited on me at the front counter, and after giving her my name she pulled the work order and read a message written on a yellow sticky note attached to the outside.

"Um, Mr. O'Brien asked me to let him know when you

stopped by. He needs to talk with you."

"Oh, okay," I said, wondering what Ben's dad would need to see me about. Maybe there were more issues with the car. We couldn't have it breaking down all the time, especially when we'd be making trips back and forth to Des Moines.

The girl picked up the phone and called back to the shop. "Mr. O'Brien to the front please."

A few moments later, Ben came into the office and broke into a big smile when he saw me standing at the counter.

"Jamie, remember you can call me Ben," he said to his employee. "Mr. O'Brien is my dad."

"Oh, I'm sorry Mr. O . . . *Ben*. My parents told me I should call adults by Mr. or Mrs., especially my boss!"

"This is Jamie's third day, and she's doing an excellent job—although she's making me feel old," Ben joked to both of us.

I took the paperwork from Jamie, and she let me know the keys would be in the car. Ben gestured toward the back and ushered me into his office. He took a seat behind the desk, and I sat in one of two chairs in front. The office was nice for being in an auto repair shop, and several framed photos sat behind his desk on a low cabinet.

"Are those your kids?" I asked, looking at the smiling faces of two adorable little boys.

"Yeah. Richie and Alec. That was a few years ago—they're ten and twelve now."

"How 'bout you? Do you have kids?" I could tell right away he wished he hadn't asked me the question.

"No. What did you need to see me about?" I replied, hoping he'd change the subject. "Is there something else wrong with the car?" It felt awkward being in Ben's office alone, and I wanted to finish our business and get home to my mom.

"No, no, I'm sorry. I just wanted to check to see how the appointment went. You were both pretty shook up the other night, and I was hoping maybe you'd gotten some good news in Des Moines."

"It wasn't what we'd hoped to hear. We have to be back early tomorrow for surgery to get as many of the tumors out as possible. Mom's in for the fight of her life, and she's probably going to lose it." The words came out at the same time as tears began rolling down my cheeks.

Ben reached behind his desk and placed a box of tissues in front of me. "Oh Cass, I'm so sorry." He started to come around his desk, but I stood up, keeping him at bay.

"No, I'm fine" I said, putting the strap from my purse over my shoulder to leave. He retreated to his chair, aware of the fact I didn't want him to comfort me.

"How can I help?" he asked.

"There's nothing you can do—but thank you."

"How 'bout we go to Sully's and grab a beer and a hamburger? It would take your mind off this for a little while. I'd love to catch up . . ."

"No, I need to get back to my mom. She hardly spoke all the way home, and I need to see how she's feeling about what's ahead. Maybe another time?" I wasn't sure if I wanted there to be another time or not but left the door open just in case.

"I'll hold you to that," he said sincerely. I could tell he wanted to say more, so I hesitated before leaving.

. "Cass . . . I'm glad you've had the life you wanted. And look at me—now I'm running the shop like I always dreamed about. Everything turned out the way it was supposed to."

He had no idea how imperfect things were in my life. I felt

sad thinking of what might have been between us under different circumstances. The only silver lining was that Ben seemed happy. I felt grateful he'd been able to move on despite the way I'd treated him.

There was no way we could achieve the resolution we needed with a discussion lasting less than five minutes, but I hoped someday we'd be able to get that closure.

"Thanks. It really is good to see you again," I said with a smile. Still the same great guy he was in his teens, Ben hadn't changed at all.

We said our goodbyes, and I walked out into the cold to find Mom's car running and warmed for me. I knew Ben probably treated all his customers this well, but it made me feel special anyway.

***

Pulling into Mom's driveway, I could see the light on above the stove through the plantation shutters in the kitchen. I remembered how she'd left the light on when I was out with my friends or had a school activity bringing me home after dark, and I appreciated it more as an adult than I ever had as a teenager.

The thought of losing her was terrifying. Panic began to take hold, and I took deep breaths to get things under control. My therapist had taught me how to curb the terrible onset of anxiety, which had been an issue for most of my adult life.

First Graham and now my mom; soon I'd be all alone in the world. Even my own daughter would never know who I was, and it was a punishment I deserved for giving her up.

A fire burned in the fireplace as Mom sipped tea in her comfortable leather chair. If I hadn't known how devastated she must have felt, I'd have thought she was having an ideal winter night at home.

"Everything good with the car?" she asked as she glanced up from reading the pamphlets we'd received at the doctor's office. "Yeah. Ben says everything's fine—something came loose from somewhere, and all I know is he fixed it. We shouldn't have any more problems with it."

"Oh, that's good. Come . . . sit with me."

"How are you doing, Mom?" I sat down on the ottoman in front of her, feeling the lump forming in my throat again.

"I've been thinking about all of this. You know, even though the doctor said it's probably terminal, it doesn't mean I don't have some time to live."

"You could have several years. There are treatments and things we can do. I'll get on the phone with any colleagues I can think of to help us."

"There's one thing I want you to promise me."

"What's that?" I asked.

"I want you to be honest with me. Don't fill me full of false hope. If things look better than what we think they might, I'm going to be the first one dancing in the street. If I don't have much time, let's make sure we spend it wisely."

Kneeling beside her chair, I laid my head in her lap and felt like a little girl again. "I can't make it without you. We're going to fight this."

"Oh, honey," she said quietly as she stroked my hair. "You're going to be without me *someday*. I don't know how long we've got, but more than anything, I want you to be okay. You've been on your own since you were eighteen.

You're stronger than you think, and I promise you, I'll always be with you. Maybe not in the physical sense, but in your heart—no matter what happens."

She had no idea how hard it had been for me over the years. "I'm sorry I've been gone for so long," I said, dreading how quickly her health might deteriorate.

"No matter when death comes, it never feels like you've had enough time. Let's promise each other we'll spend the next few weeks or months we have making up for all the time we've lost. Let's treat it like the gift we've been given and try to embrace it."

Mom remained positive even when we were facing the worst possible circumstances, and I wanted her to have more years to her life than what it appeared she was going to be given.

***

It seemed like hours passed as we waited in the prep area while at least a dozen people got Mom ready for surgery. Des Moines General was a big hospital, and the Heartland Cancer Center made up only a small part of the campus. There were many clinicians involved in the pre-op room, each coming in to assess the situation before they got started. I was glad no one knew me, because sometimes when you were a doctor, other physicians expected you to know what was going on.

I needed to be a daughter and have the medical professionals take me by the hand through each agonizing step of my mother's day. They finally asked me to say my goodbyes and go to the waiting area.

"I need to go now. The sooner you get into surgery, the quicker you'll be out," I said, kissing her on the cheek.

"I'm going to take a nice long nap, and we'll face the future in a few hours."

"Please take good care of my mom," I said to a nurse as she attached a saline bag to Mom's IV. "You have no idea what a wonderful woman you're working on today."

My aunts would be with me during the lengthy surgery, and it gave me comfort to know I wasn't going to be alone on such a scary day. I had so much love for them knowing they continued their commitment to Mom and me after my dad died. They could have lost touch with us but kept us in their lives after his death as he would have wanted them to. Having them with me made me feel as if a part of my dad was there too.

A surgical waiting area is an unusual place. For most families, there are a few relatives waiting for each patient, abiding by some unwritten rule about the number of people allowed for such a private occasion. Other families treat the day of surgery like a family reunion, complete with loud laughter and pizza deliveries.

We had the bad luck to be sitting near one of those families. The time did go a little faster listening to how one of the sons had a botched vasectomy, which led to the birth of two more children after they thought they were done having kids.

The area was intended to make families feel at home with recliners and comfortable sofas in carefully arranged pods. The colors were subdued and there was contemporary artwork on the walls. I knew the soothing decor was designed to help people deal with the fact their loved one was unconscious and being cut open by a stranger, but it wasn't enough to calm me through the hours of worried anticipation.

An information desk sat on one side of the room with a bank of vending machines on the other. You could get about anything you wanted, including cappuccino and sushi, if you were brave enough to eat sushi out of a vending machine.

I found the thought of food nauseating, but if you were waiting for someone who was having their gall bladder removed or resetting a bone after falling on the ice, you might be more apt to be hungry. My aunts weren't going to let something like a little surgery keep them from snacking all afternoon, and they came armed with enough bags of candy and packages of cheese crackers to feed us for a week.

I watched as families were taken back to meet with doctors and wondered what each person was facing. How many were waiting for results that would mean approaching death for their loved ones? I didn't know which was harder, being the family or the doctor. Broaching difficult topics had never been my strong suit, and I hated giving bad news to people.

A large monitor mounted above the information desk showed a screen with the status of each patient listed by individual number, and I watched as Josephine Garrett went from *surgery prep* to *procedure in progress*.

As the hours dragged on, my aunts told stories of when my mom and dad were first dating. " . . . and remember when Josie snuck back in at two in the morning, and her dad was sitting in his chair smoking? All she could see was the orange butt of his cigarette." They both giggled at the memory. "Well, maybe that's a story for a different time," Aunt Barb said, with a wink and a chuckle. "I can't enjoy it if Josie isn't here to add the part where her dad says, '*A little late isn't it?*'"

They resumed their laughter, which ended in a melancholy absence of going on with more of the story.

"I'm going to get some coffee. Do you two want any?" I needed a break from them even more than caffeine and figured a trip to the cafeteria might be a good diversion for me. They were driving me nuts, but I knew my lack of patience for them was unfounded. They were doing the right thing by being with me, but my anxiety made me want to retreat into myself, which was hard to do with them cackling on either side of me.

It would be at least a couple more hours before we heard anything, and I didn't know how I was going to make small talk and happily recall family memories when all I cared about was finding out what we were facing.

I had no choice but to suck it up and get through the waiting purgatory with the two of them, trying to remember to be grateful they were there. The coffees would be an apology of sorts; a peace offering they didn't know they deserved.

Chapter Eight
May 1996

Mark and Leslie Sinclair were waiting for me at the airport in Los Angeles. I'd never seen such traffic, not even when I'd gone on a field trip to Chicago in tenth grade. I was glad they were willing to park and come in to meet me, because I don't know how I would have found them otherwise.

They'd left the twins at Leslie's parents because they said they wanted me to get settled and go over some of the rules of the household before having the girls meet me again. They were nice enough, but they were all business. I was working for them over the summer, but I'd kind of hoped it would be more like my summers with Turner.

Leslie started, "I like to choose my own sitter for the girls, but because you're so important to Steve and Jess, I'm willing to do this favor for them, even if it wouldn't be my first choice." She put me in my place immediately, and I understood our relationship wasn't going to be one of friendship.

Mark chimed in sternly, "You'll need to make grades and find your own way . . . although we're here for you in an emergency as we said we would be." An insincere smile punctuated his statement.

Leslie started in again, "Our home is your home, but after dinner each night we'd prefer you go to your suite and give us some family time. Please be up and ready to go by 7:00 a.m. each morning, which is when we'll be out the door to work. We'd like for you to keep things cleaned up, and every couple of days empty the trash cans from throughout the house. The housekeeper comes every Friday, but we like the house tidied up daily."

"This probably sounds a little regimented, but we would've hired someone to work for us under these guidelines had we not been asked to consider you for this position. You're going to have to abide by our rules if this is going to work," Mark added.

I couldn't help but think of Cinderella while they were talking, even though I was grateful they were allowing me to stay with them and tried to concentrate on the positive things they were saying.

Dr. Sinclair and Jess had gone to so much trouble for me already. Helping me with the set up to go to California and work for the summer and then have Leslie's law firm handle the adoption was the perfect plan. I'd have my own space, and the girls and I would have activities to do. Mark and Leslie would be gone most of every day, so I wouldn't feel like the burden to them they were describing.

With the *pleasantries* out of the way, I was shown the efficiency apartment above the garage. Mark brought my bags up, and I began to get unpacked. The boxes I'd mailed to myself via UPS had been delivered, and they were stacked next to the queen-sized bed. The room wasn't fancy, but it would be comfortable.

There was a kitchenette along one wall with a small table and two chairs in the corner. A sofa divided the room in half, and a TV sat on top of a dresser that had been cleaned out for my use. There were ample hangers and blankets in the closet by the front door. The small apartment was sufficient for what I needed, and it would be a nice home for a few months.

The girls' grandparents arrived around dinnertime, and I was introduced as the summer nanny. The twins didn't seem to remember me from when I'd watched them on New Year's Eve, but I was confident we'd get along well once we got to know each other again.

I went to my room with a VISA card in hand and the keys to one of the cars, which would be mine to use for the summer. Leslie suggested I get a few items from the Target store not far from their home, and I looked at the credit card and saw it had my name on it. She told me the card was for necessities, gas, and anything I'd do with the children over the summer like movies or getting lunch at the pool.

Wow, I hadn't expected my own credit card!

I headed out to grab a few items and went through a drive through to pick up a salad. When the teenage boy told me my dinner would be $7.02, I handed him the credit card with my name on it. I got back to the apartment and spent the rest of the evening unpacking, falling asleep early in the comfy bed high above the Sinclair's cars and bicycles.

***

Each day I woke up early and took a quick shower so I could be in the Sinclair's kitchen by 6:50 a.m. I could tell they appreciated my prompt arrival each morning, and I wanted to do what I could to please them.

Some days Leslie headed out earlier, but Mark never left before 7:30. Sometimes he would spend time talking with me while he drank his morning coffee. It wasn't long before I realized if it were up to Mark, there wouldn't be as many rules to be followed in the household. At times, Leslie treated him like an employee too.

Emma and Libby were nice little girls and well-behaved. I enjoyed my time with them and found myself looking forward to watching them each day and taking them to the park or swimming lessons. Leslie left a list of ideas for activities each week, and we did almost all of them to keep her happy.

Since Mark and Leslie were usually home by early evening, I had several hours after being dismissed from my daytime duties to enjoy some private time. Much of it was spent talking to Ben on the phone and trying to convince him we were doing the right thing by giving up our baby.

Once a week, I'd talk with my mom and fill her in with mostly lies about how things were going in California. She wanted to know about the weather and how I liked the family I was working for. She tried to persuade me she should come out before classes in the fall to help me get settled in the dorms—but I couldn't let that happen.

I'd told her Mark and Leslie knew someone who was renting out a small apartment near campus, which would be cheaper than the dorms, and they'd told me they could help me get moved in. She was hurt by the fact I didn't want her to come to California, and it was hard to convince her of my feelings when I'd never needed her more. She also worried about me not being with other kids in student housing so I could make friends, but I assured her I'd get involved in other activities with people my age after school started.

It didn't seem feasible to move into the dorms when I was having a baby so soon after. When my child's adoptive parents offered to pay for an apartment, I jumped at the chance. It would give me more privacy, and after the baby came, I could worry about fitting into the routine of an average college student. Being the pregnant girl in a co-ed dorm would be a hard label to overcome.

Leslie's OB-GYN took care of my check-ups, and I had anything provided to me that I needed. Jess called once a week to give support and advice. Even though Leslie was working on the adoption, Jess assured me we could change our minds if we wanted to.

We could even have an open adoption where we could have contact with our little girl as she grew up. I kept coming back to the same conclusion. If I wanted to be a part of the baby's life, I'd raise her myself. Wasn't the entire point to keep the pregnancy a secret and move on with our lives?

***

The summer went by quickly, but living with Mark and Leslie had shown me they weren't as happy as they portrayed to the outside world.

Leslie was a control freak, always making sure everyone knew she called the shots in their house. I didn't know if she was threatened by the fact the girls seemed to love me, but there was no doubt she needed to have the upper hand at all times.

She insisted the family eat only healthy foods and even left a list of exactly what she wanted the girls to consume each day. If we varied from the menus, she'd get angry, acting as if serving strawberries when she'd asked me to feed them grapes was a major deviation from her instructions.

Mark usually put up with her demands, but I'd found a few junk food wrappers stuffed deep in the trash when I cleaned up his office each day, letting me know he didn't always follow her stringent rules. It was ridiculous a grown man had to sneak a Snickers bar and try to get rid of the evidence just to keep his wife happy.

Sometimes I'd hear yelling coming from the house in the evenings. I'd turn off the television to try to figure out what was going on but could never hear anything but muffled arguing. It was mostly Leslie's voice, with quieter responses from Mark—but it happened often enough I got used to it as a regular occurrence.

One night, I made a quick trip down the back stairs with a bag of trash from my apartment. I was startled to hear Mark speak to me from the behind the garage, and it made me uncomfortable to meet him unexpectedly outside their house.

"Hey, Cassie. I'm out here…didn't want to scare you," he said as he took a drag off a joint.

"Oh . . . no—you didn't scare me," I said, even though he had. I was surprised to see him puffing away, obviously hiding from Leslie's watchful eye.

"Please don't tell Leslie you saw me out here smoking," he said.

"Yeah . . . I won't. It's none of my business. Is everything okay?" I asked.

"Everything's just peachy," he said sarcastically.

"Well, I'd better get to bed." I quickly put the bag in the trash can and turned to leave.

"I'm sorry about Leslie," he continued. "She's really not a bad person." Leslie was always on my case, so I knew Mark was referring to her treatment of me. If you had to clarify someone wasn't a bad person, there was a good chance they probably were.

"Of course, she isn't. You've both been so good to me this summer." I didn't want to rock the boat when I had such a brief time left with them.

"You know, I really admire you. Getting pregnant in high school and having the guts to give the baby up so you aren't tied down to a dead-end marriage shows how smart you are."

The conversation felt completely inappropriate. I didn't know where his relaxed observations of life were leading, but I had an idea he was headed for the bag of Cheetos I'd seen hidden in his office as soon as the munchies set in.

I was living with people I really didn't know, and the uncomfortable interaction with Mark made me glad it was almost time to move on. If we were caught by Leslie behind the garage, she'd have me out of there the next morning assuming the worst of both of us.

"Goodnight," I said, heading back up the stairs to the apartment.

"Yeah . . . goodnight," he said as he inhaled again and slid down the wall to sit on the bare ground.

I didn't like the feeling of discovering another side of Mark. I locked the door behind me and pulled one of the chairs from the dining table over and placed it under the doorknob to secure it, trying to put aside the unpleasant feeling in the pit of my stomach.

***

I entered the kitchen one early morning to find Mark and Leslie sitting at the breakfast bar looking serious.

"Hi," I said. "Is everything all right?" They seemed more tense than normal as if I'd interrupted an argument in progress.

"No, things are not all right. I need to ask you something, and it's very important you answer truthfully," Leslie said angrily.

"What is it?" I asked as I quickly reviewed in my head the events of the previous few days, wondering if she was unhappy with something I'd done with the girls.

"I found some marijuana in the back of the hall closet and want to know if it's yours." She was asking a question, but her face told me she thought she already knew the answer.

"No, I don't smoke pot," I said, looking her directly in the eye. I didn't know if Mark had blamed me for his drugs, or if she was just assuming it belonged to me.

"I told her it was mine, but she doesn't believe me," Mark said coldly. "Why would Cassie hide drugs in *our* house, when she has an apartment of her own?" he continued. I felt relief at knowing he wasn't trying to pin the discovery on me and could tell his statement had her considering the possibilities.

"Maybe she stuck it in there when one of us got home early from work and was going to retrieve it later," she added, shooting an accusing glance at me.

"I don't know anything about it," I said again, pleading with her to believe me. "I don't smoke pot, not even when I'm not pregnant."

"Why are you covering for her?" she asked Mark accusingly. "I've never seen you smoke in your entire life. If she's on drugs, I don't want her anywhere around our girls."

If she found out the pot was his, did it mean she wouldn't allow

Mark to be around their children?

"Guess what? You don't know everything about me. I like to smoke, and I've been doing it for years. The fact you aren't aware of it just proves you can't control everything in our lives." Mark was taking the opportunity to stand up for himself, and it was a declaration of independence I didn't want to witness.

Leslie told me to go back to the garage apartment and she'd be up to talk with me before she left for work. I headed upstairs feeling like my days might be numbered at the Sinclair house. What if she didn't believe me and kicked me out? I wouldn't have any place to go except home, with the birth of my baby following soon after. I waited in fear for nearly an hour before she came upstairs to give me her verdict.

"It seems I owe you an apology," she offered tersely from the open doorway. "I'd appreciate it if you'd keep this between us, I don't need anyone else knowing our business. Mark has assured me this won't be a problem in the future, and I'm sorry I accused you." She turned and went back downstairs to her car and left for work without saying anything else.

When I returned to the kitchen, the girls were eating cereal and Mark was drinking his coffee. I didn't know what to say, hoping it would be swept under the rug and never discussed again.

"I'm sorry, Cassie. I tried to convince her it was mine, but she wouldn't believe me. You should never have been drawn into our problems, but thanks for keeping your mouth shut. I respect the hell out of you for not saying more than you did."

"Daddy, you said a naughty word," Libby piped in as both girls laughed.

"It's okay," I said. "Just so she believes me. I need this job and don't know what I'd do if she told me I had to leave."

"That's not going to happen. She believes you. I *did* have to give up my favorite hiding place . . . but once I showed her another stash, she knew it was mine."

I couldn't believe Mark would protect me at his own expense but was happy it looked like I could stay put for a few more weeks. We never spoke of the incident again, but I relished each day taking me closer to the time when I could get out of there.

***

It was early on the morning of September 20th, and I could hear birds singing as they announced the arrival of another ideal California day. Every single day had bright sunshine and blue sky overhead. You'd think it would be a welcome change from the weather of Iowa, but I hated it.

I'd started classes at Berkeley the second week of September, the only obviously pregnant girl on campus. I thought I would also be the only person who didn't look like they'd grown up surfing on the California coast, but my assumptions were wrong.

Berkeley had a diverse group of students. There were hundreds of new first-years from all over the world. Everyone looked and acted differently from what I was used to, and my pregnancy didn't seem to warrant a second look from anyone who might have noticed.

I tried to layer my clothing to hide my protruding stomach in the first days of classes and spoke with each professor letting them know I would be missing class for at least a week. They were all understanding and said they'd work with me if I kept in contact to let them know what was going on. No one else seemed to care, and I was grateful to be able to blend into the student body without issue.

The neon orange numbers on the alarm clock next to my bed told me there was time to snooze before I needed to head to the train station to catch a ride to class. I'd finished babysitting Emma and Libby for the summer once classes started but would continue living in the garage apartment until the baby came.

As I dozed in and out of sleep, my stomach clenched and relaxed. Braxton Hicks contractions, or so my doctor told me when I'd thought I was going into labor a couple of weeks earlier. I'd taken a cab home from school and gone directly to the doctor's office only to have Leslie pick me up later after finding out it had been a false alarm.

She was mad since she'd been working on a big trial and had to leave work early because of my stupidity, but I had no idea you could feel like you were having a baby when you weren't actually having one. Leslie couldn't cut me a break. It was my first time being pregnant, and she hadn't been the warmest of hosts. I didn't feel like I could ask her any of the important questions about the actual process of giving birth to another human being.

The alarm went off, and I leaned over to hit the snooze button again. Rolling back over in bed, I felt a warm liquid rush from inside me to the sheets below. A terror gripped me so tightly I audibly gasped. It was still over a week until my due date, and I wasn't ready to face giving birth yet.

I felt queasy, and my head throbbed. I laid there a few more minutes and thought about what to do. If my water *had* broken, I needed to get to the hospital. What if I'd peed the bed because the baby was sitting on my bladder causing another false alarm? Maybe I'd take the train to the clinic and get it checked out before I caused Leslie to miss any more work. At the very least, I could sneak to the doctor's office unnoticed and alert the Sinclairs later if necessary.

I took a quick shower and put on some loose-fitting clothes, pulling my hair back in a ponytail. I rubbed Vaseline on my dry, cracked lips. Everything about my body had gone haywire over the past few months, and it was a full-time job keeping myself comfortable.

A hard contraction tightened my belly and took my breath away. Maybe it would be smarter to drive, that way I'd have a car at the hospital if needed, and no one would have to retrieve it from the train station if this wasn't another false alarm.

Pulling out of the driveway, I could see the Sinclair's lights on in the kitchen. Leslie would be getting ready to head to work after her early morning exercise class, and Mark would be thinking about waking the girls up, which was his job now that I wasn't responsible for the children each day.

They would never notice I left early, and if they did, I would say I'd met a friend for breakfast before class.

Like I had a lot of friends....

I drove several miles before another contraction overcame me. This one was so strong I had to pull over to the side of the road. Terrified and not sure what to do, I knew there was a smaller hospital close by. It wasn't the one where my doctor's office was or where we planned to have the baby, but I needed to get to medical attention quickly.

I pulled down a side street making my way to Oaklawn Community Hospital.

Chapter Nine
December 2014

Families came in and out, leaving my aunts and me alone in the waiting room by late afternoon. As worry began to set in, my name was finally called. I was led to a small room to wait for the doctor to appear and give me Mom's prognosis. The twenty-one minutes spent in the sterile room seemed like hours, yet I didn't want Dr. Bryn to open the door and snuff out my hope for a positive outcome.

"Dr. Garrett," she started as she walked into the room, "Your mom did well, considering. I was able to get most of the tumors out, and she's in recovery now. She'll go to the ICU for the night, and then we'll get her transferred into her own room if possible. You can see her for fifteen minutes per hour and longer if you can sweet talk the nurses." Dr. Bryn wore pale green scrubs and clean white tennis shoes. A white mask dangled in front of her face revealing freshly applied lipstick on a mouth that would tell me what I needed to know.

Dr. Bryn was giving me all the basics, but I needed more. "What about the staging?" I was most interested in finding out how far the cancer had invaded my mom's body.

"We won't know for sure until the pathology comes back on the lymph nodes. We took twenty-two of them, and they'll tell us how far this thing has spread. We also put in a port, so if we need to do chemo, we won't have to go back in to place that device."

That sounded encouraging, didn't it?

Dr. Bryn went on, "To be honest with you, it doesn't look good. My best guess is late stage three as we discussed, and at worst stage four with maybe a few weeks or months to live. We'll know more after the tests come back. I've put a rush on them, and I'll plan to talk with you during rounds tomorrow when we know more."

"Thank you," I said, wondering why a person says "*thank you*" when they're given a bad report. She turned to leave, and her white tennis shoes made a squeaking sound on the polished marble floor as if she was making a break on the basketball court and not delivering a crushing blow changing our lives forever.

I sat by myself for a few minutes, knowing as soon as I left the room we'd start down a big hill. We'd pick up speed as time continued, unable to stop until my mom was dead. If I sat there and let the doctor's words sink in, it seemed like we could sit perched on that peak without moving in either direction. It wasn't fair to let my aunts wonder any longer, so I took a deep breath and headed back to the surgical waiting room.

They were holding hands as I approached them. They had each other making it easier for them. "Mom came through the surgery well. Dr. Bryn got most of the tumors, and we won't know much of anything else until the labs come back tomorrow."

I let the words hang in the air without adding more. It was all they needed for the moment, and it would give the two of them another night of hopeful sleep.

We all hugged before they got ready to leave, and I didn't feel like crying anymore. It was time to figure out how to care for my mom, not to cry over something that couldn't be changed. My mom needed me to step up to the plate, and I was going to embrace the chance to make up for years of absence.

***

The waiting room near the intensive care unit was large and set up in areas where families could sleep and gather during their loved one's stay. I chose a spot in an alcove with two chairs that could be made into beds and a small table between them. I decided to get some bedding from the nurse's station, staking my claim like a pioneer in the Wild West.

I unfolded one of the sleeping chairs and covered it with the sheets and blanket I'd retrieved from a utility closet near the head nurse's desk. Once the bed was made, I sat in the chair across from it and checked my cell phone. The phone indicated two messages were recorded, and I held it to my ear to listen.

"Cassidy, this is Janice from the law firm of Stockdale, Billings and Sommers. Please don't forget your meeting on Wednesday with Keith Sommers at 1:00 p.m. to go over the paperwork for your divorce. Thank you."

I wouldn't be making the meeting with Mr. Sommers, and his appointments were so hard to come by. The call reminded me my mom's illness wasn't the only thing that needed to be managed in my life. I'd have to call and reschedule.

The second one was from an Elmwood number I didn't recognize. I pushed the voicemail icon to listen to the message.

"Cassie—it's Ben. I wanted to check on your mom. Call

me if you want. It's okay if you don't. Know I'm thinking about both of you. "

Checking in on us was so thoughtful of him, and hearing his voice reminded me again how much I'd cared about Ben. He was the only man in my life, except for my dad, who'd ever made me feel a sense of security.

I sent him a quick text letting him know Mom had made it through surgery and added his phone number to my contacts. Something told me we weren't finished with our conversation from a few days earlier. With a sick mother and a divorce in process, I wasn't in a place where I could consider having a romantic relationship with anyone. However, Ben's friendship would be a welcome distraction.

As I put my phone away, I heard my name being called over the intercom and knew they must have Mom settled in her ICU room. I left a book and an empty cup next to the chair by my bed hoping they'd be enough to hold my place for the night.

Mom laid motionless in the hospital bed with her head leaning to one side. Her eyes were closed and her breathing steady. She had a good-sized drain removing blood from the surgery site. I checked to see how much fluid had been taken off. I didn't want any blood backing up making her even sicker.

I pulled a folding chair from the corner and sat it next to the bed. I leaned in close to her ear and whispered, "I'm here, Mom."

She moved slightly and tried to open her eyes. "It's okay, just sleep. That's the best thing you can do right now." She tried to say something, drifting off again without uttering a word. She would be this way for a few more hours, but I would take every opportunity to be in the room with her. I was sure it would be the first of many long nights.

True to her word, Dr. Bryn made rounds at 10:00 a.m. and had the pathology report in hand when she entered the room. Mom was more alert but still floating in and out of sleep due to the effects of morphine and hydrocodone.

Dr. Bryn started the conversation by saying, "Since you're a doctor, Cassie, I'm not going to pull any punches." Whenever someone started a conversation with those words, you always felt like you'd been punched in the gut.

"We've got a serious situation here," she continued. "Most of the lymph nodes came back positive, so we're at a late stage three ovarian cancer diagnosis for sure. With her age and overall health being what it is we could try a round of chemo and see what happens. I can't promise anything, and in fact, you should prepare yourself for the worst."

I looked at my mom's delicate face, only to find her asleep again. I was thankful I could take the news for both of us. She had enough to handle just getting through the surgery.

"We need to get her stabilized and healed, and then we can look at options for treatment. That will be at least 6-8 weeks, and a lot can change in that amount of time with someone as sick as your mom."

"You don't know Josephine Garrett, Dr. Bryn," I said as if all of Mom's good deeds could keep her alive despite her diagnosis.

"Well, she'll have the best care thanks to you, Cassie. I wish you both the best. I'll see you tomorrow, but I'll have her transferred to the regular surgical floor as soon as I can. You'll be much more at home there, and there won't be as many rules."

Mom slept most of the day and was moved to her own room later in the afternoon. It was a nice change, with a leather recliner for me to sit in as well as a sofa that made into a bed. I didn't plan to bring up Dr. Bryn's visit until she asked specifically, and that didn't take long.

"Did the results come back yet?" she asked hopefully.

"Yeah, Mom. They did. Lots of your nodes came back positive, which means the cancer has spread. But Dr. Bryn thinks you could benefit from chemo. I'm going to be here every step of the way making sure you have everything you need. You won't have to worry about anything, and all you have to do is concentrate on getting better."

"Oh, Cassie. What about your life?"

"You are my life, Mom. You're all I have."

The conversation ended as she drifted back to sleep. I settled on the couch and took out my laptop to begin drafting an email to the clinic to tell them I wouldn't be returning to work . . . *ever*.

***

I'd just fallen asleep when there was a quiet knock at the door. "Come in," I said cheerfully as if we were expecting guests for a party and not trying to rest after another long day in the hospital.

The door opened slightly, and Ben poked his head in. "Hey, special delivery for Mrs. Garrett!" he said as he entered the room carrying a beautiful glass vase filled with flowers and a bright colored balloon attached to it.

"Ben . . ." I got up and quickly started to tidy the room and myself for our unexpected visitor. I felt like I was in the hospital right along with Mom and knew I probably looked terrible.

Ben set the flowers on the windowsill and then went to Mom's bedside. "Hi, Mrs. Garrett. How are you feeling?"

Had Ben driven to Des Moines just to visit us?

"Thanks, Ben. How nice of you to drop by and see me. And the flowers are gorgeous—thank you so much!" Mom was more alert and was smiling for the first time in days at receiving such a beautiful bouquet.

"What are you doing here?" I asked, hoping my reaction didn't come off as rude.

"I hope I'm not intruding," Ben started. "I had to bring my boys to Des Moines. Angie's parents moved here a couple of years ago when her dad took a job at one of the big churches out in Waukee. Her mom has extended family in the area, and they're celebrating the holidays on New Year's Day this year. I'm helping out by delivering the kids so thought I'd stop by on my way out of town. I figured the two of you would be throwing a big New Year's Eve bash tonight for everyone on your floor!" he joked.

It *was* New Year's Eve. I'd lost track of time once Mom and I 'd entered the world of ovarian cancer. I hated New Year's Eve, and this year was no different. As the calendar changed over to another year with a fresh start, I was always reminded of past regrets and decisions that couldn't be changed.

We visited for a few minutes, discussing the weather and the holidays, and then Ben said it was time for him to leave.

He asked if we needed anything, and when we assured him we didn't, he headed for the door.

"I'll walk Ben out," I said to Mom as I followed behind him. We went a short distance to a family lounge at the end of the hall and sat down to talk.

"How's she really doing?" he asked quietly.

That's all I needed to dissolve into a puddle of tears brought on by lack of sleep, too much caffeine, and the prospect of being alone in the world. I felt safe with Ben, and his kindness allowed me to let my guard down and feel the honest emotions I tried to hold in when I was with Mom.

"It'll be okay, Cass. She's a strong woman; she can beat this thing." Ben put his arms around me and let me cry, and I allowed myself to be consoled by him.

"She isn't stronger than ovarian cancer. This thing is a killer. Although she may have some time—I'm going to lose her."

"Let me stay with you, you shouldn't be alone. I can sit out here in the waiting area, and you can take a break every couple of hours or so, and we can talk. I'll watch the bowl games just like if I was at home, and you won't feel so alone on a night when you're supposed to be dressed up and drinking champagne."

"No, Ben. I'm fine," I couldn't help but think of another New Year's Eve when I let Ben stay with me, and that didn't turn out so well.

"You don't have to face this alone, and I want to help however you need me to. I owe you that much . . . and I obviously don't have anything else planned for New Year's Eve."

Ben was just as wonderful as I'd remembered. Since that

night at the repair shop, I'd been going through everything in my mind that had been said and done in our past.

"Ben, it's the other way around. I feel so bad at how I handled myself all those years ago. I don't even deserve for you to talk to me. Let alone *be there for me* in this situation. I was young and immature, dealing with the most important decision of my life. I screwed up—I ran when I should've faced the problem head on. But none of it can be changed, and now we're just two people who are no longer connected, and you don't owe me anything."

"We'll always be connected. No one can take away the fact that we made a beautiful little girl together. We did the right thing for the right reasons. Everyone's a winner in this situation."

"It wasn't a game to win or lose. We could have raised our little girl. I should have listened to you instead of worrying about what people would think. I've taken so much from you, and my mom, and even myself. We could have done it if we'd only tried. I took the opportunity away from all of us."

"You're exhausted, and I'm sure your emotions are all over the place—so try to give yourself a break. I heard you're going through a divorce, too, and I just feel so bad for you to be dealing with all of this. We've moved on with our lives, but the one thing that's never changed is that I care about you. I just wanted you to know how I felt, and I wasn't able to tell you the other night."

This was a lot of information to take into my already saturated brain. I wondered who'd told him I was single again. It wasn't a secret since my entire family knew, but I had no idea my personal life was on the Elmwood grapevine.

"Ben, I'm going through a lot right now. The only thing I

can possibly consider at this point is getting to know an old friend again." I wasn't sure what Ben was trying to convey to me, but I needed to put the brakes on his feelings before one of us said something we'd regret.

Ben smiled and put his hand on mine. "If it's a friend you need, then I'm here for you. I also think you need a decent meal and a good night's sleep. I'm going to go across the street and get you some food and a reservation at the Hampton Inn attached to the hospital, and you're going to get out of here. You can come back in the morning when it's 2015—refreshed and ready to take on whatever needs to be done."

"But what if Mom needs me?" The offer was really tempting. Another night on a piece of furniture that made into an uncomfortable sleeping surface sounded awful.

"It's right across the street—they'll call you if she needs you. As a *friend*, I'm telling you that this is what you need more than anything else, and taking care of yourself will help your mom in the long run.

It wasn't a half hour before Ben came back with a club sandwich and some soup, along with the key to a room with a king-size bed, which would give me the best sleep I'd had in a long time. Mom had agreed with Ben that I needed to get some better rest, and she promised me she'd keep her cell phone with her at all times in case she couldn't get a nurse to respond to her.

With Ben on his way back to Elmwood and my mom tucked into bed with a fresh shift of nurses ready for the sound of her call button, I walked across the skywalk to the Hampton Inn.

I looked out over the city of Des Moines and could see the

hustle and bustle of a New Year's Eve just getting started. People were dressed up and going in and out of restaurants along the street below. It reminded me of a life without so many worries and soon to be ex-husbands and dying mothers.

As I'd done every year since my senior year in high school, I thought back to the New Year's Eve that changed my life forever and reflected on the conversation Ben and I had just had. Each December 31st, I took an internal assessment and always came up with the same conclusion. We'd had no choice but to give our daughter up for adoption. Everything else was just collateral damage.

At the time, it was our little girl's future that mattered the most. Ben was right, I was exhausted and feeling guilty about things that couldn't be changed.

Once settled in my room at the hotel, my mind finally shut down, and I fell into a deep sleep on the fluffy pillow top mattress of room 807. I'd been asleep for more than three hours when the rest of the Midwest celebrated the start of 2015.

Chapter Ten
September 1996

The dark-haired physician introduced herself as she entered my room. "Cassidy, I'm Dr. Ingman. What brings you here? I'm assuming you have your own doctor and have been having regular pre-natal visits?"

"Yes, I've been seeing Dr. Peters at California Pacific Medical Center but decided to come to the closest hospital. My water broke a while ago or maybe I peed myself, and my contractions and pain are getting worse. I know this could be false labor, so I wanted to see before going further."

"Let me do a quick check of your cervix, and we'll know what we're dealing with. How close are your contractions?" Dr. Ingman asked as she tried to calm me.

"Maybe 5 minutes or so. And they're getting worse, and I got scared, and..." I began to cry as another hard contraction, this one more painful than all of them combined, overtook my entire body.

Dr. Ingman helped me into the stirrups and did an internal exam. The next contraction was so strong it felt like my insides were ripping open. The excruciating pain made me feel like I'd lost control of everything.

"Okay, you're progressing quickly. There's no time to do

anything but get you into a labor room and prepare for this baby. Is there someone we can call for you? I would guess this won't take long, so whoever it is better be close or they're going to miss this birth."

Dr. Ingman didn't know me and had no idea about the adoption. In that moment of realization, I decided to have the baby by myself. After I saw her I could decide what I wanted to do. No one would whisk her away and make assumptions about my rights or what was best for all of us. All the lying, and planning, and sacrifices for this moment came down to me and my baby anyway. I could change my mind if I wanted to. Jess had made that clear to me during the entire process.

"I'm alone, so there's no one to call," I said quietly, touching the heart shaped locket hanging around my neck. It was a little piece of Ben with me for the most important moment of my life.

"Okay, well—we're having a baby today! Do you know if it's a boy or a girl?"

"Yes, it's a girl," I said proudly.

"Do you have a name picked out for her?" Dr. Ingman asked, giving the nursing staff instructions for my move to a labor room.

"I'm not sure yet. I might name her after my mom." It wasn't the truth, but it was what I wished I could do.

"Well, I'm sure your mom would be honored to have her granddaughter named after her. Will this be her first grandchild?" she inquired.

"Yes," I said with tears streaming down my face. Another painful contraction made me pull my feet up toward my stomach in agony. Jess wasn't flying in for a few days yet, and it had been the plan for her to be with me for the birth.

This little girl was coming quickly and would make an entrance without her adoptive mom by my side. I'd be the only mother she'd know for the first hours of her life.

I thought of my own mom, and wished she was with me. She would never know of this little girl's existence except to see her as the Sinclair's new baby. Mom would run into them at church and gush over the infant who would surely be dressed in pink. She'd be wearing an adorable hat cocked precisely on top of her soft head, smelling of baby lotion and Jess' expensive perfume. This child would have everything she could ever want, except for Josephine Garrett as her grandmother. Maybe it was too big of a price to pay.

When Jess came up with the plan for her and Dr. Sinclair to adopt our little girl, it seemed like the perfect solution to our problem. The fact that Leslie's law firm could oversee the legal end of things only made it easier.

I'd never known Jess and Dr. Sinclair only had Turner because they couldn't have another baby. I'd wondered why Turner was an only child when the Sinclairs had the means to expand their family. I'd thought Jess was pregnant a few times over the years when she wasn't feeling well or looked a little bigger through the middle when she wore a snug top, but nothing ever came of those suspicions.

When I told her about the pregnancy, she opened up to me, telling me how much she longed for more children. She and Dr. Sinclair had something called secondary infertility, which was when you had one child but couldn't get pregnant with another. She said she'd had some kind of surgeries to help her get pregnant, but they'd all failed.

Knowing our baby would have the wonderful life the Sinclairs could give her seemed like the best way out of our dilemma. I'd never have to worry about her at all. She'd be loved and cared for and have every opportunity she could ever want.

It all seemed like such a good plan until I started to think about handing the growing baby inside of me over to someone else. I was so grateful the Sinclairs were willing to take our baby and raise her as their own, but knowing where she was as she grew up would have its own set of challenges.

I couldn't call Jess up when I went home to Elmwood and see if she wanted to go to lunch, because now there would be this thing between us, which would be the most important tie ever but would cut me off from their love as I'd known it. I wanted my baby to have that kind of family but selfishly didn't want to be without it for myself.

The birth process took longer than what Dr. Ingman had originally thought, but the 6 hours flew by to me. I was transferred to a private room with bright lights on the ceiling and a baby bassinet in the corner. The smaller hospital's OB wing was nothing like the one at CPMC where I'd been seeing Leslie's doctor for four months, but it would have to do.

Everything was set for the arrival of my precious bundle of joy; the result of the love Ben and I shared and a night of unprotected sex that never happened again. I knew celibacy couldn't reverse the result of our actions, but I was too scared to do it again.

Our baby's imminent birth proved a pregnancy could happen the first time you had sex, and I wondered if any other girls at my high school had faced a similar circumstance.

I'd call Ben later in the day and tell him first of her birth. Even though I told him I never wanted to see or talk to him again after she was born, I'd promised him one last phone call.

His constant pleading for us to keep the baby and raise her together was too much for me to bear as the birth got closer, and our phone calls had become less frequent to avoid the topic we would never agree on.

Each day I doubted myself a little more, and as she got bigger, I couldn't imagine giving her up. Keeping her wasn't an option either. I couldn't disappoint the Sinclairs after everything they'd done for me or allow myself to toss my dreams away by going back home to Elmwood as an unwed mother with no education or job to support my child.

My labor progressed mightily, and when I didn't think the torture could get much worse, they gave me a shot in my back taking the pain away. I could still feel the pressure of the baby in the birth canal but began to relax and even fell asleep for a few minutes. Had I known how much better the epidural would make me feel—I would have asked for one hours earlier.

They lowered the lights as labor progressed, and over time the room began to fill with people. Finally, Dr. Ingman told me it was time to push. I felt like I'd tumbled into a strange twilight zone of sadness and happiness. As I pushed, inner strength like I'd never felt before came from someplace deep inside.

I strained and grunted and prayed to God to let me know what to do. Before long, I heard the shrill cry of a baby, no longer the result of a mistake or a reason to be resentful of everything I'd given up.

She was a tiny miracle, and I could already tell she'd be a smart and brave girl who might someday cure cancer or win a Nobel Peace Prize. My role in bringing her into the world seemed to make sense and gave me a calm I hadn't felt in months.

"She's so cute, isn't she?" the nurse asked me as I held the little pink bundle in my arms for those first few moments.

"She is," I replied as the perfect baby girl squirmed, and wiggled, and settled into my heart right where she was supposed to be.

It was 5 p.m. before we were taken to our room, and I had the chance to make some calls. Neither Sinclairs would be happy with the situation, but I didn't care about them. I wanted to talk with Ben and make a final decision about what to do. For hours I'd been trying to figure out how to take this baby home and be her mother.

Seeing her and holding her in my arms had made things clearer. Looking at her little face made me love her more than I'd imagined possible. That same mother's love confirmed my decision she should be with the Sinclairs. Ben and I couldn't provide the life she needed, and our baby didn't have time to wait for us to figure it out.

I dialed Ben's number, and he answered on the third ring. It was two hours later in Iowa, and Ben's mom would be off work. I hoped we could talk openly without fear of our conversation being overheard.

"Are you okay?" Ben asked as soon as he knew it was me on the phone. The sound of his voice made me cry. "What's wrong, Cass? Is everything okay with the baby?"

"Are you alone? I don't want anyone to hear you talking to me."

"Yeah, my mom's at the grocery store, and Dad's still at the shop. What's going on?" I could hear the concern in his voice.

"I went into labor this morning, and she's here."

"What? It's not time yet! Are you both all right? Is Jess there with you?"

"No, I'm alone. I kind of snuck over to another hospital and had the baby without anyone knowing. I have to call them when I get off the phone with you . . . " I could barely catch my breath I was crying so hard. My head ached as I wiped my snotty nose on the white bed sheet. "She's beautiful, Ben. We made a perfect little girl together."

The baby laid quietly beside my bed wrapped tightly in a light pink blanket, oblivious to the crossroads of her life. If I took her home and raised her, the only one who would know what I gave up for her would be me. She wouldn't love the Sinclairs or miss their impact on her life, and she would be happy being a simple little girl raised by young parents. It would be okay because she wouldn't know any better. Maybe Ben and I *could* stay together and eventually get married, and we'd be a family.

"I wish I was there. Can you give her a big kiss for me, and tell her Daddy loves her?"

"I will."

"Are you sure about this? Can't I fly out there and bring the two of you home? I can't live without you or our baby. I love you both so much."

"No, Ben. You said I could make the final decision, and I've made it. I'm going to call Leslie after getting off the phone with you, and it's all going to move on from there. We can't give this little girl what she deserves. And if you were here and you saw her, you'd say the same thing. We all have to move on with our lives and forget this ever happened. You promised me if I called you this last time, we would go our separate ways and never speak of this again."

"Even if we don't have the baby, can't we still have each other?"

"No, I can't have one of you without the other. I need to move on with my life here in California, and you need to move on with yours in Iowa. It just wasn't meant to be, but we did a good thing for a family who deserves this little girl. We need to feel good about that. After this, I don't want you to ever contact me again, okay? This is what we decided, and I need for you to keep your word. Otherwise, it's going to be too hard."

"I'm not ever going to feel good about this, but I love you enough to keep my promise. I'll always love both of you, please don't ever forget it." He was sobbing too.

"Did you sign the preliminary papers already?" I asked, part of me hoping he hadn't.

"Yes, everything's done. The attorney is meeting me to sign the final forms, and then there will just be the waiting period." Leslie's law firm had offices all over the country, and someone from their Des Moines branch would be handling Ben's paperwork while her partner in San Francisco was doing mine.

"Okay, everything's settled," I said flatly.

"It is." His voice was quiet.

"I'm sorry, Ben. Never forget how much I love you."

"Don't forget to tell her what I said. I mean it, whisper it in her ear, and make sure she knows how much I wanted her."

"I promise."

Those were the last words we spoke to each other on September 20, 1996, the day of our daughter's birth.

There was one more call I needed to make before informing

the Sinclairs that the baby had been born. I took out my calling card again and dialed my mom.

"Hello?" The sound of her voice made me want to tell her everything and take the next flight home with my new baby swaddled in a sling against my chest.

"Hi, Mom. I wanted to call and say hello." The words cracked a little as they came out.

"What's wrong, honey? You sound sad."

"I'm okay. Just a little homesick...."

"Well, guess what? I was looking at the calendar today, and there are only nine weeks until Thanksgiving," she said excitedly.

"I can't wait to see you." I was glad to know there were still nine weeks left to get myself together before going home again.

"I've been saving up for your plane ticket, and I almost have enough to book it," she said proudly.

"Well, Mom, you don't need to worry. I was able to save so much working for Mark and Leslie this summer, I have enough to get my own ticket, so you don't have to cut back on anything. I'm the one who made the decision to go so far away to school, and I'm the one who should be responsible for paying my way home."

"Are you sure? I don't want you to be short of grocery money or anything." She had no idea I'd be financially comfortable for the first time in my entire life after giving the Sinclairs my child.

"I'm sure. It will all work out. Listen, I've got to go. I just wanted to tell you I love you and can't wait to see you." Truer words were never spoken.

Mark and Leslie were at the hospital in less than an hour after I called them and had the baby moved out of my room soon after their arrival. I knew it would be the case, so I'd spent the last moments before they got there holding my baby girl, telling her everything an eighteen-year-old mom could remember to tell a child she thought she'd never see again.

Leslie was livid I hadn't called them and even more upset I'd delivered at another hospital. She said I'd gone against their wishes and endangered the baby. She added this was exactly why I wasn't mature enough to raise a baby on my own. I didn't care what Leslie thought anymore, and her insults couldn't make me feel worse than I already did.

Jess and Dr. Sinclair arrived the next day and treated me as someone who'd given them a special gift, showering me with praise and affection. They brought me flowers and my favorite dinner, treating me with the same love and respect they'd always given to me.

I told Jess I didn't want to see Mark and Leslie, and she promised me that she'd pack up my things in the garage apartment, so I never had to feel the harsh judgement of Dr. Sinclair's brother and his wife again.

I left the hospital a couple of days later, and Jess got me settled into the new furnished apartment they'd rented for me near the Berkeley campus. It was small but cute and bright, and I felt grateful to have my own place to start my new life.

I had my scholarships, and the Sinclairs were giving me $500 per month for necessities so I wouldn't have to work, allowing me more time to study in such a highly competitive program. I wouldn't need a car since my apartment was centrally located and near public transportation. The arrangement would allow me to concentrate on my schoolwork and do an internship each semester without the need to take on additional employment.

Leslie had made it clear to me that Dr. Sinclair and Jess' support was because they loved me and wanted the best for me, but it did not come in exchange for the adoption of the baby. I wasn't sure about all the legal matters—only that I couldn't connect the adoption with their financial support after her birth to protect all of us from getting in trouble. It was another set of secrets to keep, and I was getting very good at deception.

Once the papers were signed, Jess called me one last time to thank me for everything and make sure I would contact them if I needed anything. "I know we decided it would be better if we only communicated through the attorneys for any money issues or whatever, but Cassie, I'm here for you no matter what."

Before we said our goodbyes, I needed to know one more thing.

"Jess, I want to know what you named her. When I think about her in the years to come, I want her to have a name...."

"To be honest, you've shown so much courage and maturity during this process, Steve and I wanted to name her after you. We couldn't just call her Cassie, so we came up with a name we felt honored the amazing young woman you've been through this process. We named her Grace."

There was silence on the line as Jess waited for me to respond. "Thank you, Jess. It's beautiful. Thank you for being such an important person in my life. And as she gets older, let Grace know we gave her up because we loved her so much. Ben and I aren't ready to be parents. Make sure she doesn't feel this was her fault or that we didn't love her."

"I will, Cassie. I promise you she will have the best life you can imagine. We love you. Goodbye, sweetheart."

As the phone line went quiet, I stayed on listening until the recording played, *"If you'd like to make a call, please hang up and dial again...."*

As I hung up the phone, I tried to sever the connection between my past life and the future waiting for me.

Chapter Eleven
February 2015

It had been six weeks since the surgery, and Mom was feeling much better.

"Josephine, you've healed well and are ready to start chemo," Dr. Bryn said with confidence. "Ovarian cancer follows a path of destruction moving from the abdomen to the lungs and then the brain." Dr. Bryn didn't mince words. "If chemo is not effective, I would expect you might have six months to live."

There were already spots in Mom's lungs, although she wasn't experiencing symptoms yet. Dr. Bryn was open with us, people who choose treatment in Mom's condition don't always buy themselves more time, and they risk spending the life they have left feeling sick and living with a diminished quality of life.

"I understand my options, but I can't accept my cancer diagnosis without at least giving chemo a try. I've weighed the pros and cons, and if it gets to be too much, I'll opt for quality of life over quantity," Mom responded back to her.

The initial round of chemo was scheduled for the following day. We'd have to travel to Des Moines each week for the treatments, but this time we'd stay in a hotel so Mom wouldn't be so tired on her first day.

We decided to make a fun night of it and booked a room at a fancy hotel in downtown Des Moines. As a treat, I reserved a two-bedroom suite so I could lavish my mother with as much luxury as possible during what would probably be our last months together.

"Oh my gosh, Cassie. How much did you have to pay for this?" she exclaimed as we walked into the suite. "This is probably where the president would stay if he came to Iowa!"

"If it's good enough for Barack Obama, it's good enough for us," I joked, hugging her shoulders.

"We don't need all of this, but isn't it going to be fun?" she asked. "I don't want to go out to dinner, let's put our pajamas on and order room service," she suggested.

"Well, it's only 4 p.m."

"I don't care if it's noon! We can't waste time going anywhere else when we have this room for the night!" She was right about it being a stunning hotel suite.

By the time the 6 p.m. news came on, we were settled and changed out of our clothes. We brought out pillows and blankets from our bedrooms and set ourselves up on the sofa in front of a large television mounted to the wall above a gas fireplace. Mom searched for movies for us to rent, and I perused the room service menu.

We ended up watching a "Flip or Flop" marathon on HGTV as we ate grilled salmon and roasted chicken dinners from the high-end hotel restaurant. We enjoyed an expensive bottle of chardonnay I'd ordered from the bar, and it was the perfect accompaniment to our delicious meals.

We finished the night by sharing a piece of cherry cheesecake as we snuggled under a blanket on the sofa. We knew the morning would bring the necessity to face the health struggle never far from our thoughts, but we didn't waste an opportunity to relax and have a little fun.

I fell asleep feeling as if we'd cheated cancer out of at least one night of it's terrifying hold on us. It made me think about other things I could do to make Mom's life more fun during such a terrible time.

***

When the elevator doors opened on level five of the cancer treatment center, a whole new world came into view for us. Beyond the nurse's station on the infusion floor was an expansive room where chemo veterans in various stages of health were hooked up to IV bags.

An older woman sat stoically as her husband napped quietly in a chair beside her, a teenage boy played video games, and a businessman worked on his laptop as the lifesaving poison dripped into their veins to stop whatever kind of cancer they had from taking their lives.

It was clear cancer didn't care who it attacked. There were people getting treatment of all ages, cultures, and socio-economic backgrounds. Looking out over a room full of people fighting for their lives made me feel guilty for being healthy. I didn't want my mom to be a part of this struggling fraternity where membership often came with a death sentence.

I enthusiastically checked Mom in as I complimented the nurses on the color of their scrubs, trying to mask my trepidation with confident conversation. We made small talk as one of the nurses looked for Mom's files. When she commented on Mom's light gray sweat suit, I bragged about how she'd bought three of them in different colors and a new bag to carry her things in, so she'd look stylish for her treatments.

I felt naive about things I should have had a better handle on given my experience in healthcare, and the comment was stupid and thoughtless, as if how you looked could affect the experience. I was scared, and arriving for our first round of chemo brought to light how serious things were.

I would never again take for granted the feelings of my patients and their loved ones. I felt embarrassed at how I'd sometimes brushed off their deep emotions wishing they'd leave my office and figure it out on their own time. I was learning important lessons, but they came at the expense of my mother's health.

A benefit of being a new patient was we'd have our own room for the first treatment. We were ushered into the small space, and the nurse attached Mom to an IV bag. She settled in with her favorite blanket to comfort her and some ridiculous talk show tuned in on a television attached to the wall.

"I can't believe I've spent my entire life eating well and not smoking, only to find myself here . . . pumping poison into my body to try and save my life," she said quietly as the clear liquid steadily dripped into her veins.

"I'm so sorry you have to go through this," I said.

The various drugs in Mom's chemo cocktail included Benadryl to make sure she didn't have an allergic reaction to the medication. It wasn't long before she'd gone to sleep and left me to my own thoughts.

I made a mental note to be less jovial the next time we

arrived at the treatment center. I'd gone to the check in desk as if we were signing in for a pedicure. I should have quietly let them know Josephine Garrett was reporting for the battle of her life, leaving my overly optimistic attitude at home.

Seeing so many others in various stages of beating or being beat by the opponent named cancer made me feel panicked. Would we be lucky enough to get a miracle? Mom needed me to be her best cheerleader, but in doing so, I felt as if I'd disrespected those who were already on the front lines. They needed us to quietly slip in with the rest of them leaving my pep rally for another time.

Before long, another nurse came to our room, and we spent the next hour going over all the things we could expect in the coming weeks. I knew about most of the side effects, but the information was new and scary to Mom. Hair loss and nausea were almost a given, but there were several other side effects to be prepared for including neuropathy and stomach pain.

After we finished, Mom asked, "Do you think Dr. Bryn is right? This probably won't give me more time?"

"At this point, it's our only chance at beating this thing or at least keeping it at bay." I didn't think she could beat ovarian cancer, but we could hope for more time.

The statistics showed a 90% mortality rate five years after diagnosis. How much time we could give her was something I couldn't begin to predict. So much would depend on her own body's response and the aggressiveness of the cancer itself.

"I'm not afraid to die," Mom said quietly as she looked out the window. We hadn't discussed the obvious in all this yet. I was waiting for her to bring it up.

"You've lived the best life. You have such a strong faith.

I'm going to be with you every step of the way, and we'll do whatever needs to be done to make you feel comfortable. You don't need to be scared about anything."

My words of encouragement were spoken with assurance, though the thought of Mom's death struck terror in my soul. She needed me to be strong for her, so I couldn't worry about my own feelings.

"We'll see how it goes. But, I'm not going to spend the next few months feeling awful. It isn't worth it," she said quietly.

"That will all be up to you, Mom." I'd spend the rest of the time we had together finally being the daughter she needed. I would do whatever possible to make her last months the best of her life.

***

The next six weeks were spent getting ready for chemo, taking chemo, and dealing with the side effects of chemo. Mom would feel good for a day or so after her treatments thanks to the steroids added to her regimen. It would take most of the rest of the week to recover, only to find ourselves getting ready to head back to Des Moines for another round.

We'd shaved her head once her hair started to fall out, but Mom hadn't cared about it. Over the need to be vain, she embraced the simplicity of not having to do her hair every day.

She was nauseous after treatments and couldn't eat much, but the side effects were manageable. She often felt fatigued, but we enjoyed our time together watching movies, doing puzzles, and eating homemade meals brought to us by family and friends.

We hardly had to leave the house with everyone making

sure our needs were met. I reconnected with many of the people who'd been a part of my younger life from the safety of my mom's house. Because we were rarely in public, I didn't have to worry about running into anyone from my past, which made the time at home much more enjoyable.

Everyone looked a little older, but for the most part they were just as they'd always been. It was as if time had stood still in Elmwood while the rest of the world went on changing without them. I appreciated the simple life in my hometown and wished I'd spent more time in the place that made me who I was.

The craziness of living and working in California, and the constant striving toward success seemed to suck the joy out of each day. Facing the end of my mom's life gave me the gift of perspective. I promised myself I'd never again work for the sake of money or prestige. My future would include having a career and a personal life I could be passionate about. Life was short, and I didn't want to waste more time on anything or anyone that didn't make me happy.

I found pleasure in taking care of the simple needs Mom had. Rubbing her feet or painting her fingernails felt like the most wonderful gift I could give her. No matter what happened, no one could ever take those six weeks of chemo treatments away from us. It was a time when we were able to cling to each other with the common goal of beating cancer.

At the end of the first series of treatments, we met with the doctor after tests were done to determine if she was in remission. My heart sank the moment Dr. Bryn came into the room. I'd had the same grim look on my face when the test results weren't good, and I dreaded the next few moments when we'd be told *things hadn't gone as planned.*

"Good morning, Josephine," said Dr. Bryn. She wasted no time getting to the point. "I'm sorry to tell you we didn't get the outcome we'd hoped for." I squeezed Mom's hand as she sat motionless, ready to receive her death sentence with bravery and poise.

"Your numbers don't look good, which is a sign the chemo isn't working. How've you been feeling?" she asked.

"I'm nauseous, tired and bald, Dr. Bryn. All in all, I'm not feeling great, " Mom said. Her sense of humor was still intact.

"Here's the long and short of it. The cancer is spreading. We need to consider letting you have some time to get your affairs in order before your illness begins to overtake you. If you stop treatment now, my best guess is you might have a couple of months before you start to feel the impact of the disease. If we continue treatment, I'm not sure I can give you many more good days before this begins to take a turn for the worse. It's up to you, but I feel a hospice referral is probably the best thing I can give you."

"Hospice already? But you said I had some time . . ." Mom was startled by Dr. Bryn's suggestion.

"There's a misconception about hospice care. It isn't only for the last few days or hours of life. You could really benefit from the services provided, and when the time comes, you can utilize their inpatient unit if needed. It's up to you, but I can't say enough good things about the hospice in Elmwood, and I think you'd be happy with them," Dr. Bryn explained.

"If I was your mother, would you suggest discontinuing treatment or would you try to look for other therapies? What about going to one of those Cancer Treatment Centers they advertise on TV where they do all those trials?"

"Those are options, Josephine. It means an extreme amount

of travel and time spent away from home when most people want to be closest to the ones they love. And in answer to your question . . . I *did* suggest ending treatment when my mother got to where you are right now. We had four good months together where we took a trip, and she got to meet her first great-grandchild. She was able to see each of her eight siblings from across the country before she died. If she'd continued treatment, she wouldn't have been well enough to experience those things."

Mom sat on the exam table with me standing behind her, my arm around her waist. I didn't want to face we were already so close to the end, but I needed to be strong for Mom and help her to navigate and understand all Dr. Bryn had laid out for us.

"I trust you, Dr. Bryn," Mom said bravely. "Cassie, let's go home. We've got a lot to do in the next couple of months."

"Josephine, I'm so sorry. We've come a long way with research, but we haven't come as far with ovarian cancer. Good luck," she said, shaking our hands as she made her way out of the exam room.

Neither of us said much in the car, each lost in our own thoughts about what needed to be done. When we got home, Mom went straight to bed telling me she wanted to get some rest and would face everything with a good night's sleep under her belt.

I took out my cell phone and sent Ben a text asking him to meet me at Sully's. I needed a friend, and he was the only person that came to mind.

***

Sully's had been an Elmwood staple for as long as I could

remember. People made fun of it for being a dive bar, but everyone knew they had the best burgers in town. I got there before Ben, snagging a corner booth for us and ordered a pitcher of Bud Light. Ben came through the front door as the beer and frosty mugs were being delivered to our table.

He slipped his jacket off and slid into the seat across from me. "Hey, is everything okay?" he asked, surprised by my last-minute invitation.

"I felt like getting out of the house tonight, and I wanted a chance to thank you again for stopping by the hospital in Des Moines and convincing me I needed a night in a hotel bed," I said with a smile.

"I'm glad my suggestion helped. You looked so tired, and I felt awful for you," he answered back. "I'm really glad to see you again . . . what's going on? Is your mom okay?" His expression changed to one of concern.

"No. She's going to end her treatments. That means she doesn't have long to live. Maybe a few months at the most. She's being referred to hospice, and we won't be going back and forth to Des Moines anymore."

"I'm so sorry. I was hoping the chemo would have better results. I assume you're staying here for a while and not going back to California?"

"I'm staying here for as long as Mom needs me. I've already quit my job in Ventura, and I'm not sure what I'm doing after that. Between my personal and professional lives, the timing couldn't have been better for me. I'm starting my life over when Mom needs me most. I've been gone for so many years, and it's all been overwhelming. But, this entire experience has also given me a chance to put my priorities in order."

"I'm sorry, Cassie. What can I do to help?"

"How about get my mind off things? Let's order burgers and finish this pitcher of beer while you tell me about your boys and the shop. I want to know everything!" I said, hoping he had great things going on in his life.

I spent the next hour listening to Ben talk about convincing his dad to start carrying more mini-mart items and bringing in more sales than they'd ever done before. He talked about the things he did in his spare time, like refurbishing old cars and watching football. He shared stories about his boys and the activities they were in, telling me how hard it was to live separately from them. He never mentioned Angie, but I could tell how deeply their divorce had affected him.

Ben asked about my life, and I filled him in on the high points and expanded on my own pending divorce. I left out some of the more salacious parts but was sure he got the gist of the challenges I'd faced.

"What happened between you and Angie?" I asked boldly, finishing off the last bite of my hamburger. I could hardly believe they'd married, let alone figure out why they'd divorced.

"Truthfully?" he asked.

"No, tell me a lie," I joked as we smiled across the table from each other. I could feel myself relaxing as the beer kicked in and the stress of my life was set aside for a while.

"She was a good mom, and she tried to be a good wife. She wasn't you, Cass. That's the truth. I was still in love with you when I married her, and so I blame myself for not being totally into the relationship. I kept thinking it would get better, but it never did. Finally, she got sick of me staying late at the shop and keeping my distance from her emotionally, and she started seeing someone else behind my back. I didn't really blame her. She cheated on me, but she was lonely, and I didn't do anything to make her feel differently. It probably sounds strange, but now that it's all in the past, I'm happy she found someone."

I was surprised at Ben's ability to be so vulnerable with me. "I'm not ready to toast my ex and his girlfriend yet, but I suppose it's still a little fresh for me." I hoped someday I'd be able to think of Graham without negative emotions overtaking me.

"They're married now, and they seem happy. He's a good stepdad to the boys, and that's all I care about. I'm a more invested dad now that I have all the responsibility when they're with me. I do the best I can," he added.

I was flattered Ben had loved me for so long, but sad our relationship had caused him such heartache. I didn't deserve his love after the way I'd treated him as an overwhelmed teenage girl. I silently wondered if he *still* loved me.

He'd hardly changed since high school, still talking about the same friends and places. My experiences had put me in contact with so many different people and cultures. I couldn't imagine having stayed in our hometown for my entire life. I was grateful I'd been able to experience so much, although I was right back where I started.

"My ex had an affair too. But, I'm not ready to forgive him yet. We shouldn't have been together in the first place, so maybe it wasn't all his fault. Did you ever tell Angie about Grace?" I held my breath waiting for his answer. I needed to be sure the only people who knew our secret were the Sinclairs and us. I hadn't told Graham about Grace, but it didn't mean Ben hadn't disclosed our past to his wife.

"No. I never told her anything about it." Ben looked directly at me, and I knew I could believe what he was saying. After so many years, he'd been true to his word.

"I appreciate that. I'm still so afraid someone will find out what happened. Not a day goes by when I'm not thinking about that time in our lives. I'm sorry I left you heartbroken. I felt so ashamed but couldn't think of any other way out."

"It's okay. A lot of time has passed, and I'm not holding you responsible for things you did when you were backed into a corner. You shouldn't feel bad about something that happened so long ago resulting in the birth of another human being. That's a lot to hold on to for a lifetime. I'm grateful to have a chance to see you again and talk through some of these things. Not having a proper ending with you made things difficult for me, and I didn't handle it the best. There was a time when I probably drank too much and tried to date every girl in town to get you off my mind."

So that's how he ended up with Angie Stanford.

"You need to know I think we did the right thing for our little girl. *You* did the right thing for her. Hell, sometimes it's hard to be a good dad to my boys now—no telling how bad I'd have been at it when I was eighteen. I don't have anything but love for you in my heart, and I'm sorry I put you in that position in the first place."

My phone vibrated, and I pulled it out of my purse to see Mom was calling. I hated to interrupt him when he was pouring his heart out to me but couldn't miss a call from her.

"Hi, Mom. Are you okay?"

The phone call was short, but she asked me to bring her a burger from Sully's, so I knew she must be feeling a little better.

"Ben, I'm so sorry you had to face all of that by yourself.

I've thought about how hard it must have been for you, but at the time, I couldn't see past my own needs. I'm lucky you're still talking to me. You were wonderful to me, and if I started to tell you all my regrets, we'd be here for days," I said quietly, reaching across the table to put my hand on top of his. I stopped short of telling him he'd been the love of my life, and no one after him had come anywhere close to taking his place.

He took my hand in his and smiled. "That means a lot, Cassie. Hearing those words after all these years means the world to me."

The server came by and asked if we needed anything else, interrupting the moment and giving me the opportunity to place an order for a burger to go. I started to get my things together and finally got the nerve to ask Ben the most important question of the night.

"Do you ever see her around town?" Elmwood wasn't very big, and the Sinclairs had never been a family to stay in the shadows. He probably saw her all the time.

"Yeah. I see her...."

"What does she look like?" I wondered how hard it was for Ben to live in the same town as Grace and not be able to know her. I'd been so happy he and Angie hadn't had any children until Grace was about five. That would keep their boys from having much to do with her, which was good for a myriad of reasons.

"She's involved in tons of school activities so she's in the newspaper all the time. She worked at the Dairy Queen a couple of summers, and the boys always wanted to go. I'd usually wait in the car but could see her taking their orders. It broke my heart to think my sons didn't know that their sister was serving them ice cream. And I see her driving around town in a cute little red car her parents bought her for her sixteenth birthday."

I smiled at the thought of Grace being the center of the Sinclair's universe. That's what I wanted for her.

Looking at Ben, it seemed like the years had flown by. He was a good man, and he'd protected both of us from everyone in town finding out about our connection to Grace Sinclair.

The waiter returned with the bill and let me know the burger was almost ready. I reached for the check and started to get my credit card out of my wallet. Ben took the small plastic tray out of my hands and pulled it toward him.

"You're not paying the bill, Cass," Ben said as he put some cash on top of the paper with our orders scribbled across the middle.

"No, Ben. I've got Mom's burger on there, and you don't need to do that." I reached for the bill again.

"I'll get it. *Please* . . ." The tone in his voice and the look on his face let me know there was no use arguing about it.

We both got up, and I gave Ben a long hug, thanking him for meeting me on short notice. I'd needed time with an old friend on such a difficult night, and once again he'd given me what I asked for. I was drawn to Ben and grateful for emotional closure, which hadn't been possible in eighteen years.

We said our goodbyes, and I headed for the condo with a deluxe cheeseburger riding shotgun on the front seat of Mom's car.

Chapter Twelve
October 1996

I'd returned to classes one week after Grace's birth, feeling better physically, even though my emotions were all over the place. I began to assimilate back into the normal life of a college student but at night felt restless and filled with anxiety, and the solitude of having my own apartment only added to my sense of despair and loneliness.

I'd have nightmares about leaving Grace in a dark basement. Hearing her cries in my bad dream, I'd search my subconscious for her, suddenly remembering she hadn't been changed or fed in days because I'd forgotten about her.

After I woke, it would take a few minutes before I'd remember Grace was safe and sleeping in an adorable pink nursery at the Sinclair's home back in Iowa. The recurring dream made me want to stay awake all night so I wouldn't have to face the terror within sleep.

I didn't know how to go on and live my life without all the people I loved back at home. The lies I'd told my mom and the distance I'd put between myself and Iowa may have been necessary, but they were also devastating. Knowing I could never go home without Grace's existence staring me in the face made me grieve for the life I'd never have again.

The soft spot in my heart where the memory of Grace lived felt like a scab ripped off every time I saw a baby or a family reminding me of what might have been. Seeing students and their children at a nearby park, raising families and pursuing their academic goals at the same time, made me feel like other options should have been considered for baby Grace. Maybe I'd been too quick to decide I couldn't keep her.

I looked forward to and dreaded weekly calls with my mom when she asked me questions about how classes were going and who my friends were. It exhausted me to make her feel secure about my well-being when I was struggling to hold it all together.

It didn't take long until the stress of my studies and the effort to fit in at Berkeley moved to the lead on my list of things to worry about. I couldn't distinguish between anxiety over the loss of Grace and emotions caused by being alone for the first time in my life at a college far from home.

The first real connections I made with my fellow students came from a seminar class. I was assigned to a cohort of ten students, and we began to meet a few times per week for a project. Sometimes we met for coffee at the student union or at one of the dorms where we could check out a room with space to spread out and plan our presentation. It turned out to be the best thing for me, as it gave me a handful of friends and regular meetings forcing me to spend time with other college students.

I hit it off with a couple of girls who lived in a dorm not far from my apartment. They introduced me to friends from their floor, and suddenly I was being invited to parties or to catch a movie and dinner with some of them on the weekends.

As I got more involved with students who didn't have any idea I'd recently had a baby, I didn't have to tell lies to them and could relax and be myself again. I'd kept such a low profile at the start of the school year that my new friends believed me when I told them I'd joined the semester a little late because of a summer job commitment.

It was early on a Saturday morning, and I lounged in bed and thought about what to do with my weekend. I had a paper due on Tuesday and planned to do some studying at the library later in the day. As I rolled over and pulled the comforter up around my neck, there was a knock at the front door.

I wondered if it might be the mail carrier. I'd begun to receive letters from Ben as soon as I got out of the hospital and figured maybe he'd sent me something bigger than an envelope. I couldn't imagine who else would be at my door so early on a Saturday morning.

Lying in bed, hoping the knocking would go away, I thought about the first letter I'd received from Ben. I'd opened it eagerly, desperate for a connection to my old self.

Reading affirmations from the boy who loved me so deeply helped my fragile self-image. I couldn't continue a relationship with him but desperately wanted to feel the security I'd had with him. I didn't hold it against my mom that she gave my new address to Ben, even if it made things more difficult.

Over a couple of weeks, I'd received a letter almost every day. Finally, I sat down and wrote a note back, telling him how much I still loved him, but that I couldn't move on with my life unless we broke up. I didn't call him because the conversation would have been too hard and would only delay the inevitable. It had been more than two weeks since I'd received a letter, and I was both relieved and devastated at the thought of no more contact.

The knocking started again, this time harder and louder. It didn't sound like the person was going away. I pushed the covers back and found my robe in a heap on the carpeting. I tried to fix my hair as I headed to the front door, hopscotching my way through the living room over books and empty pop cans. I made a mental note to clean the apartment later in the day.

There was a window at the top of the front door covered by a small white curtain. I pushed it aside, looking out while standing on my toes. When I saw who was at my front door the blood drained from my face.

The untidy status of my apartment, and my own bloated body made me take a quick assessment of how I would get through the next few hours of my life. I took a sharp breath in and opened the door to my mother waiting to enter the apartment of her only daughter, who'd given birth to a baby she knew nothing about just weeks before.

"Mom?" I said as if I wasn't sure who she was.

"Cassie!" she exclaimed, pulling me into her arms.

Stunned to see her and unprepared for the surprise visit, there was no time to review the lies I'd told and the changes I'd been through over the past months. I thought it would be Thanksgiving before we saw each other again, and now she was standing at my front door for an unexpected reunion.

"Since you said you had enough money for your ticket home for Thanksgiving, I used what I'd saved to come out and surprise you! I took the red-eye and have Monday off too, so we have the entire weekend together. Isn't that great?" she asked, hoping for a positive response from me.

I was left open mouthed and silent, trying to think of an answer that didn't expose my utter shock at seeing her.

She went on, "I've had the feeling something isn't right with you, and I couldn't wait until the holidays to make sure you were okay."

"Oh my gosh, Mom!" They were the only words I could come up with. "Come in," I said, wishing I'd cleaned the apartment the day before.

As she entered my small residence, her eyes showed the uneasiness at what she saw. It would take less than an hour to get the place cleaned up, but I'd neglected to take the hour to do it in some time. Mom's arrival made me realize I wasn't doing well at all.

I needed to go to the counseling office I'd seen advertised on a bulletin board in the student union where I could get help processing everything I'd gone through. It was something I'd been considering, but seeing my mom helped me to make the final decision. There was nothing like reality to bring you back to reality.

"Mom, I'm so sorry this place is a mess. I've been working on a big paper, and I kind of let things go the past few days. If I'd known you were coming...."

"Oh, honey, it's okay," she said sweetly, though it clearly was not okay. "I missed you so much and came up with this idea to surprise you. It's been five months since I've seen you, and I couldn't wait another day!"

I started to tidy the apartment, figuring up in my head how much I'd weighed before leaving Elmwood and compared it to my current weight. Still more than ten pounds heavier than before I'd gotten pregnant with Grace, I thought maybe it could be blamed on the freshman fifteen, although most college students didn't gain it all in the first few weeks.

"I'm so shocked to see you!" I kept saying, continuing to clean and try to pull myself together.

"I hope in a good way?" she asked apprehensively.

"Well, of course," I replied, faking sincerity. "I'm so astonished you're here; I can hardly think straight." It was the most honest thing I'd said to her in months.

"Your place is bigger than I'd expected. This is less expensive than living in the dorms?" she asked as she looked around. She had no idea this little perk was because I'd given her granddaughter up for adoption, and the Sinclairs were footing my bills because of it.

"Well, Mark has a lot of connections at Berkeley, so he knows the property owner, and they gave me a really good deal. Plus, preparing my own food is so much cheaper than eating in the cafeteria," I added. Maybe she'd think my weight gain was due to my cooking rather than giving birth to an eight-pound baby girl.

Mom put her suitcase next to the sofa, and I finished cleaning up. By noon we'd settled into a comfortable rapport allowing me to finally be happy to see her.

We walked around campus, and I showed her where my classes were and took her to some of my favorite places. I'd been so overwhelmed since Grace's birth that I'd begun to settle into my new life without even noticing.

In a crazy stroke of good luck, we ran into some of the girls I'd recently met, and their introductions to my mother made it seem like things were better for me than what they were. Mom was happy to know I had friends and a nice place to live, which was the reason for her trip in the first place.

Mom took me out to eat and bought me a new outfit at the mall. Although I wouldn't have chosen a surprise visit from my mom—it was just what I needed.

The weekend was spent catching up on family gossip and making plans for Thanksgiving. The only time our conversation became tense was when the Sinclair's new baby came up.

"You should see the darling baby girl the Sinclairs adopted," Mom said unknowingly. "Did you know they were in the process of adopting?"

"No, I didn't." It felt like my heart stopped beating.

"I had no idea until they brought the baby to church. She's so cute and has dark skin and hair like you did when you were a baby. I wonder if her biological parents are Italian or if she's biracial?" she wondered aloud.

"No idea . . . but, what do you want to do tonight?" I needed to get off the topic of the Sinclair's baby as soon as possible.

Mom didn't seem to notice my discomfort, and we moved our conversation along to something else before spending the rest of the evening playing cards and working on a puzzle.

We ended our weekend with a trip to the store and an afternoon of my mom's cooking, which would stock my freezer for a long time.

When she left Monday morning, I felt relaxed and happy. Mom had made the nearly two-thousand-mile trip to find out for herself what was going on with her only child, and she'd seen enough to be satisfied. I was happy we'd had the time together before facing everyone in my hometown again.

***

I'd made the most of those few weeks after Mom's trip to California by starting sessions with Dr. Miller at the Student Health Center. I'd seen fliers on campus encouraging new students to seek help for a variety of issues from eating disorders to homesickness. Even though they didn't specifically advertise assistance for students who'd given up a baby the second week of classes, I was sure they'd be able to offer support.

I'd only had three sessions before heading back to Iowa, but they were important ones with guidance on how to manage my engulfing anxiety and discussions about how to begin to forgive myself for something that couldn't be changed. I planned to continue for as long as Dr. Miller would see me and looked forward to the sessions, though parts of them were painful for me to endure.

The unplanned visit from my mom had helped to rush the semester along, and before I knew it, it was time to head home for Thanksgiving.

As the plane landed in Des Moines, I felt panic at returning to Elmwood for the first time since Grace's birth. Breathing deeply as Dr. Miller had taught me, I exited the plane feeling calmer and searched the crowd for my mom's face in the mob of people picking up their loved ones for the Thanksgiving holiday.

As we headed down the highway, the drab color of harvested cornfields contrasted sharply to the lush landscape I'd just left. Our 90-minute drive to Elmwood went fast as I eagerly told Mom more about my new friends and the project we were working on for class.

We talked about making it a priority to keep my apartment clean and about the thrift store I'd found after she'd left where I bought a few things to make my place homier. She reacted with pride at some of the deals I'd found, telling me I was a "chip off the old block" when it came to finding the best secondhand treasures.

I'd also started walking every day, thanks to the suggestion of my counselor, and I'd lost five pounds since Mom's surprise visit. I was starting to look and feel more like me again.

"We've got five days before you have to go back. What do you want to do?" Mom asked as we traveled through the Iowa countryside. Farms with grain silos and old-fashioned windmills dotted the landscape and reminded me I wasn't in the city anymore.

"I'd kind of like to stay close to home and relax." I wanted to spend quality time with her *and* avoid a chance encounter with those I didn't want to see.

Mom knew I'd broken up with Ben, but she didn't know the real reason we weren't together. I'd led her to believe a long-distance romance had caused our split, and she'd accepted it at face value.

"Don't you want to spend some time with your friends or visit the Sinclairs?" she asked. "I thought you'd want to see their new baby."

"No. I'm sure they're busy, and since I have such a short time at home I don't want to spend it with anyone but you." If she was surprised about my housebound vacation plans, she didn't show it.

***

After sleeping in my own bed, Mom and I had coffee and homemade banana bread while we watched the Macy's Thanksgiving Day Parade. We had to leave by noon to head over to my Aunt Lynn's house for dinner.

We hauled my grandma's sage dressing in a big roaster and brought two more disposable pans of sweet potatoes covered in brown sugar and marshmallows. Mom had made her famous pumpkin bars with cream cheese frosting, and I was excited at the thought of eating some of my family's favorite dishes.

The house quickly filled with my closest relatives, and the mood felt festive and fun. There wasn't any place to sit, and my cousins snagged up extra floor space if they could find it. We'd outgrown a normal sized house but didn't want to break tradition, so we kept cramming in family members year after year.

It relaxed me to be surrounded by people who loved me. I visited with my cousins and ate comfort food prepared by the loving hands of my mom and aunts. Whenever we spent time with my dad's side of the family, his presence was palpable, and his reflection was visible in the faces of those who shared his DNA. For the first time in nearly a year, I felt good and happy to be alive.

We drove home with our stomachs filled with turkey and green bean casserole and a leftover pumpkin pie balancing on my knees. We decided to stop at the video store to get some movies to sustain us for several days. I handed the pie to Mom and ran in to pick out our entertainment for the long weekend.

The video store was packed; one of the only places open at 5 p.m. on Thanksgiving Day. I stood in the New Release section trying to decide between "Mr. Holland's Opus" and "The Bridges of Madison County." I hadn't seen either in the theaters so put both in my basket and headed toward the front to pay. Rounding the corner toward the counter, I heard a familiar voice call my name.

"Cassie?" Turner was standing next to the kid's section holding the movie "Babe."

"Hi, Turner!" I said, wanting to scoop him in my arms and swing him around, but holding back in case Jess stood nearby with a bundled Grace in her arms.

Turner came toward me, and I had no choice but to open my arms to the hug he was already giving me. "Did you know I have a new baby sister?" he asked proudly, oblivious to the way those words would slice into my heart.

"I heard!" I said, trying to keep it together and maintain an emotional distance from the little boy I'd taken care of for years. Dr. Sinclair came around the corner. It seemed we were both surprised to run into each other at Blockbuster.

"Hi, Cassie," he said quietly as he told Turner they needed to get their movies and go home. It was an awkward moment neither of us were prepared to deal with.

"Dad, can Cassie come over and see Grace? Can she babysit us while she's home?" he asked hopefully.

"Turner, I'm sure Cassie's only here for a few days and doesn't want to babysit. Come on, let's get going. We need to get home before Mom wonders where we are."

"Can't we stay for a few more minutes?" he asked.

"Turner, my mom's waiting for me so I have to hurry. We can talk another time." I hated to be so unfriendly to Turner but wanted him to obey his dad and leave the store as soon as possible so I could do the same.

"Okay," he said sadly. "Will you call me before you go back to college?" he asked.

"I'm sorry, Turner. I don't think I'll be able to this trip. Maybe next time."

The disappointment showed on his face, and it killed me to be so rude to him. He was a little boy and had no idea of the situation. It hurt me to know I'd never have a chance to tell him how sorry I was, and he might carry the exchange with him for the rest of his life, wondering if I cared about him at all.

I waited until Dr. Sinclair and Turner left the front of the store before I moved to the line to pay for my movies. I wanted to get out of the video store as soon as possible and return to the safety of home.

I opened the door to the car and quickly buckled my seatbelt.

"What's that all about?" Mom asked.

"What do you mean?"

"Well, it was an awful big sigh for someone who ran in to get a couple of movies."

"Yeah . . . it was just busy in there, and I'm ready to get home," I replied flatly.

"What movies did you get?" she asked, and I told her the ones I'd selected.

"Oh, those sound great. I've been wanting to see *The Bridges of Madison County*. Some guy from Iowa wrote that book...." she continued talking on the way home, but I wasn't listening.

All I could think about was Turner's face as he tried to connect with me and how cold I'd been to him. I felt such sadness knowing that the Sinclairs were out of my life forever. I'd loved them like my own family but would never again be a part of their lives.

The rest of my time at home was spent in the security of our little house where Mom and I stayed in our pajamas, pretending the rest of the world didn't exist.

Chapter Thirteen
April 2015

When I came in the door from Sully's, Mom was sweeping something from the kitchen floor. I saw the vase that had held flowers from Mom's St. Cecelia's church circle shattered on the ceramic tile.

"I hope you weren't rushed," she said, cleaning up the shards of glass. "How's Ben?"

"Good, " I answered, putting her hamburger on the counter. I was more interested in how the vase had fallen than updating Mom on Ben's life.

"It was nice to visit with him for a little while. I'm glad you called. If you feel like a Sully's burger, then that's what you need!" I was happy to do something to make her feel better.

"What happened?" I asked as she put a dustpan full of crystal into the trashcan.

"I was having a little pity party and had the brilliant idea to throw my mother's antique vase to the ground to make myself feel better. Now I'm dying, *and* I've broken one of my favorite family heirlooms," she said calmly.

I took the broom and dustpan from her hands, setting them aside, and wrapped my arms around her. "I'm sorry, Mom. I shouldn't have left you alone."

"It's okay. I wanted a little time to myself to cry and curse God and this damn cancer. I feel so cheated to have to deal with this right now—just when I was starting to enjoy my life. It's so unfair."

"I wish there was something I could say or do to change things. I'll be with you every step of the way. We have each other, and I'll help you get through this as comfortably as possible."

Knowing she needed my support more than I needed hers made me pull myself together and had shaken me out of the dark place I'd been since the moment I'd found Graham with another woman. We couldn't both be out of control at the same time. Considering her diagnosis, I'd let her be the one who needed to be taken care of.

"I realized I'd worked up an appetite after hurling that stupid vase onto the floor and decided on a Sully's cheeseburger. I haven't had one in years, and they used to be your dad's favorite. The longer I felt sorry for myself, the more I craved one of those burgers," she said.

I helped get her food onto a tray as she settled in the recliner. "It was a big day; how can I help you process all of this?"

"That's not the kind of news you're used to getting. Strangely, it's an answer without a lot of question marks. I'm dying. And I'm dying sooner rather than later. I got to thinking *why am I wasting this evening in bed*? I don't have much time left, and I better get up and start living before it's too late."

"Oh, Mom . . ." My heart was breaking for her.

"When I went in the kitchen, I had this huge desire to chuck that vase into the air—and to be honest, it felt fantastic! Once

I heard it crash, my tantrum was over, and I was ready to move on with what needs to be done."

"I hated that vase. If it made you feel better, I'm glad it's broken into a thousand pieces. We're going to handle things the way you want to. And if it means doing something dramatic like breaking a vase, then that's what we'll do," I said, secretly hoping she'd refrain from breaking things as it scared me to see my mom out of control.

"Dr. Bryn said you have several months. Let's sit and figure out what you want to do with them. You're right, the more time we waste being upset, the less time we have to do things together."

"You've been gone for so many years. We have a lot to make up for, and I want to start doing it right now."

"Let me grab a pad of paper, and let's make a "bucket list" for you. We'll try to get everything done on the list before you start to feel bad, and it will give us fun things to look forward to every day. How does that sound?"

"That's a great idea," she said through a mouth full of hamburger. "To be honest, there won't be much on the list."

"Surely there must be things you'd like to do before you die. Do you want to go on a trip somewhere? Maybe visit Italy and see where your grandparents lived?"

"I'd love to see Italy. But, let's not go so far away. I'm not going to spend my last months away from my home and loved ones. I'm happy with the simple life I've been living and want to spend each day doing more of the same. I don't have a lot of unrealized dreams, and now that you're home, I just want to be with you. There's only one *big* thing I'd like to do before it's my time—I want to go to Disney World," she added without hesitation, popping a limp french fry in her mouth.

"Disney World?" I asked. "In Florida?"

"Well, yes. It seems easier than going to the one in Paris, and you don't want to go back to California right now—so Orlando it is," she said cheerfully.

"Why Disney World?" I asked.

"I felt bad your dad and I didn't get to take you before he died. And then money was tight, and I couldn't afford it. Now it doesn't matter; I've got money in the bank I won't need to live on for the next forty years. You've got your own money, so you don't need mine. Let's go for an entire week and see all the parks. I want to stay in the best hotel, watch the fireworks at night, and visit the countries at Epcot."

"Mom, if Dr. Bryn says it's okay, I'll happily take you to Orlando. But, you're wearing me out with your plans, and I'm not even sick! I'm not sure you'll be able to do all of those things," I warned.

"That's okay. If we get there and I can't do everything, I'll do what I can. Will you help me make it happen?"

"Of course."

I was happy to know my mom had lived her life in the way she'd wanted to, and if the only thing on her bucket list was a trip to Disney World—that's where we'd go. I planned to call Dr. Bryn to get the approval and then a travel agent to plan our vacation as soon as possible.

***

I was up early and out for a walk as my internal clock seemed to be off. Sometimes I slept later than I should, or I'd wake before the crack of dawn because of a necessary nap the afternoon before. I was dealing with a lot of issues, and sleeping was difficult.

Although I was fine during the day when Mom needed me to be strong, my subconscious wouldn't let me rest at night, just like after Grace had been born. My lifelong struggle with anxiety had only worsened during Mom's illness, and sometimes I would wake up with night terrors causing me to stay awake for hours.

I was losing my mom and didn't know how I could go on after her death. We'd always had each other, and the thought of being alone terrified me. In the darkest hours of my marriage with Graham, I'd known my mom was there for support and love back at home. Looking toward my future, the lack of direction gave me an unsettled feeling, which was difficult for someone who needed to be in control.

What I did know was Mom and I were going to Disney World. There wasn't anything else of significance on Mom's bucket list.

Some things had been easy to check off, like driving to Cedar Point to eat dinner at the same restaurant where she and Dad had always gone and heading to church early on Easter Sunday so she could get a good seat in front to hear the choir sing the "Hallelujah" chorus at the end of the service.

We'd gone shopping for a red swimsuit and matching cover so she could take it to Florida. She'd always wanted a red suit but thought she was too old to wear such a bright color.

As the end of her life came into sight, she pulled her credit card out buying the $150 set without hesitation. The joy and freedom her end-of-life adventure brought was invigorating for me and made me continue to reevaluate the way I'd been living my life.

Dr. Bryn had suggested letting a few weeks pass so Mom could get her strength back before heading to Florida. I'd been busy making all the reservations for our trip and putting the plans in place. If she was feeling okay, we were set to leave in a little more than a week.

Things were looking up in my personal life as well. I was getting close to being divorced from Graham. The law firm set a meeting for all of us, and Graham's team had agreed to let them Skype with me due to the situation with Mom. This allowed us to keep the ball rolling without having to travel back to California to do it in person.

We'd come to an agreement, although I was currently unemployed and had no idea what my future earnings might be. I hadn't intended to be without a job when we were at the end of our divorce, it just happened that way. Graham felt Mom's illness and my breakdown were a little too convenient and a way to get out of giving a larger financial settlement. Only someone as selfish as Graham would see himself as the victim in such a circumstance.

Luckily for me, Graham was also impulsive. He didn't want to wait any longer than I did for the divorce to be finalized. He wanted to get his money quickly so he could move forward with whatever he was planning.

I didn't care what he thought anymore and was too exhausted to consider his latest rantings of how others had wronged him. I planned to offer him more, but after he said my mom's ovarian cancer had cost him money in the divorce settlement, I told my attorney to cut the deal in half and send it over for his side to review.

It took several days before we heard back. After taking my job status into account, Graham's attorneys had suggested he settle. Finally, we'd agreed on something.

Graham and I were able to complete the divorce process in

a matter of months when sometimes it took years for couples to disconnect their lives from one another. I couldn't help but come to the realization that we were easily divided because we were never very connected to begin with.

The final paperwork was being completed, and all it would take was a signature from both of us to finish it. Just like Grace's adoption, a few marks with a pen legally dismantled complicated personal relationships, even though the emotional ties would bind us forever.

I grabbed a bottle of water and headed for the deck. The morning sunshine brought the promise of spring. The grass was getting greener, and I could see flowers beginning to peek their colorful heads from the dark ground. Mom's condo backed up to woods, and tiny moss-colored buds were beginning to cover the thickness of the trees making it look like someone had taken a paint brush and flecked the canvas with avocado green.

I'd been listening to music on my earbuds during my walk and hadn't noticed a text message had come in. My heart skipped a beat when I saw it was from Ben.

Stop by the shop today? Need to talk.

I wasn't unhappy to hear from Ben. The few times we'd been together since my return to Iowa had reminded me that Ben hadn't left my heart, and each conversation drew me closer to him. I still didn't think it was a good idea to consider the possibility of anything but friendship with him when so much was going on in my life.

I'd be lying if I didn't admit that it *had* occupied my thoughts as I fell asleep at night and let my mind wander from Mom's condition. I wanted his attention, and the thought of spending time with him was exciting and made me forget about my problems.

Was that what Ben wanted to talk about? Even if it would be a fun diversion, I couldn't risk hurting him again. Eventually, I'd have to take my life back, and the time was coming soon. I'd spent years trying to get Elmwood out of my head, only to be back in the same spot facing everything I'd left behind.

"Good morning!" Mom's cheerful voice interrupted my thoughts as she opened the sliding glass door to let me know she was awake. "You're up early!"

"You know me...either sleeping too much or not enough!"

"I wish you could get that figured out. You need your sleep. Maybe you should see a doctor and get it checked out. I'm adding *you getting your sleep issues figured out* to my bucket list." We both laughed at her attempt to make me feel better.

"Mom, *I am* a doctor. I'm fine." I wasn't able to tell her my real problem had to do with her illness and approaching death. "I'll take a little melatonin to get on a more regular sleep schedule. There's nothing to worry about!"

"Okay, honey. Doctor knows best," she said. "Do you want some coffee?"

"I'm one step ahead of you. There's a fresh pot on the counter, and I made some blueberry muffins. I'll come in and join you."

There we sat on an early Saturday morning sipping coffee and eating warm muffins. It made me happy, and I was sad to think of the years I'd spent avoiding the only place that could bring me such joy. I wanted to soak up every moment we had together and keep the memories in a special place to cherish in the years to come. But first, I needed to find out what Ben needed to discuss with me.

O'Brien's Auto Repair buzzed with activity. It was one of the only places in town with donuts, so there were plenty of people who made a stop each weekend to pick out their favorite glazed and sprinkled sweets. Mom had raved about them herself, and one of the first days I was home, I'd snuck out to get several for us to enjoy for breakfast.

It was easy to see success had come to the O'Briens, and I was proud of Ben for bringing what he'd learned at community college back to his dad's shop. It had been his dream to run the place, and it made me happy to see he'd been able to achieve his goal.

I walked into the front office and asked for Ben.

"I'll let him know you're here," the high school girl said.

I wondered if she knew Grace.

"Tell him Cassie's here to see him."

She raised the shop phone and dialed three numbers. "Ben, someone named Cassie is here to see you . . . Okay, yes, I'll send her back. He said to go back to his office. It's the last one on the left."

"Yes, thank you," I said as I began to make my way through another door to the hallway. Ben appeared at the doorway to his office and ushered me in as he closed the door behind us.

"Wow, a shut door. This must be serious," I joked. Ben didn't seem to be amused. Maybe he *wasn't* going to profess his love for me.

"Thanks for coming over, Cass. How's your mom doing?"

"She's hanging in there, but now you have my attention. What's up?"

"I have something serious to discuss with you. There's no

easy way to say it," he said, almost whispering.

"Are you okay? What's going on?" His demeanor was solemn, and it alarmed me.

"I got a call from Jess Sinclair yesterday."

"Oh, no. Is it Grace?" My heart sank as my mind raced to everything that could be wrong. Even though I wasn't Grace's mom in the traditional sense, she was never far from my heart.

"Grace wants to meet us," he said matter of factly.

"She wants to meet you and me?" I asked, shocked. He'd had some time to process the request, but I was just learning of the possibility of a meeting with her.

"Yes."

"Does Jess know I'm back in Elmwood?"

"She knows. I don't know who told her, but she didn't want to contact you herself with Josephine being sick and all. By the way, she told me to tell you how sorry she is about your mom."

"What else? Tell me everything you know," I quickly dismissed the message from Jess, though my heart soared when thinking of how kind she'd always been to me.

"Well, I've talked with Jess over the years. She's brought her car in on a few occasions and asked me to keep an eye out for a used car for Grace when she turned sixteen."

"You're responsible for the little red sports car?" I asked, wishing he'd found something safer and slower. "Whatever, it isn't important right now." I continued, "You and Jess have been talking all these years without me knowing about it? You know things about *our* daughter you haven't shared with me?"

"Cassie, I have my own relationships with people. You made it clear years ago you didn't want to have anything to do with this. I respected your decision, but it doesn't mean I felt the same way. I've kept in touch in an appropriate way to make sure our little girl was okay. And she's really good, so you don't need to worry about that."

I was surprised Ben hadn't mentioned any of this when we'd been together but knew I had no right to feel slighted.

"She knows who we are?"

"No. She knows she's adopted, but she doesn't know any of the details. Jess said she started asking more specific questions around her sixteenth birthday, and she hasn't let up since. Jess feels since she's eighteen, maybe it's time she had some answers. More than anything, Grace is at an age where she's trying to figure out who she is, and knowing this piece of the puzzle would help her to do that. Jess has assured her she had good birth parents and told her we were too young to raise her. She knows her parents weren't drug addicts or had their parental rights taken away, or whatever else a young girl can make up about something like this."

It was a moment I'd dreamed of and dreaded my entire life. It's not that I didn't want to meet her, but I had so much on my plate with my mom and the divorce looming.

We sat for a few minutes, each lost in our own thoughts. Finally, he broke the silence. "I told her we'd be there at 6:00 on Thursday."

"What? You spoke for both of us? I'm not sure—I need time to think about this," I said nervously.

"Cass, our daughter wants to meet us. We can't say no. I can't imagine you haven't been thinking about this for eighteen years. This is a dream come true for me."

"What are we going to say to her? I wanted to become a doctor and get out of Elmwood, so I gave her up? That I couldn't see myself marrying her father at eighteen, so we decided it was better to have someone else raise her?"

"Is that the truth?" he asked. I didn't know if he was asking for Grace or himself.

"Yes . . . no . . . I don't know. There *were* other options, but I didn't want to explore them. If I heard that from my mom, I'd think it was selfish and short-sighted."

"The Sinclairs made the offer to *us* to meet Grace," he added. "We're in this together. You don't have to be scared. Grace has had a wonderful life. One I doubt she would change even if she could. The Sinclairs are her parents. Turner is her brother. This wasn't a mistake, and I don't think she's going to blame us for what happened. She's the same age now as we were when we gave her up. If there was ever a time for her to understand our decision, it's now."

I felt trapped. I'd never liked the feeling of being forced into a decision. I liked to take my time and think about difficult things before having to make a choice. I didn't like to have them thrown on me like a bucket of ice water leaving me wet and shivering with no chance to avoid the uncomfortable sensation of surprise.

I thought of my mom and how this would affect her. If we met Grace, could we be sure she wouldn't tell the entire town? We couldn't very well meet her and make her promise to keep it to herself. Grace was the most important person in the situation, and she would have to have the privilege of telling whomever she wanted.

I'd have to tell my mom about Grace. Josephine Garrett didn't know the most important thing about her beloved daughter, and I couldn't leave it unsaid and risk someone else telling her she had a granddaughter. How would this revelation impact her already failing health?

"Did you ever tell your parents?" I asked, hoping he hadn't. "No. I didn't see where it would do anything except make it more difficult. She's beautiful and smart, and she's always doing something awesome. She's just like you, and everyone loves her. If I'd told my parents, it would have only hurt them to know she existed, but they couldn't be in her life."

I was far from the naive overachiever I'd been in high school but was touched Ben still saw me that way.

"Please say yes, Cassie. We need to do this for Grace. We can handle whatever happens. Don't make me go alone and explain to her why you aren't there." He was right, but I didn't want him to be.

"Okay," I said, knowing the decision would change our lives. My heart beat out of my chest. I was so wrong about Ben's desire to declare his love for me and beg me to go out on a date with him. I felt silly to have thought he'd still be pining for me after so many years, when what he really wanted to discuss was our daughter.

"Where are we meeting?" I asked, wondering where we could have this encounter without calling attention to ourselves.

"Jess wants to do it at their house. She thinks it would be the most private spot for all of us. I'll pick you up, and we can go together."

"I don't want to go to their house, but it makes sense. Are you going to contact Jess and tell her we'll do it?"

"I didn't give her any reason to think we wouldn't be there, so it's all set."

"Okay, but my mom can't know anything about this yet. I'll just tell her we're going to dinner again, and you can pick me up early so we can prepare a little before we go over there."

I was freaking out inside but also wished the meeting wasn't five days away. I could make myself crazy with worry in that amount of time, but it would also give me a chance to figure out what to say and how to eventually share this long-kept secret with my mother.

"What is there to prepare for, Cass?" he asked. "We tell Grace the truth."

Giving up Grace was the defining moment of my life. It gave me my freedom back and took it away at the same time. I had no idea what seemed like the easy way out would rob me of my own happiness in the years to come.

I wanted to give my daughter the answers she deserved, even if it meant my entire life would unravel around me.

Chapter Fourteen
May 2014

It was early on the morning of my thirty-sixth birthday. I sipped herbal tea and looked through a stack of newspapers for articles that didn't make me too anxious about the plight of humanity. My practice kept me so busy it was often the weekend before I could get updated on current events. My attention was easily drawn away from the headlines with news of my own taking precedent over other topics.

Graham had a special day planned to mark another trip around the sun for me. We didn't always have the marriage I'd hoped for, but he never let my birthday pass without some sort of grand gesture.

His excitement for life and the things he was interested in drew me to him, but keeping him at a level of contentment proved to be exhausting. He had two moods, exuberance and despair. The more he experienced such profound highs and lows, the more I found myself pulling away.

I often felt like Graham's mother instead of his life partner, always in the role of encouraging an immature and self centered man who couldn't find his place in the world. I was beginning to realize Graham was somebody who needed to be coddled and dealt with instead of someone I loved and admired.

Ironically, the more negatively I felt toward him, the harder I tried to make our relationship work. Marriage was permanent in my opinion, and I'd been committed enough that I hadn't seriously considered leaving him. I was excited about the surprise to be shared with him at my birthday dinner and optimistic it would be a welcome change in direction for us.

After I'd graduated from Berkeley, I'd done my four years of medical school at USC and then moved on to UCLA to do my residency. I was thrilled to work at such a prestigious hospital, and I'd met Graham during that busy but exciting time in my life.

Jill Bailey and Scott Kramer were medical students I met the first week at UCLA, and we'd hit it off immediately. Good friends made the long hours easier to survive and made the difficult years of medical school more enjoyable.

When I moved in with them, the bedroom arrangement wasn't hard to figure out. Jill and Scott had started dating each other right after meeting, and by the time we all moved in together, they were a serious couple but needed another roommate to help pay the rent.

I was happy to share their well-located apartment, which provided me my own bedroom and adjoining bath. Occasionally I felt like a third wheel, but we were putting in over 60 hours a week, so *who* I was living with wasn't as important as how comfortable my bed was.

On the infrequent occasions when we did have some time

off, we'd often order take-out and watch movies or grab a beer at a local bar. It was on one of those rare nights out that Graham came into my life.

We'd just ordered a double cheese and pepperoni pizza when I noticed a group of guys coming through the doors of Benji's, one of our favorite watering holes within walking distance of our apartment.

I recognized several of the med students who'd obviously had a few drinks before they arrived and were ready to blow off some steam on a Friday night. We exchanged greetings, and the group of rowdy guys found a corner booth and started ordering pitchers of beer.

One of the residents headed toward the jukebox asking us what kind of music we wanted to hear. Despite our suggestions for something mellow, Justin Timberlake's *Sexy Back* began to play over the speakers with its electro rhythm and blues beat filling the bar with sound. The bass reverberated off the walls, and I began to move to the music as a relaxed mood washed over me.

Jill motioned to me, and we abandoned Scott and our rum and Cokes for the small dance floor in the corner. She took my hand, and we began to dance to the beat of the music, doing our best to transform ourselves from the exhausted and overwhelmed residents we were, to two sexy and alluring twenty-something women out on the town. We were quickly joined by several of the guys from the corner booth, and I was drenched in sweat after a few songs.

I was happy when our pizza was delivered to the table where Scott still sat. He was giving us a less than pleased look as he began to douse his pizza with parmesan cheese and crushed red peppers. I started toward the table following behind Jill who was already making excuses for leaving him alone in the booth.

"Hey . . ." said an extremely attractive blond guy who'd been dancing with us for a couple of songs. "Where are you going?"

"Time to eat," I said, making an eating motion with my hands to get the message across above the loud music.

He grabbed my hands and pulled me close to him as he said in my ear, "I want to keep dancing with the prettiest girl in the place!" His handsome smile made me want to forego pizza and spend the rest of the night looking into his piercing blue eyes.

I turned toward him and said loudly, "I don't even know your name!"

"I'm Tom's roommate—Graham," he said. I knew Tom from the surgical rotation; it was hard to forget a guy who fainted during the first observation as soon as a cut was made into the patient's chest.

"I'm Cassie Garrett," I answered, shaking his outstretched hand.

"Why don't you get some food, and then let me buy you a drink so we can get to know each other better. You come highly recommended by Tom…and he's pretty critical of the ladies," he said with a charismatic wink.

After pizza and a couple more drinks, Scott and Jill headed for home and left me sitting at the bar talking to my new friend who'd promised to walk me home after Jill had protested about leaving me behind.

We weren't far from the apartment, and I felt secure staying out with a bunch of guys from work. Once they got some food in their bellies and the music got a little softer, they settled down and were the respectful young doctors I was used to being around.

By the end evening, I'd learned Graham was a first year professor of creative writing at UCLA and had a published collection of short stories and was just finishing his first full-length novel. He was two years younger than me, but since he wasn't a student anymore, he seemed older and more mature than the residents I knew.

He'd done his graduate work at The University of Iowa Writers' Workshop. Once he found out I was originally from Iowa, our conversation turned more personal, and by the end of our time together, we'd already made plans to see each other the following weekend.

As a writer, he was creative and open with his feelings, including sharing on that first night he didn't want kids. When I told him I didn't want children either, he looked at me like he'd just scratched a winning lottery ticket. I'd never met anyone quite like him and was completely head over heels in love within a few weeks.

Graham had a zest for life like I'd never seen and had dreams to travel the world and become a New York Times bestselling author. Mostly, all I wanted to do on my weekends off was sleep, but Graham kept our relationship exciting by planning getaways and surprising me with gifts and flowers when I least expected them.

When my residency was over the following spring, I took a job at a clinic in Ventura, and Graham and I moved to our dream home after a simple wedding at a vineyard we frequented.

The occasion had also been the first meeting between my mom and Graham. She hadn't felt completely comfortable with the relationship moving so quickly, but she'd accepted it anyway.

I couldn't remember much of the advice Dad had given during my childhood, but one phrase stuck in my head. He'd always told me *"If something seems too good to be true, then it probably is."* My whirlwind romance with Graham was an example of what he was warning me about, even if the advice hadn't sunk in deep enough to keep me from making a huge mistake.

Graham's unhappiness started after my job took us to Ventura. He'd spent the first couple years of our marriage commuting to UCLA to teach, but work travel wasn't as much fun as other kinds of travel. After several disagreements with the dean of his department over a variety of minor problems Graham seemed to turn into major disputes, he decided to take a job at a smaller university closer to home.

The commute was shorter, but he hadn't been fulfilled with his career change. I made ten times as much as Graham did, and we both knew our life needed to be in Ventura to accommodate my job commitments. His lack of passion for his position caused him to pull back from teaching and spend more time writing. He had several books going but never seemed to be able to finish a concept or get his ideas accepted by an agent. With more time on his hands, he became increasingly restless.

Marriage was difficult enough without having to micromanage the mental health of your spouse.

As time went on, it became a full-time endeavor for me. It was a main topic of discussion with my therapist who I'd been seeing for a year this time around; still working through the anxiety I'd dealt with since college.

I'd begun to think our marital troubles had as much to do

with some of *my* issues as they did with Graham and his unhappiness. Maybe the answer for both of us was to get the focus back on *us* instead of each of us pursuing our individual interests.

So, when Graham and I'd gone camping in the Sequoia National Park, if you can call staying in a cabin with room service *camping*, I was feeling good about myself and open to new adventures waiting for us.

We seemed to be going through a better time as a couple. Graham had been asked to serve on an arts board with the city of Ventura, and this made him feel more respected and professionally fulfilled for a change. He'd been writing in a new office we'd set up in the pool house, and he was finally happier in his career after taking on another new role at Ventura Community College.

Graham had loaded the car the morning of our trip, accidentally leaving my toiletry bag on the bathroom vanity. I'd been able to replace the makeup, toothbrush, and other necessities at a Walmart outside Fresno. The one thing I couldn't replace was the diaphragm in the bottom of the bag, waiting for the perfect romantic moment in the California wilderness. With this dilemma in mind, I'd grabbed a box of condoms off the shelf to make sure we were protected.

After we watched the sunset from our cabin's private hot tub and finished a bottle of champagne, Graham had seductively dried me off with the plush resort towels. He'd carried me to the king-size bed and began to explore my body with his mouth. "Remember, you have to use a condom," I reminded him, knowing he wasn't happy he'd left my birth control device on the counter either.

"I'm not using one of those damn things," he said

breathlessly as he persisted in seducing me. As the romance continued under the leaves of some of the oldest trees on record, I silently hoped having sex above what must be very fertile soil was good luck.

Graham didn't realize he was making love to someone who's biological clock had been ticking loudly. We'd never discussed having kids since we'd been married; those conversations had taken place before we took our vows. I assumed his actions were a sign we'd both had a change of heart.

It had been six weeks since that night in the California forest and eight days since I'd confirmed my pregnancy. I was nervously excited about this change in life circumstances but not so sure about telling Graham. He had to know of the possibility, and I assumed he must've been open to parenthood, or he wouldn't have taken such a risk when protection was available. I hoped he'd softened to the idea of a baby—because we were having one.

If our problems as a couple came from having nothing to connect us, a child would bridge the gap. I had an elaborate plan for revealing the pregnancy at my birthday dinner and hoped it would be a happy memory when we looked back on the night starting us on our most exciting adventure ever.

***

We had a dinner reservation at Bistro 1426 and Graham had the limousine pick us up early due to rush hour traffic. With soft lighting and a fully stocked bar, the ride to one of the city's swankiest restaurants supplied part of the fun.

I was touched that Graham had made all the arrangements for my birthday celebration and hoped my announcement would make it an unforgettable night for both of us.

Graham filled our glasses and made a toast. "To the most beautiful birthday girl in the world!" He kissed me softly on the neck and handed me the crystal champagne flute. I appreciated his effort to make me feel special. Even though things weren't the best between us, we did have moments when things felt right.

I barely touched the champagne, telling Graham I'd rather wait and have drinks at the restaurant, and he didn't question me about it further. I never drank much, so he wasn't suspicious of my motives. The ride went quickly as I went over in my head again how I planned to share my unexpected news with Graham.

When we arrived, the driver opened the side door and offered me his hand. The fresh air hit my face, and my senses were awakened to the sights and sounds of the city. I loved living in Ventura, but having access to Los Angeles was so much fun.

Graham got out on the other side of the car and handed the driver some cash instructing him to come back when we called. Graham took my hand and led me into the dimly lit restaurant. He liked feeling important, so when I told him a patient's son owned one of Los Angeles' most popular hot spots, he was more than happy to take advantage of the connection.

We were seated at a nice table in the back corner near the patio. There were small lit trees lining the railing of the outside space, and the tiny white lights made it look festive. It was romantic and perfect for what I had planned.

We ordered a round of drinks, and I excused myself to use the bathroom. Before entering the restroom, I found our waiter and asked him to change my order to tonic and lime, without vodka, and to keep them coming.

I smiled coyly, patting my stomach and slipping him a twenty. The handsome young man shoved the money into his pocket and winked at me saying, "Your secret is safe with me, ma'am."

When I returned to the table, our drinks had arrived. As I sat down, my attention went to a small box placed on the appetizer plate in front of me. Graham reached over and squeezed my hand and said, "Happy birthday."

I unwrapped the delicate red box encasing a pair of diamond earrings. "Oh, they're beautiful!" I said, quickly taking out the earrings I was wearing to put the new ones in.

"They looked like you," Graham said, smiling proudly from across the table.

"This was so thoughtful. Thank you." Graham could be so charming, and at times like this, I felt like the luckiest girl in the world.

"It's been a lovely birthday . . . more than I expected," I started.

"You liked my homemade blueberry pancakes this morning? I promised you when we got married, I'd make sure your life was interesting, and I've done a good job keeping that pledge. What do you think is the best adventure we've had?" Graham asked playfully. "Golfing in Scotland? Or what about when we skydived over the Grand Canyon?"

The conversation was common between the two of us as Graham loved when I praised his adventurous spirit. He'd planned plenty of fun-filled outings and unique day trips to places I'd never heard of. He never got tired of hearing how great he was at planning surprises. Tonight, it would be Graham who would be surprised to find out he was going to be a dad.

"Well, it was the most terrifying for sure." I remembered how frightening skydiving had been, and I'd vowed never to do it again. "We've had such an amazing life so far. Do you ever wonder what our lives will be like when we get older?"

"As long as I'm physically able to do things, I'm going to do them. I thought next year we could take an African safari. A guy at work told me the other day about his brother-in-law who took a month off and stayed in these deluxe yurts right by a game reserve."

"It would be difficult for me to be gone a month . . . it wouldn't be the worst thing to slow down a little bit, would it? Sometimes I'd like to relax at home on the weekends. With work being so busy, more down time might be nice," I added, still waiting for the opportunity to share my surprise.

"I guess . . . we'll slow down when we have to. We've got a long time before that happens."

Graham wanted to be able to jet off to Vail for the weekend when snow was in the forecast or take a last-minute flight to Maui just because they were predicting perfect ocean swells for surfing. He'd never wanted the constraints of a family, and until recently, I felt the same way.

"Well, I know it's *my* birthday, but I have something for you too." My heart was racing.

"Something for me?" he asked with a confused look on his face.

"You'll understand when you open it."

The waiter appeared again, although our cocktails were

only partially gone. "May I bring you another round?" he asked, giving me a knowing smile.

"Cassie, another drink?" Graham asked.

"Sure, maybe one more...." I replied as the waiter began to share the dinner specials. With our orders placed and an appetizer on the way, I reached into my purse and pulled out a small box and slid it over to Graham.

"I can't imagine what you'd be giving me on *your* birthday," he said. He removed the green ribbon and unwrapped the gift covered in brown paper. He opened the box to reveal three small leaves I'd saved as a keepsake from our weekend in the Sequoia National Forest.

"Hey, aren't these the leaves you picked up from our trip?" he asked. I nodded as he unfolded the thin tissue paper revealing a framed poem I'd typed and cut from cardstock so it would sit precisely in the middle like a photo.

"What's this?" he said, cocking his head in confusion.

"Read it . . . " I sat in quiet anticipation.

"Okay—*ten little fingers and ten little toes, two little eyes and one little nose, put them together and what do you got? Our baby on the way, ready or not . . .*"

His head jerked up as he read the last phrase, and he stared at me without expression.

I smiled and reached for his hand. "We're going to have a baby.
"

Chapter Fifteen
April 2015

I got into the car and let out a heavy sigh.

"Are you okay?" Ben asked.

"Yeah, I just want to get this over with."

"Cassie, I wish you weren't dreading this. I'm so excited I can hardly stand it! Do you think Grace wants to meet us so she can yell at us, telling us how much she hates us? She wants to know who we are and confirm in her own mind she came from something good. And she did. We loved each other, and she came from us."

Years of self-loathing bubbled to the surface, and I couldn't hide my insecurities. The therapy I'd had over the years had helped, but I just couldn't shake my belief that I didn't deserve to be happy.

Ben reached over and squeezed my hand, and I took it gratefully. "It'll be okay. I promise. Let's go meet our daughter," he said with confidence.

We rang the bell, and I could hear footsteps and the bark of a dog somewhere in the house. When the door opened, Jess stood smiling as she welcomed us in. She looked older but more beautiful that ever with her hair pulled back and a turquoise sweater paired with dark-wash jeans. Jess had always been simple and classic and the definition of what the ideal woman should be.

She shook Ben's hand, thanking him for coming, and opened her arms wide for me to embrace her. As I fell into her, we began to cry. Jess had promised me they would give Grace the best life possible. When she put her arms around me, I knew they'd kept their word.

Dr. Sinclair joined us and was friendly, if not overly warm like Jess. Those were their personalities, so it didn't surprise me that he seemed a little reserved. We were all feeling uneasy at not knowing how the evening would go.

The house had the same homey vibe as it did nearly two decades before, although the furniture and colors had been updated in the formal living room. I saw a framed photo on the table behind the sofa of a grown-up looking Turner on his wedding day and another right beside it with he and his wife and what looked like a baby boy smiling between them. The Sinclairs were grandparents.

When Turner found out his sister had been my little girl, I knew it would all make sense to him why I never kept in touch after I'd headed off to college.

We exchanged some pleasantries about it finally being spring, and they inquired about my mom expressing their sadness at her terminal diagnosis. They asked what my plans were, and I told them I wasn't sure.

"I want you to know that we're extremely grateful the two of you were willing to do this for Gracie," Dr Sinclair started. "She's had a lot of questions, and quite frankly, she's been making up her own story about what probably became of her biological parents to the point of obsession. We think this meeting is the healthiest thing for her."

"We thought the two of you might want to meet her as well, so we're hoping this wasn't a selfish request. When I heard Cassie was here caring for her mother, it seemed like we'd been handed an unexpected opportunity," Jess added, taking Dr. Sinclair 's hand as they sat together on the loveseat looking unsure of what was about to happen. "Being Grace's parents has been one of the most incredible gifts we've ever been given, and we're so thankful the two of you chose us to raise her."

I appreciated her words, although they sounded rehearsed and stiff.

"Cassie and I are happy to be here and are looking forward to talking with Grace," Ben replied, filling up the uncomfortable silence between all of us.

Ben had seen Grace many times, but for me the thought of finally seeing her again was overwhelming. I recalled the last moments she and I shared before the California Sinclairs arrived and made sure she was moved permanently from my room.

I remembered the way she looked and smelled. Her skin was soft and pink, and she snuggled close to me as I whispered in her ear the message I'd promised Ben I'd give her about how much we loved her. After so many years, all I wanted to do was take her in my arms again and tell her the same thing.

"We wanted these few minutes to talk alone with you, and we asked Grace to stay upstairs until we invite her to join you. Grace asked us to give the three of you some time alone if both of you are okay with it. We'll stay in the game room, and

Grace can come up and get us after the three of you are done talking."

"Sure, that works fine for us," Ben said, looking to me for confirmation.

"Whatever Grace needs. We'll answer any questions she has, and I hope we can ask her some things about her life too. I'd love to hear about her college plans if that's something she's willing to share," I added.

"Great," Jess said as the two of them started to get up. "We'll let Grace know you're here and make ourselves scarce. Thank you again, and Cassie, please let me know if there's anything we can do for you or your mom while you're here."

The two of them left the room, and I glanced over at Ben who looked terrified. He raised his hands out in front of his body and showed me he was shaking. I smiled and closed my eyes tight in anticipation. I heard footsteps on the stairs and straightened up, so Grace didn't walk in on the two of us acting like crazy people.

She rounded the corner apprehensively. "Hi, I'm Grace," she said softly. I looked at her face and could see Ben's nose and my mother's smile looking back at me.

We got up, and there was an awkward moment when we didn't know if we should hug or shake hands. We ended up doing neither, and I began the conversation.

"Grace . . . it's so nice to meet you. I'm Cassie Garrett. And this is—"

"I'm Ben O'Brien."

We'd decided earlier we would introduce ourselves and let her talk, so we didn't inundate her with information. We thought it was best to let her take the lead for the direction of our conversation.

"Can we sit and talk for a while?" she asked.

"Of course," I said.

"Yes, whatever you want," Ben replied on top of my words. We were talking over each other and jockeying for position. We ended up sitting where the Sinclairs had sat, and Grace took one of the chairs beside the loveseat.

Grace was a beautiful young woman, and her name fit her perfectly. She was poised and confident, qualities I knew were a result of having Jess for a mother.

Although she was taller than me, I could see a resemblance to my former high school self. I wondered how nature and nurture worked together to make a person who they were when they were adopted.

"Well, I'm excited to meet both of you," Grace said quietly and with some trepidation. "Are you married to each other?"

"No . . . I still live here in Elmwood. Your mom—I mean Cassie, lives in California. She's a doctor!" Ben looked so proud of me, and it touched me he wanted Grace to know that about me.

"Well, I don't live in California anymore," I offered, letting that bit of information trail off since I didn't want to expand on it anyway.

"How did you know each other?" she asked. "I mean, how did you end up having me?"

Ben started this part of the conversation, and I was grateful for it.

"Well, you see we were together in high school. We dated each other for more than a year and were in love. We were young and as sometimes is the case, we got pregnant with you at a time in our lives when we weren't equipped to be parents. Cassie babysat Turner, and when we were faced with this situation, your mom helped us to figure out what to do. They wanted to have another baby and weren't able to, and they agreed to adopt you."

"Did you ever think about keeping me?" Grace asked. I couldn't read the look on her face. Was she glad she'd had the life the Sinclairs had given her, or did she resent us for taking what she might consider the easy way out?

There was a pause in the conversation. Ben had been so unwavering in his desire to raise our baby girl, and I didn't want him to have to answer this difficult question on his own.

"Grace, we wanted you to have everything you could ever want, and at the time, we were just too young to be good parents to you."

I didn't feel like Ben should bear any of the responsibility for having other people raise our little girl, and I was going to make that clear to Grace.

"Ben wanted to get married and raise you together, but he allowed me to make the final decision for all of us. It seemed like the right thing to do back then. We never told anyone about the adoption, not even our own parents, out of respect for you and your new family. We loved you so much, and when you were born, I almost changed my mind. You were so special, and I wanted to keep you even though it would have been difficult. When I thought about what was best for you, I decided the Sinclairs could offer you so much more than we could."

"Wow, that must have been really hard," she said. "I couldn't have grown up in a better family, so thank you for choosing them for me." Knowing she understood and was happy with the life she'd been given released a burden from my heart I hadn't realized had been so heavy.

She continued, "Would you both tell me some things about yourselves? I wanted to kind of find out who you are. Not only your names but things like what you like to do and if I have any brothers and sisters or anything like that."

Ben started telling her about his boys and his job. He told her to stop by anytime, and he would check her car for free. He told her how proud he was of her when he saw her name in the newspaper or heard of another award she'd received at school through a customer simply sharing the news of the town.

She asked about our parents and if they were still living. Ben told her his parents lived in Elmwood. He told her my dad had died many years ago, and my mom was battling terminal cancer. I loved him for telling her what she needed to know and realizing how difficult it would have been for me to share that information in the highly emotional setting.

She asked if she could meet her biological grandparents, and we agreed that with her parents' blessing we could arrange it.

Grace told us she'd been excited to hear I was a doctor because she'd been accepted into the nursing program at St. Ambrose University. I loved this choice for her; I'd considered the liberal arts college in Eastern Iowa for my undergraduate work during my own college search in the mid-nineties.

Grace said she'd be rooming with her best friend from high school, and they were excited to decorate their room and be on their own for the first time. She talked about her school activities and her love of animals and how she'd considered going to Iowa State to become a veterinarian. It was the best conversation I could have hoped for, and I began to feel the years of regret fall away.

We spent nearly two hours together before Ben finally said we should go. I couldn't believe he was ready to end such a wonderful evening but knew if one of us didn't bring it up we might never leave. The Sinclairs didn't come back to join the conversation, and I didn't think it was our place to try to include them.

"How long will you be in Elmwood?" Grace asked me.

"I'm not sure. I'll be here as long as my mom needs me." I hoped it would be a long time, but I knew better.

"This was so nice, Grace. Thanks for asking to meet us. If you ever need anything, you let us know," Ben said with tears in his eyes.

"Grace, you are as perfect today as you were on the day you were born. I'm so proud of you, and we want only the best for you," I said, my own tears welling up.

I should have told her that I'd spent my entire life loving her in my heart, but I couldn't get the words to come out over the lump in my throat.

"Thank you for giving me a great life. I love you both for that, and maybe I can see you again, and we can get to know each other better," Grace said, her eyes searching ours for direction of how to proceed in what would be our new lives after the meeting.

I put my arms around Grace, and Ben came up behind her and hugged both of us. It was the first time our little family had ever been together.

Meeting Grace had given me the gift of peace, and I had a feeling it would be the first step on the long road back to finding myself.

***

I woke up on the last day of our Disney holiday with sore feet and a sunburned face. We were staying at the Disney Beach Club Villas, but being right in the middle of the happiest place on Earth couldn't take away the feeling of foreboding that Mom didn't have much time left.

Since we'd met Grace, I needed to find the right time to tell Mom about the grandchild she never knew she had. Although I'd planned to tell her in Florida, we'd been having such a good time I decided to wait until we got home.

I opened my bedroom door and saw Mom already sitting on the sofa in the living room of our suite. She was still in her pajamas, and she didn't look well.

"What's wrong?" I asked, taking her hand.

"I'm not feeling the best," she said. "I'm short of breath and having some pain in my abdomen."

"Should I get your hydrocodone?" I knew she hadn't been taking it because it made her drowsy, and she wanted to be alert and ready for fun.

"No, I don't want to ruin our last day of vacation," she said through tears.

"Let's get some medicine in you and have you rest. We can go out later if you feel better. Things are open until midnight." I wanted her to sleep and not worry about seeing another Disney attraction when she wasn't feeling good.

"Cassie," she said as I helped her into her room, "I'm getting weaker. I can feel it. Maybe this trip was too much for me." It devastated me to see her losing hope.

"We've been careful not to do too much, you'll be okay if you lie down for a while. I'll order some breakfast for us, and when you get up, you can have some fruit and maybe some toast." I was tired too. Mostly because I'd been pushing Mom around in a wheelchair since we left Elmwood.

She'd dreamt of going to Disney World, and I wanted her to be able to enjoy her last day. Even though her condition had its perks, like going to the front of the line for every attraction we visited, it wasn't enough to keep her from getting worn out quickly.

I helped her into bed and covered her with the comforter, closing the curtains tight so it would be dark for her. "Do you want some tea?" I was hoping to do something to help her feel better.

"No, sweetheart. Just let me sleep."

I closed the door behind me and went out on the balcony to collect my thoughts. I watched families eating breakfast by the pool and children swimming in the early morning sun.

We waited too long. Even though we'd had a good time, Mom had been worn out most of the time and wasn't able to fully enjoy it.

I embraced the gift of seeing Mom so happy at being able to take this dream vacation together but wished we'd taken lots of trips over the years. I'd had the money to take her wherever she would have wanted to go. I'd been too wrapped up in my own life to think of what I was missing with her and had no idea our time was short.

We'd visited the Magic Kingdom, Hollywood Studios, and Animal Kingdom already. It was our last day, and we'd planned to go to Epcot where we had a reservation for dinner at an authentic Italian restaurant. I wanted Mom to feel like she was visiting the homeland of her grandparents, and with her health deteriorating quickly, visiting Epcot was the best I could do in the time we had left.

Mom didn't get up until late in the afternoon. She was

feeling better, so she put on her new red swimsuit, and we sat by the pool for a while. We ordered frozen drinks with umbrellas in them and enjoyed the warm Florida sunshine.

In the evening, we took the tram to Epcot and made our way to the country of Italy. Mom was smiling and happy as she talked with the servers dressed in the traditional colors of green, white, and red. She told them about her grandparents leaving Italy to come to America, oblivious to the fact that the Epcot cast members were probably college students from the drama department at the University of Central Florida.

I pushed Mom's wheelchair through the cobblestone streets, and we ordered gelato from a street vendor. I knew it would probably be one of the last fun outings she would have before her illness started to take over, and I was happy we'd been able to make the trip at all.

As we made our way out of the theme park, we took a quick detour through France. A character dressed as a mime came up to Mom and handed her a red rose. Mom breathed in the scent of the fresh flower and smiled as he bent to give her a silent kiss on the cheek.

It was such a small gesture, but it brought tears to my eyes to see how happy it made her. Cancer would steal so much from us in the coming weeks, but it couldn't take our memories of a tropical vacation.

***

We'd only been home for a couple of days when our hospice nurse suggested ordering some oxygen for Mom. The cancer was spreading, and she wasn't getting the air she needed in her lungs due to the growing tumors. Mom did her best to try to hide how she felt, but her body revealed what couldn't be denied.

It was time to tell Mom about Grace. I'd thought about it and weighed my options for telling her or not telling her. It would be easier to let the years of deception stay hidden like a page ripped out of the scrapbook of my life; the remnants of paper attached to the binding, and only I would know what should have been there.

I'd decided I couldn't allow my mom to die without knowing she had a grandchild. She deserved to know what happened all those years before and all the years since. As I was coming to terms with the end of Mom's life, my gut told me she would want to know, and my secret couldn't be kept any longer.

How to bring it up was the biggest challenge. You don't just casually say, *"By the way, I had a baby you never knew about, and she's been living across town from you for eighteen years."* There would be questions and disappointment, and thinking about it made me feel like a scared teenager all over again.

I'd come to treasure our after-dinner talks when Mom was comfortably settled in her favorite chair. I knew the conversation about Grace would be different than the rest, with neither of us feeling at ease when it was over.

"Mom, there's something we need to talk about." I drew a jagged breath and began.

"What is it, sweetie?" she asked softly. She had a quilt over her legs, and her feet were propped up in the recliner. She looked as if she could drift off to sleep, which made me feel worse knowing what I was about to tell her.

"I need to tell you something that's going to be difficult for you to hear. It's something that could impact the way you feel about me." As I prepared to reveal the truth after so many years, I worried she might be so angry that she'd never want to see me again.

"There's nothing you could tell me that would change the way I feel about you. A mother's love for her child is infinite. From the moment I knew I was going to be your mom, you had my eternal love and support. You are my one true accomplishment and the reason I've lived at all."

I would carry those words with me for the rest of my life. I wasn't sure she'd ever said something so meaningful to me.

"Do you remember back when I left early for college and went out to California to live with Dr. Sinclair's brother and his wife?"

"I've got cancer—not Alzheimer's!" she joked. "I still wish you'd taken the scholarship at The University of Iowa instead of Berkeley. Maybe you'd have come back to Elmwood to practice medicine."

"Mom, I'm so sorry to tell you this now . . ." I began to cry. She stared at me, unable to figure out where the conversation was leading.

". . . I left because I was pregnant. I went to California so no one would know I had a baby and gave it up for adoption."

I'd thought about this conversation for years, and I'd seen it play out in a hundred different ways in my mind. I was about to find out if my fears measured up to the reality of her response. Mom was silent for a few minutes, and I could see her brain trying to grasp what I'd just told her.

"Tell me everything."

I started with the Sinclairs adopting Grace and worked my way back. Then worked my way forward again and explained and apologized repeatedly for avoiding home and abandoning her over the years because I couldn't face my own mistakes.

I told her of the conversations I'd had with Ben over the past few weeks, and that we'd met Grace. I added that she was the most beautiful girl in the entire world.

"Of course she is," Mom said proudly. "You were her mother."

I began to sob. I'd been so afraid of my mom's reaction, only to have her embrace and love me the way I'd hoped she would.

We talked for more than three hours with Mom asking me any question she had about the situation. Her emotions ranged from surprise she hadn't had a clue, to anger at the Sinclairs for not telling her about the pregnancy.

It felt so freeing to get everything off my chest and be able to have a truthful conversation with my dying mother about the most significant thing that had ever happened in my life.

Before I helped her to bed, she spoke the sweetest words I'd ever heard.

"When do I get to meet Grace?"

Chapter Sixteen
May 2014

The waiter said, "Here you go. One for the lady, and a dirty martini with extra olives for you, sir." He gave me a quick wink with our drinks. "I'll be right back with your appetizer, and your dinners will be up in a bit."

He left quickly, and I wondered if he realized I was right in the middle of telling my husband that he was going to be a father. Graham sat with his hand over his mouth looking shocked. I couldn't tell if it was a good shock or a bad shock, but it was definitely shock.

"Say something, Graham. Isn't this wonderful? We're having a baby." I said it again, thinking the second time would elicit the reaction I hoped for.

"I don't want a baby," he replied flatly, looking directly at me with a cold stare. His emotions were somewhere between fury and bursting into tears.

"Well, we're having one, Graham. It must have happened when we were camping. It's the only time we didn't use protection and..."

"And I don't want a baby. You knew that. I've told you from the beginning that I didn't want to have kids. How could you do this to me?"

I grabbed my purse and headed for the door. The birthday celebration was over.

Standing outside in the warm evening air, my stomach churned, a mixture of pregnancy and despair at Graham's reaction. Watching through the glass, I could see Graham paying the server and calling for the car. The limo arrived moments later, and I got in before Graham came outside.

"Is everything okay, ma'am?" the driver asked as he opened the heavy black door for me.

"I'm not feeling well."

If I'd thought the driver would pull away, leaving Graham to find his own way home, I would have had him drive me to the airport allowing me to catch the first flight to anywhere else.

Graham got in and slumped in his seat. He'd left the handmade gift and leaves from our trip sitting on the table to be discarded. Apparently, the gift wasn't going to be a treasured keepsake like I'd hoped.

My mind raced, and I felt scared like when I was pregnant with Grace. This time was different though. I could raise this child on my own and didn't need Graham in my life and neither did our baby.

We drove for miles before either of us spoke.

"Why would you have done that?" he asked quietly.

"Well, the last time I checked, it wasn't possible for me to impregnate myself."

"No, I mean why would you tell me this in a public place and on your birthday of all days," his voice grew louder, and I wondered if the driver could hear us through the partition.

He was processing information I'd had some time to think about, but his repulsed reaction left no room for clarification.

"*Shit*, Cassie. Neither of us want kids. What are we going to do? You don't want this baby, do you? Because if you do—I'm not sure what it means for us."

He'd said it. The words he could never take back.

"Yes, I want this baby. I was hoping you'd want it too. You knew when we had unprotected sex that this could be the outcome. I thought since you didn't seem to have any issue with it you'd changed your mind."

"Just because I wanted to screw my wife without using a rubber doesn't mean I wanted a baby! *Dammit, Cassie* . . . this isn't something you do on a whim. You've known since the first night we met I didn't want to have kids. *You* didn't want to have kids. And now you're trapping me into this, and I'm going to be the bad guy for standing up for what I've made clear to you."

"I'm trapping *you*? Because it didn't seem like you were trapped when you were on top of me having sex without a condom I asked you to use . . . You're being a complete jackass, and I don't care if you want to be a part of this child's life or not. I'm having this baby, and you can go straight to hell for all I care. I don't need you, and right now, don't even want you in my life. As soon as we get home, you get your stuff out of our bedroom and move to the pool house. You can stay there until we figure out what to do."

We didn't speak for the rest of the ride home. I was planning the next eighteen years of my life as Graham did shots from the mini bar. It was typical of the way we each dealt with life, and it had never been clearer to me that we were not the right fit as a couple.

For the first time in years, I felt in control of my life and certain Graham wasn't going to be a part of it anymore. Like my therapist had said, I'd made the best decision possible when I was a teenager. As an adult, I wanted to embrace happiness and my chance to be a mom.

Grace had a great mother in Jess Sinclair, and I could be someone else's mom without hurting her. I was ready and didn't need a man to make a wonderful life for a child.

Graham slept on the couch that night and moved to the pool house the next day as asked. The small apartment was a nice perk we'd sometimes rented as a furnished studio when the opportunity arose. It had been empty since our last tenant left without warning when we asked him to refrain from late night skinny dipping with his many overnight visitors. He'd caused such a ruckus, police had to be called to our house twice after the neighbors woke to loud music and late-night parties taking place when we were out of town.

We'd cleaned it up recently when Graham decided he needed a creative space for writing more than we needed the rental income. Thankfully, it provided the physical separation we needed while we let our emotions cool.

***

It was nearly a week before we spoke. Graham didn't enter the main house at all in the first few days of his stay in the backyard. He'd taken some bedding and towels from the linen closet, but he couldn't stay out there forever.

We needed to discuss things, and I'd already decided if Graham continued to feel the same way as he had so eloquently expressed to me the night of my birthday, I'd file for divorce. Nothing would change my decision to have the baby.

On Friday night after work, I noticed he'd made something

on the stove because the dishes were in the dishwasher. I'd worked a late shift, so by the time I got home, I could see the pool house was dark.

Over the weekend, he'd been in the house several times to get clothes and a fresh tube of toothpaste. I'd heard him watching TV in the den when I got home Sunday morning after being on call, but I'd gone straight to bed.

Every day I felt stronger about my decision. I didn't want to be a single mom but was ready to do it if necessary. I didn't know how long we could go on without discussing our baby's existence, but I'd decided it wasn't going to be me to make the first attempt at a conversation.

I was up early before work making a cup of decaf when the back door opened, and Graham stepped into the kitchen without saying a word. He looked awful, unshaven, and distraught. My heart softened when I saw how devastated he looked. I hated him for the way he'd treated me but wasn't surprised at his reaction and felt responsible for blindsiding him at the restaurant.

Regardless of how he received the news, I'd expected him to be a mature man and take responsibility instead of acting like a selfish child throwing a tantrum about having to do something he didn't want to do.

"Hi."

"Hi," I said, continuing to make my coffee with my back to the kitchen island where Graham had taken a seat.

"I'm sorry about how things went the other night. You took me by complete surprise. It was unfair of you to hit me with something like that at an expensive French restaurant. This isn't your fault, and I'm sorry if I made it sound that way. I was so damn taken aback . . ." he continued to take one step forward and one step back during his flimsy apology.

"So, you said," I replied firmly.

"I'm trying to be honest with you. This isn't something I would choose. If you've decided you're having this baby, I'll try to get on board and do the best I can."

"Wow, Graham. I appreciate the lackluster offer, but parenthood isn't one of those things you just attempt. A child's life is at stake. This isn't like taking up tennis and deciding you don't like it, so you drop your club membership and sell your racket on eBay." I wanted to accept his apology but didn't know how to do it considering all the terrible things he'd said to me.

"What do you want me to say? I love you, and don't want to be without you. I'm doing the best I can here."

Graham came up behind me and put his arms around me. I didn't want to give in, but it was hard not to. Although I didn't need him to raise our baby, I wanted him to be a part of its life. I'd adored my father so much and didn't want my baby to be without one.

"Could we try to start over?" he asked. Something had changed between us, and I wasn't sure it could be fixed. The accusatory way he reacted to the best news any person could get in their lives had scarred me, and I didn't know if I'd ever feel the same way about him. But, I had to try, for the baby's sake at least.

"I love kids. You know I adore my nieces and nephews— I'm not a monster. I just never imagined myself as a father and don't think not wanting to do something has to make me the villain in this. I wanted a different lifestyle than what everyone else has. I wanted to experience everything life has to offer instead of stunting my growth as a human being to think about daycare, and preschool, and little league. There are things I *still* want to accomplish. You know I've started to write that new novel. How am I going to finish it with a baby on the way? How are we going to do the things we want and be parents too?"

"Everyone else seems to figure it out. Whether you like it or not, we *are* having a baby. We can do this. Life changes, but I honestly believe it's going to change it for the better. You can't be on board for my sake; you have to love this baby. There's no gray area in this thing. You decide."

"I promise I'll do my best to make all of this up to you and be the dad this kid needs," he said with tears in his eyes.

Could I believe him?

Graham pulled me close again, and I allowed myself to be held. Feeling my belly touch Graham's body, I thought of the new life inside of me and made myself be happy he'd decided to stay.

Graham moved back to our bedroom, and we put the words we'd spoken and the private thoughts we'd had about each other aside to face parenthood together. We were fractured as a couple but willing to struggle through preparing our lives for the arrival of a baby neither of us had planned for, because at the end of the day, we wanted to make it work.

In the following weeks, I loved seeing Graham getting excited about the prospect of our new family. He was trying, and I found myself regretting the way I'd treated him and the thoughts I'd had toward him.

Maybe the baby would be the key to our happiness as a couple. Everything felt new and good, and we were closer than we'd ever been before. I was looking toward the future with a renewed sense of expectation. We decided to keep the pregnancy private until after my first trimester, and it was fun having such an intimate secret between the two of us.

Unfortunately, our new-found passion for each other was fleeting. One morning I woke up and noticed I'd started spotting. It wasn't long before an intense physical pain set in resulting in a miscarriage just before my twelfth week of pregnancy.

After the loss of our child, all I could think of was another little girl with Grace's tiny face and curly dark hair ripped from my life again. We hadn't known the sex of our child before the miscarriage, but I knew in my heart it was a girl. It wasn't until after we lost the baby, I realized I'd been preparing myself for the exact same experience I'd had in 1996. A redo of sorts, only this time with a husband and impeccable house waiting for our daughter's arrival.

The tiny life growing inside of me was taken, along with my final chance at motherhood. I felt betrayed by my own body, as if it worked against me to eliminate a child it knew I didn't deserve.

Any words or actions Graham and I had set aside for the good of our growing family were quickly remembered and found a prominent place in the emptiness of a marriage that wasn't going to last much longer anyway.

***

Summer went by quickly, and as the calendar turned to fall, I was ready to settle in for another season packed with fake pumpkins and orange and gold leaf garlands making me miss the colors of autumn in Iowa.

It was October, which meant Graham was celebrating another year of life, and I was faced with trying to make him feel special when I could barely look at him.

I picked up the cake from my favorite bakery and finished decorating while one of Graham's friends kept him busy with birthday cocktails. Once everything was set, I would text his friend letting him know he could bring Graham home to the surprise party.

Things hadn't been going well for us lately, and the get together was an excuse to spend the occasion with a group instead of coming up with a more intimate celebration for the two of us. The outcome of my own birthday dinner in the spring had left us clawing for solid ground as a couple, but I couldn't let Graham's birthday slip by without at least trying to make an effort for him.

The funny thing about Graham and I was that we were never on the same page. I was in a constant state of depression, and even Graham seemed to be grieving a baby he never wanted. But, we weren't dealing with it together, and the wedge between us was growing deeper every day.

The words we'd spoken in anger a few months earlier kept running through my mind, and I'd started to imagine what life would be like on my own. I'd discovered the baby had been a reason to stay, and without that connection, I wasn't sure what the future held for us.

I'd invited our neighbors, several of Graham's friends from the gym, and the entire English department at Ventura Community College. I didn't know who should be included from Graham's work, so I'd made a blanket invitation to everyone, allowing his colleagues to make their own decision about whether they wanted to come or not. I was hopeful at least a few of his co-workers would attend, but the only one to show up was his graduate assistant.

Drinks were flowing freely, and everyone was having a good time. Pictures of Graham from various times in his life were enlarged and hung throughout the house, and a chocolate cake embellished with a colorful *Happy Birthday* sat in the middle of the dining room table.

"Hi, Becca," I said, trying to make Graham's co-worker feel welcome. "I'm so glad you could make it tonight. Graham will be happy you were able to be here."

All I knew about Becca was that she was doing a semester as a department graduate assistant, which was part of her master's degree studies at the University of California.

"I wouldn't have missed it. Graham has been so good to me. I wasn't sure choosing an internship at a community college was right for me, but once I met Graham, I knew I'd made the right decision. He's so smart and funny, and I'm lucky to be able to learn from him."

I didn't see Graham the way she did.

"What do you want to do after you get your M.A.?" I asked, wondering how Graham's apparent genius would serve her future goals.

"I don't know, maybe be an academic advisor for a big university. Right now, I'm making good money as a bartender at Tito's downtown . . . it's going to be hard to leave a job that pays me so well to mix drinks and flirt with guys."

I questioned her goal setting abilities, but it wasn't any of my business.

"I love Tito's, they have great nachos!" I replied, trying to relate with her on some level.

"Hey, I'd be happy to help you mix drinks tonight if you need me to. I see you've got a bar set up, and I could make sure everyone has what they want so you don't have to worry about it," she offered.

"That would be helpful, but you're a guest tonight, and I don't want to make you work!"

"Oh, it's no problem. I'd love to help out."

"Okay, that would be fantastic. Thank you," I said, feeling relieved I could put my attention to other things at the party, and she could handle the booze. I moved on to setting out the rest of the appetizers and mingling as people arrived.

I could see from across the room that Becca was making herself an extra stiff martini as she mixed drinks for the other invitees. Dressed in a pair of tight jeans and a red halter top accentuating her voluptuous body, I wondered if she'd hit it off with one of Graham's single friends from the gym.

She was beautiful in a way that was young and innocent, and it made me want to go back a few years and enjoy life without the limitations of being a doctor and wife.

Once the festivities were in full swing, I sent a text to Graham's friend. I asked everyone to find a spot to hide while we turned the lights off and waited for them to arrive.

Fifteen minutes later, I saw lights coming up the street and turn into the driveway. The guests had been asked to park one street over and walk through the yard so Graham wouldn't be suspicious of the surprise awaiting him.

There was a dull roar as forty semi-drunk partiers tried to be quiet, and when the door opened, I flipped the lights on, and everyone yelled, "Surprise!"

"Happy birthday, Graham!" I exclaimed, throwing my arms around his neck and planting a big kiss on his lips. He smelled like whiskey, and I could tell he was ready to have a good time like the rest of the attendees.

I took Graham's hand and made the rounds so everyone could wish him a happy birthday. Graham whispered through clenched teeth that he didn't need to be led around like a puppy, but I let it go, knowing it wasn't the time to let his remark offend me. After all the work I'd put into the party, it surprised me he could be so inconsiderate toward me.

It was after midnight, and the last of the appetizers were beginning to harden on the kitchen counter. Things were winding down, and I started to rinse out glasses and cover food with tin foil. There were still plenty of people mingling throughout the house and around the pool.

I hadn't seen Graham for a while, but laughter was coming from a group sitting outside around the fire pit. Knowing there would be plenty of time to clean up the mess the following day, I decided to join in on the fun.

I started up the stairs to grab my sweater before going outside. Glancing in the guest room, I could see there were jackets and purses strewn on the bed. The true sign of a good party was having it go late, and that made me happy.

The door to the master was closed, and I figured Graham had shut it to keep guests out of our personal space. I opened the door and entered the quiet room bathed in soft light from two tortoise shell lamps sitting on each side of our king-size bed.

Our bedroom was massive and decorated in white with gold and silver accent pillows and a cream-colored chair in the corner. We'd knocked out a wall after buying the house to expand the master bath and closet, and our personal belongings found their home in a large space, complete with a crystal chandelier and a leather ottoman in the center. The closet light was on, and it reminded me of the constant annoyance I had with Graham who never turned off a light. My upbringing made me into a person who didn't like to throw away money, and the inability of him to do something so simple made me feel like he was wasteful. There wasn't much about Graham that didn't annoy me.

When I opened the door and entered the bright closet hoping to quickly find a jacket, I stopped dead in my tracks.

Becca was leaning against the shoe rack at the back of the closet as Graham kissed her passionately. His hand quickly moved from under her top, and he jumped back in a panic looking wild-eyed and caught. All three of us stood there staring at each other. Graham broke the moment of stunned silence for all of us.

"This isn't what it looks like," Graham said.

I didn't say a word, wanting to believe him, but my brain couldn't come up with any scenario making what I'd seen anything other than what it looked like.

My sweater hung on a hook, and I grabbed it before shutting the door and heading back downstairs. My throat started to hurt, and tears formed as I struggled to catch my breath.

Should I go downstairs and make an announcement I'd found my husband and his graduate assistant making out in the closet, and the celebration was over? Would I grab one of Graham's cute friends and shove him in the laundry room and start making out with him? Could I make a scene to embarrass the guest of honor as I screamed and cried and shouted for him to get the hell out of our house for good?

Instead of choosing any of those options, I simply joined the remaining guests at Graham's birthday party, pausing only to grab a bottle of Cabernet and a fresh wine glass. Nobody else seemed to notice or care that Graham never returned to the gathering in his honor.

I'd had no idea Graham was teaching Becca things not covered by her tuition. How long had this been going on, and how could this inappropriate relationship impact his career?

Wouldn't this be considered sexual harassment since he was one of her professors? They certainly seemed like consenting adults when I saw them kissing with my pricey handbag collection looking on in disgust, but this relationship could cost Graham his job. I couldn't believe even he would stoop so low.

The irony of the evening's events was that I'd had the biggest surprise of all. I trusted a man who didn't deserve my loyalty, and the result of his indiscretion would set my life on a new path I'd never imagined possible.

Chapter Seventeen
May 2015

I heard the shower come on and knew Mom was up and getting ready for the day. She could still get around in the mornings with the help of her walker and frequent hits off her O2 tank. The oxygen once present at her side as reassurance had become a lifeline so vital that we never left home without it.

When she had visitors, Mom would leave the oxygen sitting idle beside her. She'd often say she was getting tired when she needed air in her lungs. Mom had to rely on something other than her own body to be able to breathe, and she didn't want others to know the truth. It wasn't that *she* couldn't accept her illness, but Mom didn't want to see the look on the faces of family and friends when they came to realize how bad her condition had become.

On this day, three generations of Garrett women would sit together for the first and probably last time. The injustice of it all stuck in my throat like a rock. I'd never imagined this meeting would come at all and never dreamed it would happen because of the circumstances at hand.

I knew Grace wanted to meet Mom, and when I'd asked

Jess if she thought it would be okay, I was touched by her positive response. It had been a couple of weeks since I'd told Mom about Grace, but their meeting couldn't be put off any longer if it was going to happen at all.

Everything was ready for our important visitor, and a fresh floral bouquet I'd picked from the blooms outside Mom's condo sat in the middle of the kitchen island. The smell of lilacs floated through the house and reminded me of playing in the backyard of my own grandmother's house. The scent had always filled me with expectation and now seemed strange in a house slowly preparing for death.

Grace rang the doorbell, and I greeted her with a hug and a heart full of gratitude. "Good morning, Grace. Thanks again for coming, it means so much." I was nervous and needed to relax.

"I'm excited to meet your mom," she replied as I saw her face begin to fade into something else. Was she angry and hurt I'd given her up without trying to be her mother, or sad a woman she'd only known as Mrs. Garrett from church was dying?

Grace's brown hair was streaked with highlights, and I couldn't tell if they were natural, or the work of an expensive colorist paid for by the Sinclairs to make their daughter even more attractive. Grace wore a cotton jumper, which looked adorable on her and showed off her long legs already tan from being out in the spring sun during soccer and tennis practices.

She was everything you'd think a sweet, smart, and ambitious young woman would be. I felt proud of her, though I couldn't take any amount of credit for the way she'd turned out—unless you counted good genes. I saw in her a reflection of the way it was supposed to have been for me. But, I had no regrets about bringing a magnificent human being into the world despite the personal price I had to pay.

Mom sat in her favorite chair dressed in a comfortable summer dress. Her skin was pale, but she'd done her best to make herself up for such an important introduction. When we came into the room, Mom motioned for Grace to sit beside her.

"Hi, Mrs. Garrett," Grace said quietly, as if a louder voice might cause injury to such a fragile woman.

"Grace, it's so good to meet you." I wasn't sure if I should stay with them or give them time alone. I felt like an intruder but didn't want to miss a second of something that would never happen again.

I took a seat on the sofa, and Grace sat on the ottoman close to Mom. She held her hands out to Grace, and they leaned together in an embrace. I didn't make a move or utter a sound for fear I would interrupt the moment, and it would disappear like a daydream.

"Grace, do you know I've had my eye on you? There was something so familiar to me about you, and now I know what it was . . . I've felt a connection to you although we didn't know each other. It's a real pleasure to finally meet you. Your parents have obviously done a wonderful job raising you, and I'm so glad you were willing to stop by to say hello while I'm still able to...." She hesitated and changed the subject. "Tell me about yourself, what are your plans for college next year?"

Grace and Mom talked together, and Grace shared her plans to get her BSN degree and to work as a traveling nurse for a few years to be able to see different places she'd never been to before. I couldn't help but wonder if her career ambitions were genetic or environmentally learned from Dr. Sinclair. It didn't matter, she was headed in a good direction and seemed excited about her future.

They talked for nearly an hour, and I joined in on the conversation when invited. I tried to give the two of them enough time together to sustain them for their lifetimes, however short that might be for my mom.

I knew it was time for the three of us to say goodbye as I could see Mom was getting anxious to use her oxygen again. Grace must have sensed her grandmother's need to conclude the visit and began to move the conversation along. As she rose to leave, she asked if I would mind taking a picture of the two of them with her phone, and I obliged with tears in my eyes.

"Cass, let's get a picture on your phone too," Mom said.

I hadn't thought about preserving the moment in a photograph. It was one of the last gifts Mom gave me, and I'd treasure it forever.

Grace sat close to my mom on the oversized chair, and I went behind them putting my arms around both as I leaned in to complete the picture. Grace moved the camera from her vantage point so we were all in the frame. We smiled, and the only photo ever taken of me with the two most important women in my life was captured; a permanent reminder of what might have been.

***

Summer was beginning to take hold, and the June evening was warm as I entered the Southern Iowa Hospice Home after taking a short break from caring for Mom.

As I entered her well-appointed room, I could see an aide rubbing her feet with lotion, and the look on Mom's face let me know it felt good. There was nothing left to do but make her as comfortable as possible and wait for the end. Knowing my mom had done so much for other people during her lifetime made me appreciate that at the end of her life she had the simple joy of a foot rub to ease her suffering.

Because of Mom's example for how to live life, I would no longer settle for an existence that didn't honor such pure and simple happiness each day.

During the time spent at the hospice home, family and friends came to say their final goodbyes. Father Burk visited and gave Mom her Last Rites. Even Jess and Grace stopped by with a bouquet of flowers and some homemade cookies for all the families staying at the hospice home to enjoy. Everyone in our life had done what they needed to, and now it was only Mom and me waiting for death to decide the final moment.

I knelt at her bedside and whispered in her ear, "I'm here, Mom." She moved slightly, letting me know she heard me. Her eyes were closed, and I knew she wouldn't respond in words. She was in a deep sleep for a good amount of each day, but at times would wake up and want to talk or have me show her family photos from the album I'd brought at the suggestion of the social worker.

I kissed her lightly on the cheek and rubbed the soft hair growing back on her head. Mom had always had straight hair, but after chemo treatments were over, her new hair had grown back in little curls like a baby, which seemed contradictory for a person who was dying.

I quietly asked the hospice aide if she thought it would be much longer. "We never know for sure," she said quietly. "There are usually signs, and I don't see those signs yet. She's beginning to disconnect, and that's why she seems so distant from you at times. Enjoy every minute with her and let her know you love her."

I'd spent the last three nights by her bed waiting for her to wake up for a few minutes. The syncopated rhythm of air going in and out of her oxygen tank lulled me to sleep like ocean waves. I'd drift off in the recliner beside her bed, ready to spring into action and get whatever she might need like ice chips or a cold cloth for her forehead.

I had a reason for asking if her death was imminent. I'd agreed to let my aunts take the nightshift while I got some rest in a real bed, but as the time drew closer, it didn't seem like a good idea.

What if something happened to her during the night? I couldn't think of traveling the end-of-life journey with her and not being there at the end. My aunts had convinced me I needed to keep my own strength up, but I wasn't sure I'd get any better sleep across town.

Concentrating on the steady breaths going in and out of her open mouth, I tried to memorize every part of her so I wouldn't forget a single detail in the years to come. It was unsettling not knowing if we had hours or days left together.

"You never know," the aide continued, "I've seen death come quickly without many signs. More than likely, things will progress slowly . . ."

I wasn't sure what I wished for but knew what I wanted or needed didn't matter anyway.

I heard a quiet knock on the door as it opened slightly. I'd gone to sleep in the chair again and woke up with a jolt just as Ben's head popped in through the opening. I motioned for him to come in, and he smiled at me and took the chair on the other side of Mom's bed. He reached over and touched her hand as he let his attention fall on me.

"How are *you* doing?" he asked. He looked so sad, and I could tell he wasn't prepared for what he saw. She'd lost so much weight. Her thin hair matted and her face pale, the only thing looking remotely like my beautiful mother were her perfectly polished nails. We'd painted them a few days before she'd been admitted, and they were flawlessly suspended in time.

"I'm tired," I answered honestly.

"What do you need from me?" Ben asked.

"Just being here is enough. Thank you." Tears began to well in my eyes, and I wiped a single drop away before pulling myself together.

"Come on," he said. "Let's get a cup of coffee." Mom was stable, considering her status, so a few minutes away with Ben wouldn't matter.

We fixed ourselves coffee from the kitchen of the hospice home, and Ben placed two brownies on a plate. We chose a small table overlooking a wooded area outside, and when I allowed myself to relax the tears began to flow.

Ben moved to the chair next to me and took my hand. He rubbed my back and let me cry, and as sobs began to take over my body. He put his arms around me, giving me the support I desperately needed.

"Your mom is so lucky to have you, Cassie. She's very proud of you and all you've accomplished."

It was something I could finally acknowledge. She knew about Grace, and she loved me anyway. I could accept she'd been proud of all the other accomplishments I'd achieved in my life. Before, it felt like her words of praise were because she didn't know who her daughter really was.

"Why does it have to be over with so soon? We had more things to do together. It just isn't fair," I said through my tears.

"Sometimes a challenge is too big to overcome. All you can do is deal with it and move on to the next part of your life. Instead of being sad for everything you're losing with your mom, try to concentrate on all the good times you've already had. You were lucky . . . so many mothers and daughters don't have the kind of relationship the two of you have shared. No one can take that away from you."

I knew Ben was right, even if I didn't want him to be. Feeling grateful was difficult when Mom was lying on her deathbed, and I was about to be very alone.

If it hadn't been completely inappropriate timing, I would have kissed Ben. I looked at the love of my life sitting next to me and wondered if there was any way we could rekindle the feelings we'd once had for each other.

It felt like Ben still loved me, but maybe my state of vulnerability was impacting my aptitude to read people. The only thing I was sure about was that I couldn't take another loss in my life, and romantic rejection from Ben would be too much for me to handle.

I wanted to spend more time with Ben, but needed to get back to Mom, and then try to get a good night's sleep away from all the machines, and hourly checks, and death so I could prepare myself for what was coming.

***

I heard laughter as I got closer to Mom's room. I opened the door to find my aunts sitting on either side of the bed with Mom propped up on pillows looking better than she had in weeks.

"Cassie, we were just talking about you," Mom said as I entered the room. "Remember when you caught that tiny little fish at the lake, and you asked us if we could get it stuffed to hang on the wall in the living room?" All three of them erupted in laughter, and I noticed some of the color had returned to Mom's face.

"Mom!" I exclaimed, running to hug her.

"I'm not dead yet, Cassie. It takes more than a little cancer to beat Josephine Garrett!"

I couldn't believe in the nine hours since I'd left my mom, she'd pepped up and was acting like her old self again. It briefly crossed my mind that maybe I'd be able to take her home for a few more weeks, and the possibility filled me with a renewed sense of hope.

My aunts stayed a while longer and went home with a promise of returning later in the day. At Mom's suggestion, I made us each a cup of tea, and we settled in to watch TV and visit.

When the staff asked Mom if she'd like some lunch, she'd requested a grilled cheese sandwich with tomato soup on the side. It was a short-lived gift of time I hadn't expected, and we enjoyed the afternoon together.

The following morning things took a turn for the worse. It was early, and birds were singing outside of Mom's room. It would be a beautiful day, and thoughts about what we might be doing if we weren't waking up at the Southern Iowa Hospice Home came to mind.

I thought about how fun it would be to have lunch on the deck or take a ride out to the country to see how tall the corn had grown before getting an ice cream cone at the Tasty Freeze on old Highway 30. I wished this day would be like any other summer day in Iowa, but it wouldn't be. This would be the day of my mother's death.

We'd had an uneventful night, and except for visits every few hours from the staff giving Mom her morphine, we'd slept well.

I'd taken my overnight bag to the family bathroom to shower and get ready for the day. I contemplated taking Mom outside for some fresh air if she felt up to it. When I got back to her room, three staff members were attending to her.

"Is everything okay?" I asked, putting my things in the closet and moving toward the bed to see what they were doing.

"Your mom is running a fairly high fever," the nurse said, repositioning her stethoscope.

Mom's cheeks were flushed; this wasn't something I'd noticed earlier. The other nurse pulled back the blanket covering her small frame and looked at her feet and legs.

"She's starting to transition," she said quietly.

They showed me how the skin on her feet was beginning to turn dark and pointed out that her respirations were much weaker than the day before. Although I had only been present at a death during my years in residency, I knew what the signs were.

Mom was so much smaller than I'd ever remembered her as she laid in the hospital bed, which seemed incongruent with the person she'd been throughout her life. She looked peaceful, and I took a moment in my heart to acknowledge the beginning of the final stages of her life.

She had experienced such great improvement the day before, but now she was close to death. How could I be appreciative for the extra time with her and heartbroken too? Mom's rally was one of the poignant stages of the end-of-life process, and we'd been given those hours together even if they'd be our last.

The staff members began to clear out of the room telling me to let them know if I needed anything. I'd been aware this time was coming for weeks, but it felt unexpected and raw. I wasn't ready.

Mom went in and out of consciousness. She talked about meeting my dad at the skating rink. She asked if I'd delivered donuts to her mom and dad who'd both been dead for years. Each moment I spent with her was filled with begging her in my heart not to go.

"Cassie, are there a lot of Chinese people here?" she asked me.

It was such a strange thing for her to say. We lived in Elmwood, Iowa, which wasn't exactly diverse. The only Asian people I knew of in our little town owned the restaurant out by the mall with the amazing egg rolls.

"No, Mom. We're at the hospice home, and there aren't any Chinese people here. Why do you ask?" I didn't think I'd get an answer from her. It seemed like an odd question, even given her state of mind.

I played her favorite songs and rubbed her feet again, telling her how much I loved her and was going to miss her. I prayed the rosary for her, knowing she'd be saying those comforting words if she was able and followed it up with The Lord's Prayer, which I prayed for both of us.

She was already slipping away, and my mind went to all kinds of thoughts about dying. I wondered if my dad would be waiting for her when she got to heaven and even questioned if there *was* a heaven. What if life just ended and her death would be nothing but darkness? I hoped it wasn't scary for her and that she knew how much she was loved.

In the afternoon our hospice social worker, Kelsey, stopped in to check on us. She asked how we were doing, and I understood her visit was more for me than my mom.

Mom stirred when she heard an unfamiliar voice. Her eyes opened, and she reached out to the young woman who gently took her hand.

"How are you doing Josephine? Are you comfortable? Can I get you anything?"

Mom looked directly at Kelsey. "I'm waiting for the Japanese people to get here," she said.

Kelsey looked at me and smiled, neither of us knowing what Mom meant.

"That's so strange, because she just asked me if there were a lot of Chinese people here. I can't figure out what she's talking about," I said, hoping the social worker would have an answer.

Even if Mom's mind was all jumbled because of what was happening to her body, why would she have such a strange preoccupation?

"At the end of life, it isn't uncommon for there to be confusion. She must have something on her mind repeating itself in her thoughts. It isn't anything to worry about," Kelsey assured me.

"I'm not confused," Mom said firmly. "I'm waiting for the little girl."

"Mom, what do you mean?" As if I could make sense of what didn't make sense.

"Josephine, it's okay. You wait as long as you need to wait. We're here for you, and your daughter is right by your side. You take all the time you need." Kelsey had been in this position before, and I trusted her professional instincts.

I was glad to be where we were and didn't know how I would have handled things by myself. Mom settled down and fell back unconscious. Her words about the little girl would be her last.

***

Mom's respirations came evenly and then slowed to nothing. Each time she took a breath, I wasn't sure if it would be her last, and my grief settled in like an unwanted squatter.

Everything had been said and done, except for experiencing the final moments of Mom's life. Exhausted, I wanted it to be over with as much I never wanted it to end.

Flushed and going in and out of fever, Mom's pink cheeks reminded me of when I was a little girl and would put too much blush on her soft skin when she allowed me to do her makeup and fix her hair on a Saturday night at home. She'd been such a good mother, and I hoped I'd made her feel as special as she was.

She moved slightly, and I told her I was there. The nurses would describe Mom as unresponsive, but she acknowledged what I'd said in her own way. The unspoken between us as she lingered between life and death made me almost believe she'd be with me forever.

The clock read 5:00 p.m., and I doubted she'd make it

through another night. There was nothing different at the hospice home overnight. People didn't die on a schedule respecting convenience for their families or the staff taking care of them.

Every morning, some families were gone, and others had been admitted. I thought about how death didn't come with the same celebration of birth with handshakes and cigars handed out. Death came with quiet acceptance and the realization that none of us were in charge of the amount of time we had to live.

The space between my mom's shallow breaths continued to lengthen, and at one point I counted thirty seconds between them. I continued to whisper words of love near her ear, telling her everything would be okay. I asked her to tell Daddy hello for me and to stay close to me if she could.

Her eyes were focused on something other than this life. They were gray and cloudy without human cares, and her breathing was labored. I found myself becoming more tense as she became weaker, and my breathing mimicked hers. My head throbbed from holding in emotions ready to explode and holding my breath longer than was comfortable for me.

Her expression changed slightly, and her gaze fell on me as the color returned to her eyes for a moment as if she was taking my face in for the last time. She relaxed, and her eyes turned forward again. I held my breath as I'd done so many times before, until it couldn't be held any longer. The sound of my own sobs startled me, and I laid my head on my mother's chest, breathing in her scent for the last time.

I'd never felt closer or further away from her than at her death. I'd be lying if I said there wasn't relief when it was over. For a few minutes, the sacred secret of her death was held between the two of us until I could fully accept it.

***

I pulled the covers up under Mom's chin and closed her eyes, kissing her forehead and brushing her soft hair to the side. I opened the door to the hallway filled with families still waiting for the moment I'd just experienced and entered a new world where Josephine Garrett no longer existed.

I made my way to the nurse's station to inform them Mom was gone and begin the tasks necessary following a loved one's death. I noticed a dark-haired man talking with one of the aides at the front desk. He was crying as a nurse spoke softly to him, and my heart went out to him.

Glancing over to the family room and kitchen, I saw several people talking in a small group. A little boy with silky black hair broke free of his mother's hand and ran up to me. He raised his arms for me to pick him up.

His mother quickly came over to retrieve the little boy. "Oh, I'm so sorry. I wasn't paying attention. Here, I'll take him," she said apologetically as I handed the small boy over to her. I suspected her accent to be Vietnamese.

Although I had known many Asian people living in California, I couldn't always identify dialect. But, one of my favorite nurses at the clinic had the same distinctive tones in her speech pattern as the young woman, and she was from Hanoi.

"Do you have a family member here?" I asked.

"Yes, my younger sister was just admitted."

"I'm so sorry," I said with compassion.

The age of the woman led me to believe her sister must be young as well, and I felt bad for a family to lose a young person like I had lost my mom.

"My sister is only eleven; she has a brain tumor," she offered sadly. "She got here about an hour ago."

Her words shook me as I looked around and saw at least twenty people of Asian descent in the main area of the hospice home. Her sister would have arrived just as my mom entered her final moments of life.

Could there be a connection between the two? Was Mom waiting to die until the little girl and her family arrived, even if she couldn't physically see them wandering around the hospice home? The only thing I could be sure of was that something incredible had happened, and I couldn't explain it.

The words of my mother in her last hours and the Vietnamese family coming together as the young girl was dying gave me a sense of peace. I knew there was something greater than any of us could see or know at the time of death.

It gave me confidence my mom was still out there somewhere doing her good deeds and helping to bring a little girl to heaven in the proper order and timeframe destined for both of them.

I'd grown up in a Catholic home and believed in God and the afterlife mainly because of what I'd been taught. I'd never seen it before and felt it in my heart like on that warm summer afternoon when Mom left me physically and became my guardian angel.

***

I called my aunts and asked them to let the rest of our family know of Mom's death. As promised, I sent a quick text to Ben and then went to the pictures on my phone and brought up the one of Mom and me with Grace.

The fact it existed made me smile, and I copied and sent it to Grace along with the same message I'd given to Ben.

Since meeting Grace several weeks earlier we'd been in contact a few times, and I'd met Jess and Grace for coffee one day at their invitation. Grace wanted to show me pictures from her prom, and I didn't want to disappoint her or miss an opportunity to see her again. Our interactions had gone well, so when Mom died, I felt comfortable in sharing the news she deserved to hear from me.

As I took care of paperwork and coordinated final details before leaving, I could see the Vietnamese family going in and out of the little girl's room. I wanted to talk with them and ask if she'd said anything connecting her to my mom, but I didn't want to intrude and had no idea what to say to them that would make any sense. I wasn't sure what their religious or cultural views were about death and didn't want to say anything that would cause them more pain.

It was nearly 8:00 p.m. by the time I drove out of the parking lot of the Southern Iowa Hospice Home and headed for Mom's condo. I'd packed up the few belongings we'd brought for our stay while I was waiting for the funeral home to arrive and take Mom's body.

The goodbyes to the staff were harder than I'd thought they would be. The life changing experience was still so fresh, and I didn't want to leave the people who had made the last days of my mom's life so special.

As I drove toward Mom's condo, the warm breeze of a summer night breathed new life into me. The fear of how and when Mom would die had vanished. She'd died peacefully and with dignity, and I'd been with her.

Those had been my biggest worries, even if I hadn't

realized it until she was gone.

Pulling into the driveway, I saw Ben's car parked on the street in front of Mom's house. As I came around the back side of the vehicle in the garage, Ben was already headed up the driveway. He had a pizza in one hand and a bottle of wine in the other.

"I thought maybe you could use a friend tonight," he said, making his way toward me. "And I was sure you could use a pizza."

He was right about both.

Chapter Eighteen
July 2015

I woke up in California because the house I'd shared with Graham had been sold, and I had to clean out my personal items and take care of some final business to close things up.

Ben had taken me to the airport in Des Moines and had offered me a copy of the newspaper to read on the plane. When I opened it up once I was settled at the airport waiting for my flight, I realized why he'd given it to me. I turned to the classified section and saw he'd taken a bright red marker and circled an ad for a medical director for Southern Iowa Hospice.

It had been over a month since we'd buried Mom on a beautiful summer day with birds singing and butterflies landing on the spray of flowers covering her casket. Her funeral was attended by many people from different parts of our lives, and I knew she would have loved such a reunion had she been there.

Her body laid next to the spot where my dad had been for more than a quarter of a century. I remembered how terrible I'd felt for my mom when we drove out of the cemetery after Dad's service. It had been winter when he died, and Mom was worried about the ice and snow piled on top of his grave. I'd made the trip to Elmwood Memorial Gardens every day with her in those first weeks after his death to help her shovel snow off the fresh mound of dirt.

I'd never really grieved for my dad to protect Mom from the sadness I felt as a little girl. Even as a child I'd known dad's death was a devastating loss for Mom and worried about how she would be able to go on. The tears shed on the day of Mom's funeral were for both of them, although I had a sense of contentment knowing they were together again in death.

I'd been coming to terms with Mom's death and dealing with my grief since the moment she'd been diagnosed with ovarian cancer. The actual death felt more like a starting point for me than an ending, but depending on the day, I could still be brought to tears easily.

The difficult months of her illness had given me the opportunity to achieve closure in so many areas of my life. I was ready to move on, even if the direction of my new life was still up in the air.

When Mom's obituary ran in the Elmwood Gazette, Hue Pham's ran right below hers. I'd never have the answers to my questions about Mom's link to the little girl who would die in the room next to hers only a few hours later. Something had happened between them, and it was more complex than what I could comprehend.

Was it a coincidence I'd chosen white lilies to cover Mom's casket, not realizing at the time that the little girl's name meant "lily" in Vietnamese? I knew those secrets would stay hidden until the universe chose to reveal her mysteries to me at the time of my own death, but it didn't keep me from thinking about it constantly.

I was drawn to reading more about what happens during the dying process. I'd spent hours in those first days after Mom's death researching anything I could find about those topics and had met with Father Burk to get his input about what Mom had gone through. It might have been a strange obsession, but it gave me something to do besides dealing with the emptiness in Mom's condo.

From a medical perspective, I'd always been more interested in keeping people alive than thinking about helping them die. This new awareness would change the way I practiced medicine, and I was excited about becoming a more compassionate physician because of what I'd gone through with Mom.

I intended to stay in Elmwood until the condo was cleaned out and put on the market. Grief and sheer exhaustion took over, and though it had been several weeks, I'd done little more than write the thank you notes for the flowers and food people had given us. I'd get busy on the rest of the projects after returning to Iowa, but there were other things to take care of first, and I had a lot to do while in Ventura for the last time.

Ben had been wonderful to me since Mom's death. He'd listened to me talk about my experiences as I shared with him some of the interesting things I'd found in my research about the end of life. He checked in with me every few days to make sure I was doing okay and helped me with projects at Mom's condo, which usually ended with a night at Sully's.

I knew Ben wanted us to take our relationship further, but my departure from Elmwood was inevitable, and I couldn't bear to break his heart twice in a lifetime. It had become a joke between us, and I didn't know if the job listing he circled in the newspaper was his way of ribbing me a little, or if he really thought it was a viable prospect for me. The opportunity did give me an option I'd never considered.

As I began packing boxes in the guest room of our California house to send back via FedEx, I found myself daydreaming about what it would be like to get the job and settle in Mom's condo for good.

I was captivated by Ben and the possibility of a future between us but wondered what it would be like living in the same town as Grace and the Sinclairs. I'd spent so many years avoiding Elmwood, and I didn't know if coming home was the right choice.

Graham was aware I'd be in Ventura for few days, but I didn't know if I'd run into him. We'd left plenty of things unsaid, and once I left California, I'd never see him again. It seemed odd to have lived a life with someone, and then never speak to each other again, but it appeared that was the most likely end to our relationship.

I told Graham he could take any of the furniture and household items for himself, and the empty rooms and bare wall space told me he'd taken the offer. I couldn't easily get much to Iowa or wherever I'd eventually end up anyway. He'd always been into material things, and giving him most everything from the house made him feel like he'd gotten away with something and moved the divorce along quicker.

I filled several boxes with personal items, making decisions about what to keep and what to give away as I continued to think about what it would be like to run a hospice. Even if I didn't get the job, there would be similar positions across the country, and any of them would be a good fit for my new life. Although none of the others would be within dating distance of Ben.

I went downstairs and took the newspaper out of my carry-on bag and read through the qualifications again. The salary wouldn't be close to what I'd been making, but did it matter to me anymore? I took my laptop out and pulled up the hospice website, looking at the programs and services they provided. The more I read, the more excited I was about the possibilities. The last room I had to go through was the master bedroom. After cleaning out the dresser to be picked up by St. Vincent De Paul, I opened the closet door to begin going through my clothes and accessories. I didn't need much but wanted to pack my black suit for interviews and take some of my favorite pieces of jewelry.

Standing in the closet, I remembered finding Graham and Becca together that night almost a year earlier. So much had changed in my life, and the loss of an unfulfilling marriage seemed like a stroke of good luck. The decision to grab my sweater on a chilly evening had changed the course of my life forever. It felt like a lifetime ago, but the memory still brought up feelings of humiliation.

The past months had made me feel as if Graham was a stranger to me. How different things would have been if we hadn't lost our baby, and we were still together with a decorated nursery taking the place of the office down the hall. How would I have dealt with my mom's illness and the birth of our child at the same time? Would I still be married to Graham and living life with naïve contentment?

I'd just returned from getting a coffee at Starbucks and was beginning to close up the kitchen boxes when I heard Graham yell my name at the front door. Pulling the tape tight and tearing it off quickly, I headed for the front of the house and saw Graham standing in the foyer looking uneasy.

"Hi," he said.

"Hi," I answered back cautiously.

"Could we talk for a few minutes?"

"I've got a lot to do here and little time to do it in."

"This won't take long . . . *please*, Cassie."

I didn't need to talk with Graham to get perspective on the situation but was interested to hear what he had to say.

"You've got five minutes," I said with my arms folded across my chest.

"First, I'm really sorry about your mom. I know how much you loved her."

"Thank you," I said quietly.

". . . and also . . . this thing between Becca and I really *wasn't* what it looked like that night in the closet," he continued. "I'll admit we'd been flirting with each other for a while, and I had a pretty hard crush on her, but it hadn't been some blown up affair. She was hitting on me, and we'd had way too much to drink. I was lonely . . . even at my own birthday party."

"I caught the two of you kissing for the first time in the closet?" The thought was highly improbable.

"Yes . . ."

"I don't think so." How dare he insult my intelligence.

"It was playful teasing at first. We never intended for it to go further. The kiss in the closet was a terrible mistake. We took something harmless to the next level."

"I guess it wasn't all that harmless then, was it? She's your graduate assistant and could sue you for sexual harassment."

"No. She's not going to do that. We're together, Cassie. She gave up her position and left the college completely. She's doing another assistantship at the U of C now. And there's something else I need to tell you . . . she's pregnant."

Now it was me who felt blindsided about a pregnancy. "You've got to be kidding me. A baby, Graham? Wow. How are you going to travel and write your novel and all those other things you said were so important to you when it was *us* having a baby?"

"Life changes. Wasn't that what you said to me?"

I couldn't tell if Graham was being sarcastic or not, but I was reeling. Graham was getting what I'd wanted so badly for us, only he was doing it with a twentysomething graduate student instead of me.

How did we get to this place?

"So, what you're telling me is now you're ready for a family. You just hadn't been ready for one with me a few months ago. That's quite a change of heart." I was crying and didn't want to let Graham see I still felt such emotion where he was concerned. I guess I wasn't as over him as I thought.

"How old is she?" I asked in disgust.

"She's twenty-three, but she'll be twenty-four next month," he said sheepishly as I laughed out loud at the ridiculousness of it all.

I thought of Graham's selfish immaturity and remembered how Becca had spoken about him at the party. She adored him, and I was sure he must be relishing the experience of being idolized by his young lover. Becca wanted an education from Graham, and I was sure she would soon be getting more than she bargained for.

"Cassie, you know we'd been on the verge of splitting for months. Maybe years."

I hadn't been aware our relationship's demise was imminent, but I did know there hadn't been much right between us for a while. It was the betrayal that hurt the most, not the outcome.

"I'm sorry," he continued. "There's nothing I can do about it now, but it was wrong, and I didn't mean to hurt you." An apology from Graham was something new.

Even as I saw the two of them together in the closet, a little voice in my head whispered, *"you're out of this."* It had given me a valid reason to get Graham out of my life, and I was grateful for it.

If I accepted his apology, it would be hard holding on to the grudge I'd been harboring. The feeling wasn't a good one, but it was something to feel other than grief and uncertainty—giving it a prominent place in my heart. I didn't know if I wanted to give it up and allow a space for other emotions to take hold.

I recalled the mistakes I'd made in my life, and how forgiveness had been my redemption. Did I owe that to Graham? Was I willing to give it to him simply because it would help me to move on with my own life?

"If it's closure you want from me, know I'm happy about where my life is right now. I'm finishing the work on Mom's estate and have several solid job prospects. And I'm seeing someone fantastic . . . so I couldn't be happier."

It wasn't the entire truth, but I could have that life if I chose it. I was in charge of my own destiny, and maybe staying in Elmwood could be an option. I wanted Graham to feel the sting of losing someone desired by someone else. And at the very least, I knew that much was true about Ben and me.

***

I was back in Iowa by the weekend and on Monday sent in my application and resume for the job at Southern Iowa Hospice. I didn't tell Ben I'd applied and never even mentioned to him I'd seen the ad he circled for me. When the phone call came telling me I'd be one of three finalists for the position, I was ecstatic.

I spent every day researching palliative and hospice care and thinking about how I would answer questions at the interview. I presumed I'd be up against others with more direct hospice work on their resumes, so I'd have to rely on my experiences with Mom and my instincts as a doctor to do well.

I considered how to answer the tough questions about my unemployment. I could easily tie leaving my position to care for my mom back to the philosophy of hospice care. Her illness *was* the reason I chose to quit my job and come back to Iowa . . . it just wasn't the *only* reason.

It was hot and humid the day of the interview. My sensible business suit stuck to me in all the wrong places. I hoped once I got into the air-conditioning that the perspiring would stop.

The interview would be held in a conference room at the hospice home. I hadn't been back since Mom's death, and although it had been three months, my emotions were running high. All the memories of sitting with my mom as she spent her last days came flooding back to me and made me miss her more than ever. I silently asked for Mom's strength to get me through the interview.

The receptionist led me to the meeting room, and I had a few minutes to myself before the interviewers came in to join me. Nervous and excited, I took a few deep breaths and dabbed the sweat above my lip with a tissue from my purse.

The door opened, and three people filed in and sat across from me. I recognized the head nurse from the hospice home and a member of the board of directors I'd seen on their website.

The third interviewer was the Elmwood Regional Medical Center director, Dr. Steven Sinclair. As our eyes met, Dr. Sinclair smiled warmly. I hadn't thought about the possibility he would be one of the interviewers.

How would his involvement affect my chances to get the job?

They each greeted me and shook my hand. I tried to pull myself together, thinking about what this career change would mean for me. Surely Dr. Sinclair would have known I would be one of the finalists for the position. Wouldn't he have reviewed the resumes and had a hand in choosing who would be considered?

I took a deep breath and tried to concentrate as they asked the first question.

"Dr. Garrett, why are you considering coming back to Iowa to practice medicine at this time in your career?" the nurse asked me first. My head was everywhere. I needed to take a cleansing breath and be as honest as possible.

"I've been in general practice for the past few years and have enjoyed my work with patients and families. I've always been passionate about helping people. So far, my vocation has been focused on healing. My mom recently died, and her experience at the end of life has ignited my interest in hospice care."

The interview continued, and I was asked a barrage of questions about my work ethic, my management skills, and my willingness to take weekend shifts when needed. Once I began talking about my experiences with my mom and how it changed my priorities and goals for my future in medicine, the nerves subsided. I talked freely about my eagerness to lead the hospice staff and my desire to move back to Elmwood permanently.

For so long I'd avoided Elmwood, and now I was asking a panel of three people to allow me to dig my roots back into a place I wanted to call home again.

The only hesitation I had was about Dr. Sinclair serving on the search committee. Did he want me to live so close to his beloved daughter? Did my previous relationship with the Sinclairs help or hinder the most important job interview of my life?

Often people got an opportunity because of *who* they knew, and now I was terrified the job would be taken away for the same reason.

***

I'd cleaned out Mom's guest bedrooms and taken a load to the church bazaar committee. There was still a lot to do before the house could be sold, but with my job status still up in the air, I couldn't consider getting rid of it yet.

It had been two weeks since my interview at Southern Iowa Hospice, and I was placing pumpkins on the front steps of the condo when I heard my ring tone and saw their phone number come across the caller ID. My heart skipped a beat, and I was excited as well as guarded at the call I was about to take.

"Hi Cassie, it's Steve Sinclair. How are you today?"

"Good," I responded, my throat suddenly as dry as cotton.

"We've completed our interview process, and I'm happy to tell you we'd like to offer you the position if you're still interested."

I squelched a tiny scream of joy from within, realizing just how much I'd wanted to get the job. I was more than qualified, but my self-esteem had taken a beating over the past year, and my confidence had been shaken.

"Yes, I definitely am!" I responded excitedly.

"This is hospice, and you probably know we don't pay as much as you would make in another medical director's position, but the work is extremely rewarding. I think you'll be happy here."

Dr. Sinclair went on to explain the details. It paid far less than what I'd made in California, but it was still more than most people earned. I'd be able to live comfortably on the salary considering the lower cost of living in Iowa.

When he finished giving me the job offer, I thanked him and asked for a couple of days to make my final decision. I wanted to accept the position on the spot but thought it sounded more professional to let him think there might be other offers.

"Take the time you need," he said. "And Cassie, I hope you didn't think it unethical for me not to excuse myself from this interview process because we know each other. After reviewing the other applicants, you were by far the most qualified. I wanted to make sure you got this job if you wanted it and felt the best way to guarantee that happened was to be part of the process. You handled yourself beautifully in this most unusual situation, and you will make an incredible impact on the patients and families we serve. We need you in this role."

It was the most Dr. Sinclair had ever said to me, and I felt proud to know he respected my medical credentials. I hung up the phone and dialed Ben's number, asking him to meet me at Sully's for dinner.

***

Sully's was busy for a weeknight, and the music was loud. I ordered a glass of wine, and by the time the server brought it over, I could see Ben coming through the front door. He stopped at a couple of tables as he greeted people. He was friendly and well-respected, and I could already imagine the life we'd have together.

I'd been thinking about what to do if I was offered the job since returning from California. It was strange to make my final trip out West thinking the entire time how badly I wanted to get back to Iowa.

Ben had been my best friend and confidant for months. From the night of Mom's death when he'd brought dinner and stayed until the early morning hours holding me as I cried, to weekly dinners at Sully's and helping me clean out Mom's condo—he'd never left my side.

We'd fallen in love with each other all over again, but neither of us had allowed ourselves to speak the obvious aloud or bring up the topic of a future together.

"Hi," he said, sliding into the booth across from me. "I'm so glad you called. Gave me something to look forward to while I worked on a new engine this afternoon."

"It was so nice out today, wasn't it?" I said, making small talk.

"Yeah. Hey, is everything okay?" Ben could read me, and

tonight was no different.

"Yes, everything is fine. I had some news to share with you and wanted to do it in person."

"Well, here I am," he said. He seemed anxious to hear what I had to say.

"You know I've been sort of stuck in a rut, trying to figure out what to do next with my life."

"Yep, you've got a lot of options because you're such an amazing woman." Ben was my biggest fan.

"I've been doing a lot of thinking and some serious soul searching about what I want for the rest of my life. I've put out a few resumes and thought about where I'd like to practice medicine, and I've come to a decision."

"You know I'm going to support you no matter what. Just like when we were kids, all I want is for you to be happy." He looked sad, and I didn't think it was fair to keep it from him any longer.

"Well, I have a job offer I'm excited about, and I'm thinking of accepting it. But, I wanted to know what you thought about it first."

"What is it?"

"I've been offered the medical director position at Southern Iowa Hospice," I said, searching his face for the response I was hoping for.

"Wait . . . really? The one I circled in the newspaper and gave to you the day you left for California?"

"Yes, that one!" I exclaimed. "Dr. Sinclair called me today and offered me the position."

"Dr. Sinclair?"

"Yeah . . . that's another story . . . he directed the search committee I interviewed with a few weeks ago. And I got the job!"

"So, you're taking the job and staying here in Elmwood for good?" He smiled from ear to ear and reached across the table and took both of my hands in his.

"And there's one more thing I have to tell you," I said, drawing in a deep breath as I prepared to reveal my heart to him.

"How could it be anything better than that?"

"I love you," I said with confidence. "And I want us to be together."

Without saying a word, he got up from his side of the table and moved into the booth beside me. He wrapped his arms around me and gave me the best kiss I'd had in eighteen years.

Chapter Nineteen
June 2016

I looked longingly at Ben's coffee. "I'd kill for a sip of that."

"I'm sorry, but there's no reason for both of us to be miserable." Ben gave me a big grin as he took another drink. He took my hand and squeezed it as he put his other arm around my shoulders protectively.

I shifted in the waiting room chair and moved closer to him, breathing in the delicious scent of the dark roast. I couldn't have anything to eat or drink after midnight and needed a caffeine fix in the worst way.

Ben was right, there was no reason for the love of my life to be without coffee just because I couldn't have any. He was the kind of person who would dump the steaming hot beverage out if he really thought it would make me feel better. He was lucky my deep love for him kept me from asking him to make such a sacrifice so early in the morning.

We'd been a couple since the night at Sully's when I'd told Ben about my new job as the Medical Director at Southern Iowa Hospice. It hadn't taken long for us to fall completely in love again once we'd allowed ourselves to accept the inevitable. He felt like the best part of home to me, and I was relishing the happy life we were building together.

Mom's illness had revealed she carried the gene for ovarian cancer, meaning I would likely be susceptible to getting it too. Once she was gone, I'd done my own genetic testing, which gave me the bad news that cancer was likely in my future. Although I was devastated, the information allowed me to act before ovarian cancer had a chance to begin its attack. I'd eventually die of something, but it wouldn't be the disease that took my mom from me.

It had been six months since I'd found out I would need surgery, but I'd only been at my new job a short time and wanted to get a few months under my belt before I took several weeks off for medical leave. The time had come, and after a few hours, I would be recovering with Ben by my side for support.

We'd arrived at the hospital before 6:00 a.m., and the operation would follow whenever my slot in the rotation came up. I was nervous; I'd never been under general anesthesia before and hadn't even been in the hospital, except to have Grace.

The surgeon would perform a complete hysterectomy, putting me in an immediate state of menopause. The removal of my womb would take away the fear of having ovarian cancer down the road but would also eliminate any future opportunity to be a mother.

Considering my age and new career path, having a baby seemed unlikely. But, I'd rather have had the chance to make the decision myself instead of feeling like I had no choice but to purge the time bomb ticking away in my uterus.

"Cassidy?" the nurse called from the open door leading back to the surgical prep rooms.

"I'll be waiting right here," Ben said quietly.

"It shouldn't take long for them to get me ready, and then you can come back with me."

I wanted him by my side every second of the day, but the hospital didn't allow visitors until patients were completely prepped. I knew it made it easier for the doctors and nurses, but I needed Ben's strength and support more than I felt they needed extra space in the exam room.

I remembered learning in biology class that a female has all her egg cells at the time of birth, essentially carrying around the potential for thousands of babies inside her body. As I faced the removal of those eggs, along with the rest of my female reproductive organs, I found myself feeling sad for the loss of those unborn children. I thought of the connection to all the females in my family and how this would end the possibility of continuing my parents' bloodlines. Of course, there was Grace, but her family tree would always be attached to the Sinclairs without regard to biology.

The nurse got me settled, and I answered a barrage of questions about my health and habits. After she double checked my wrist band and verified my procedure, I was given a small cup of medication to relax me, and I downed it like a shot of tequila.

As the drug began to take effect and I felt sleepy and warm, Ben appeared at my bedside. He kissed my forehead and pulled a chair up next to the hospital bed. He stroked my arm and assured me everything would be ok. The nurse continued to do some paperwork at the counter, her back to us as she worked.

"Thank you for being here with me today," I said quietly, feeling emotional as my body began to shake from a chill in the room and fear of going under the knife.

"It'll be okay, Cass. I'm going to take good care of you. You'll just take a long rest, and then it will be over with." That sounded more final than I wanted it to.

"You're the only man for me." I said, my tongue starting to get thick as my eyelids got heavier. "I don't know what I'd do without you."

"Luckily, you aren't going to have to find out, because I'm never going to leave you."

"Never?" I asked.

"Never."

I looked directly at Ben and pulled him near me, kissing him on the lips. As drugs surged through my bloodstream making me feel uninhibited, I knew what I wanted to do. I didn't care if it wasn't the most romantic time or that there was another person standing two feet from us.

"Ben O'Brien, will you marry me?" I asked boldly.

My question took Ben off guard, and he hesitated before answering.

"If you still want to marry me after you get these medications out of your system, I'll marry you as soon as possible. But, I can't take advantage of a women who's drugged and ready for surgery, so I'm not going to hold you to this when you wake up...."

I could hear the nurse laugh quietly at our exchange. She probably heard lots of crazy things out of people who were under the influence.

"You can hold me to it, I promise," I said as the nurse made final preparations before taking me to the surgical suite.

"I'm sorry, it's time to say goodbye. This lady has a date with a doctor down the hall," the nurse joked.

"See, you're already interested in someone else," Ben

teased.

He kissed my hand gently before leaving. "I'll be waiting for you after you wake up. You're going to be just fine, and now we'll have many years together without the worry of ovarian cancer."

"I'm scared," I whispered.

"You don't need to be. I love you, and I've got you right here," he said, touching his heart.

The nurse began to move my bed toward the door. I'd seen her ID badge and called her by name. "Jill," I said, "this is my fiancé, Ben O'Brien." She smiled and gave Ben a wink, both of them wondering if I was serious about my proposal.

After she wheeled me back to surgery I took my place at the center of the room, lights and equipment everywhere within my sightline. The doctor asked me to count backwards from ten, but I didn't get any further than eight before I drifted off to sleep.

***

I was lying in a field of wildflowers when I heard heavy panting. I couldn't place the sound until I sat up just in time to see the big brown dog jump into my lap and begin licking my face.

"Butch!" I exclaimed. I wrapped my arms around my old friend and breathed in his canine scent. "Good boy . . . how are you, buddy? What are you doing here?"

I scratched behind his ears as the warm sunlight illuminated the colors around me. I didn't know where I was, but it was the most beautiful place I'd ever seen.

I laid back down in the fragrant bed of flowers and felt the dog's hot breath on my cheek. I'd missed him so much, and now he was in this warm and sleepy space with me.

"Cassie? Cassie? Do you want some lemonade?" I could hear my mom somewhere in the distance. I sat up and Butch started to run toward the horizon in the direction of her voice. "Butch, don't leave me!" I yelled. I wanted to stay with him longer and sleep with him by my side.

I heard my mother calling my name again, and I got up and started to walk toward the sound, hoping to find her and tell her about Butch. I saw both of them sitting on a blanket with my dad. She motioned for me to join them, but her other arm was holding a little boy. I could see the baby's olive skin and dark hair and could hear him cooing softly.

Dad was wearing his favorite plaid shirt and was lying on his side with his head propped on one arm. Mom had on a white eyelet dress and was barefoot. I'd seen them like this before, in a photo sitting on my mom's dresser for more than thirty years. It was like the photo had come alive; the only difference was that there wasn't a child in the picture I remembered.

"This is your son, Cassie," Mom said proudly.

"My son?" Could the baby she held be the one I'd lost to miscarriage? I was confused. I'd been sure I was pregnant with a girl, just like Grace. I reached for him, and Mom handed the infant to me. As I looked into his eyes, I felt a mother's love and knew he was mine.

He smelled like lavender and his skin was as soft as satin. I kissed him on the cheek, and he snuggled close to me with an instant connection only a mother and child could share.

He *was* my son.

"You've been taking care of him?" I asked my parents.

"I had him first, until your mom got here. We've been enjoying the most wonderful time together," Dad said happily. Butch rolled on his back, and my father scratched his belly.

"Am I dead?" I asked, suddenly worried that something had gone terribly wrong. I didn't want to be dead, not when I'd just asked Ben to marry me.

"No, honey," Mom said. "You're just resting, but it gave us a good chance to visit and let you know we're all right."

"Okay," I said, suddenly feeling very drowsy again. "I need to go now, but will you come to me again?" I asked, not wanting to leave them but feeling too tired to stay.

"We're always with you, even if you can't see us," Mom said.

**

I felt like I was waking up, but I was so exhausted I couldn't open my eyes.

"Cassie?" I could hear my name being called.

"Mom?" I said, feeling myself regaining consciousness. I could see the outline of her white dress at the end of my bed but was too weak to reach out to her.

"Mom?" I said again as the figure became a little clearer.

"I'm here, Cass. It's Ben."

"Did you see my mom at the end of the bed?" I asked, knowing it couldn't be possible.

"No, it's your nurse hooking up some equipment to monitor you."

"But I saw my parents and the baby," I explained. "And Butch was there too."

"She may be out of it for a bit," the figure at the end of the bed replied. Now I could see it was a nurse in light colored scrubs adjusting some cords.

"Cassie, it's just me . . . you did really well, and it's all over now," he answered close to my ear. He took my hand, stroking the top with his thumb.

I felt sore and barren.

I tried to hoist myself up, but the pain kept me from going any further.

"Do you want me to put your bed up a little?" Ben asked. I nodded and felt my back incline slightly as I allowed my eyes to open.

"You're all done. All you have to do is rest and recover, and we'll be home before you know it."

"I need some water," I said. My throat was dry and sore from the intubation tube. I was still extremely groggy. After a few sips of liquid, I fell back into a deep sleep, hoping to spend more time on the picnic blanket with my family.

It was late afternoon before I started to wake up again. I wasn't usually a person who took naps, but the deep sleep after anesthesia was one of the most enjoyable things I'd ever experienced. The hospital room was warm and quiet, and the drugs remaining in my bloodstream made me feel relaxed and sluggish.

"Can I get you anything?" Ben asked.

"No, I just need to lie here. It will be a while before I'll be much company. You can go home if you want to and come back later." I didn't want him to waste the entire day watching me sleep, even though knowing he was there comforted me.

"I'm not going anywhere. You go ahead and sleep. I'll be

right here when you wake up," he replied.

By early evening I was feeling better, and the nurse helped Ben get me up for the first time, and we went for a walk in the hallway.

When the drugs wore off, I felt better than what I had expected. I had a small dinner and even a bowl of ice cream before Ben kissed me goodnight and finally took a break for himself and went home to sleep.

***

After a restless night due to being woken up every few hours to have my vital signs taken, I was anxious to see the doctor and get released. My procedure had been laparoscopic, so a long hospital stay wasn't necessary.

Ben was at the hospital early and came bearing a large coffee and a blueberry scone. It was the best medicine I could have asked for, and before I knew it, I was settled on the couch at home after being released with instructions to take it easy for a few weeks.

Home was Mom's condo, where I'd stayed since her death. Ben still had his house for when his boys were with him, but he'd spent most other nights with me after we'd become a couple.

We cooked together and read in front of the fireplace with a glass of wine after dinner, and occasionally I'd let him beat me at gin rummy. Our life together was simple and happy, and I'd never experienced such bliss.

I was glad to be back where I could sit on the deck and get some fresh air, and Ben could help me take short walks outside to gain my strength back. It was much better than making a loop around the surgical floor alongside others who were dragging an IV pole with them like a reluctant friend.

"How are you doing?" Ben asked me after we'd been home a few days.

"So much better," I replied. Once the pain had subsided, it felt nice to have time off with nothing to do but relax.

"How are you feeling about tomorrow?" he asked.

"Tomorrow? What's tomorrow?" I answered, wondering what I had to do taking me away from the comfort of home and convalescing.

"Maybe I shouldn't have said anything. But I don't want you to forget what tomorrow is unless that's what you're trying to do."

I still had no idea what he was talking about.

"I'm sorry, I don't know what's going on tomorrow. I've been thinking of nothing else but sleeping and Netflix," I joked.

"Tomorrow is the one-year anniversary of your mom's death," he said quietly.

"Oh . . . I can't believe I forgot. I thought of it at the beginning of the month, but with everything else going on, I just lost track of what day it was."

I didn't know how I felt about the anniversary. My emotions had been up and down since the surgery, and even with the revelation a year had gone by without my mom in it, I didn't really feel anything except gratitude that I'd survived it all.

"Would you like to do something special to remember your mom? Maybe visit her grave or go out for a nice dinner?"

"I'm not sure. I don't want to spend time feeling upset. Mom wouldn't want me to do that. I'm in a good place with my grief so I don't think crying all day would be the right thing to do. I'd really like to do something fun, making the day memorable but not sad. How about you plan something for us?" I was feeling better but didn't have it in me to think about dinner reservations or planning an outing for the two of us.

"Okay, you're putting this in my hands, and I won't disappoint you. Do you want to go out somewhere or would you rather stay home and have me cook for you?" Ben asked.

"Surprise me." I trusted Ben and knew he would come up with something we'd both enjoy.

***

Ben wouldn't tell me what was on the agenda for our day of remembrance. He'd gone out first thing in the morning to shop but didn't let me see what he'd purchased and made me promise to stay out of the kitchen all day. He couldn't hide the smell of something cooking on the stove, but all I knew for sure was that it had a lot of garlic in it.

I was still sore and bruised where the incisions were, but a hot shower made me feel rejuvenated. Our special night would be the perfect opportunity for me to put on some real clothes and forget the lose fitting pants I'd been wearing for almost a week.

A sundress would give me the room I needed on my abdomen but also make me feel like I was a contributing member of society. I was surprised at how good it felt to get out of my pajamas and feel cleaned up for the first time in days.

I sprayed perfume on my wrists and put a little makeup on. My hair was damp and clean, and I ran a brush through it, pulling it to one side with a clip. I added a pair of simple earrings and some sandals, and the ensemble was just right for a quiet night at home with the man I loved.

As I finished getting ready, Ben returned and told me he was ready for me to come out to the deck. He led me to the sliding glass doors, and I could see he had candles lit everywhere. Some were in mason jars and others were in lanterns, but all illuminated the deck beautifully as the summer night's sun began to get lower in the evening sky.

Ben led me to a table prepared for two. There were white roses in a vase and a few petals laying on top of the lace tablecloth, which was set with Mom's good dishes. A bottle of champagne was chilling in a bucket of ice, and crystal glasses sat next to them waiting to be filled.

"Wow, this is beautiful . . . and so thoughtful of you," I said. I'd never been treated so well. Mom would have been impressed with his efforts to honor her in such a thoughtful way.

"Cassie, I love you more than anything. I wanted this day to be special for you, and I tried to think of how we could memorialize your mom's life in the most meaningful way. It got me to thinking . . . the one thing Josephine wanted more than anything was for you to be happy. She'd be thrilled you took the job at Southern Iowa Hospice, and I also think she'd be over the moon at knowing the two of us are together."

I shook my head in agreement, smiling as he held his hands out to me and I took them in my own. My eyes got big when I realized what he was doing as he got down on one knee and looked up at me through tears.

"I've been in love with you for my entire life. I'm sorry it's taken so long for us to get to this point, but . . . I'd like to accept your proposal if you still want to marry me."

I felt a little embarrassed about my drug induced declaration of love a few days earlier and had intended to bring up the subject when the time was right.

" . . . and I'm choosing today for our engagement because each year when you remember your mom's life, I hope your sadness will be tempered by the joy of knowing this was also the date we made a lifetime commitment to each other to become husband and wife."

I let go of him and put my hands over my mouth as he reached in his pocket and pulled out a small box holding an exquisite emerald cut diamond ring to celebrate our impending union.

"Yes, yes, yes!" I exclaimed as he put the ring on my finger and took me in his arms for the first time as his official fiancé.

Epilogue
September 2017

Mom's condo was scheduled to go on the market, and I was almost done getting things cleaned out and packed up. It had been a good place for us to stay following her death, but it was time to move on.

I knew what I was looking for but couldn't remember where I'd put the old banker's box with the lid marked *Cassie's Senior Year* in my mother's precise handwriting. Most of the boxes left in the basement were labeled with a black magic marker like the one I searched for and would go with us to the new house in the final moving process.

I shoved a storage bin to the side filled with Christmas decorations, and hidden behind Mom's old sewing machine was what I'd been looking for. I pushed the lid off the top of the box, and a musty smell permeated my senses as I began to pull things out from more than twenty years earlier.

I was sure what I was trying to find would be there but didn't know what else I'd find that would take me back to the spring of 1996. There were several dried corsages and a photo of Ben and me taken by a professional photographer before our senior prom.

I remembered how much I'd hated prom night. Everyone else was having the time of their lives as I tried to hide a growing baby bump under my pink strapless dress. Looking at the photo reminded me of how far we'd come.

There was a napkin from my graduation party and a church bulletin from St. Cecelia's with all the names of the graduating seniors on the front. There were a couple of report cards and a letter congratulating me on being inducted into the National Honor Society.

I dug through a variety of mementos until I found the green box I'd been looking for. I opened it, eager to see how the years had treated the special gift received so long ago. Inside sat the heart-shaped locket with the gold letters of Carlson's Jewelry still visible behind it.

I smiled as I looked from the necklace to the wedding ring worn on my left hand. Father Burk had married us in St. Cecelia's Chapel on a cold and snowy New Year's Eve nine months earlier, making my least liked holiday of the year my new favorite. Grace, along with Ben's boys and parents, had been our only guests. My mom's absence was deeply felt and reminded me she'd never been able to see me genuinely happy before she died.

Both Ben and I had married our former spouses outside of the Church, so our annulments came quickly. It had bothered Mom that Graham wasn't Catholic, and I knew she'd be happy I'd finally been able to receive the sacrament of matrimony in my union with Ben.

After our wedding, Ben had sold his house and moved into Mom's condo with me where we lived while the construction on our new house in Lincoln Estates was completed. I was excited to finally start moving in, but the first thing I'd taken over was the framed photo from the day Mom and Grace had met. I placed it on the mantel of our stacked stone fireplace along with a glass bowl filled with dried rose petals saved from the night Ben accepted my marriage proposal.

I looked back in the box and saw the notes from my high school graduation speech. I started to read through them and couldn't believe my prophetic words. *"As we say goodbye to Elmwood High and go our separate ways, let's remember though time and opportunities may change us, we can always come home."*

How true those words from years before had been. Coming back to Elmwood was the catalyst for overcoming years of shame and guilt. I thought I had to keep running from my past, when coming back home had finally given me what had been missing from my life for so long.

It had been almost two years since I'd taken over as the Medical Director of Southern Iowa Hospice. My work there had given me so much to be proud of. Helping families understand and prepare for the death of their loved ones was a challenging and rewarding career. Even in dying, Mom had given me a new direction for my life; a final gift of love I would always be grateful for.

Each day I lived without her became more manageable, but I would never allow myself to forget the slant of her smile or how her laugh started out quietly and built to a crescendo, sometimes ending in a little snort. I needed to remember the important things that made up the essence of her so she would never fade from my memory.

I finally felt like I belonged in Elmwood again after spending so many years worrying about who might know the secrets from my past. Now, I wasn't sure who knew the truth and who didn't, but I'd come to a place in my heart where it didn't matter anymore. I was sleeping better than I'd ever slept before and had put on ten pounds of happiness weight. I knew Mom would be glad to know I'd never felt better in my life.

Today was another example of life coming full circle. I searched for the special locket because Ben and I had decided it would be the perfect twenty-first birthday gift for Grace. I'd written in her birthday card that Ben had given it to me on our one-year anniversary, and we hoped it would be a special memento for her to keep. She didn't need to know she was conceived the same night in the den of her childhood home.

Later in the evening, we'd join the Sinclairs and a few close friends in the private dining room of the Elmwood Country Club to celebrate Grace's big birthday. Ben and I were so touched to be included, and the invitation was more than we could have ever dreamed of when we gave her up for adoption.

So often I'd had the pieces to the puzzle of my life in front of me, but I couldn't make them fit together to form something meaningful. There was always a missing part keeping me from having the life I wanted.

When faced with the need to return to Elmwood to care for my mom, the pieces shifted into place, pointing me in the direction of love and happiness that I'd been searching for my entire life.

Time and opportunities *had* changed me, but I was finally able to come home.

Acknowledgments

The journey of writing a book isn't traveled alone. I'd like to thank the following people for serving as beta readers and being a part of the creation of *Giving Up Grace*: Lori Johnson, Kendra Richman, Kathy Bailey, Lisa Boyer, Lisa Wall, Emily Rollins, Lauren Nelson, Martha Carroll, Jan McClintock, Tracy Kahl, Kathy Wedding, Cris Perry, Shannon Melcher, Michaela Vandersee, Abby Turpin, Holly Grund, Rachel Jones, Suzzanne Shelton, David Edgar, Rob Nelson, and Morgan Potts. Also, thanks to my Florida readers: Kathy Beachum, Kitty Beachum, Brenda Endelman, Patti Herron, Linda Steele, and Dusty Maddox.

The early versions of *Giving Up Grace* were pretty rough, and I thank you all for sticking with it. Your willingness to give input was greatly appreciated. If I've forgotten anyone who should be on this list, I'm so sorry!

Thank you to Lori Johnson and Elizabeth Evans Editorial for the contributions necessary to complete this project. It's hard to critique your own work, and the insights you offered were most valuable.

I'd like to thank New York Times bestselling author and fellow Iowan, Tracey Garvis Graves, for responding to my emails and encouraging me to self-publish. Thank you for sharing your knowledge with aspiring authors like me through zoom calls and author presentations. You'll never know what an inspiration you've been to me.

All my love and appreciation are extended to my personal book club, The ABC (Audubon Park Book Club) and members Lori Johnson, Kendra Richman, and Kathy Bailey. We've been through a lot together, and you've listened to me talk about writing books for way too long! Your friendships and encouragement mean the world to me.

I can't thank Lauren Nelson and Emily Rollins enough for their help in launching this book. I couldn't have done it without your proofreading abilities, design talents and social media savvy. I'm so grateful for the two of you, even if you don't always laugh at my jokes.

My sincerest gratitude goes out to the lovely people with whom I share my life. Our family has grown during the writing of this book to include spouses, significant others, and another grandchild. Emily, Nick, and Olivia Rollins; Lauren Nelson and Riley Rue; Rob Nelson and Morgan Potts; Holly, Jeff, Jake, and Morgan Bradley—I love you all!

Finally, I want to thank my amazing husband, Doug Olds. His boundless love and support have given me the confidence and courage to chase my dream of becoming an author. Writing a book takes time and energy, and having a life partner who understands the need to follow a creative passion is one of my life's extraordinary blessings. Thanks for loving me in a way that makes me feel as if I can do anything!

In Memory of
Marilyn Jo Carroll Edgar

Although *Giving Up Grace* is a work of fiction, it was inspired by my mom, Jo Edgar. In 2012, she was diagnosed with late-stage ovarian cancer. Although her terminal illness was a devastating blow to everyone in our family, it also provided an opportunity to make some very special memories, which changed our lives forever.

Mom was a retired English teacher, and she'd been editing my first novel (coming soon!) when she got sick. One of the things on her "bucket list" was to finish the book we'd started together. Although I may have chosen to put that project on hold, I moved it to the top of my to do list, and we spent many wonderful hours together finishing the manuscript during the early months of her illness.

Mom fought cancer for nearly three years and spent her last days at a hospice home in Des Moines. During one of our late-night talks, she encouraged me to keep writing and told me my next book should be about a mother and daughter facing the end of life together. I told her I didn't like how that story ended and she said, "But you could write it because you've lived it."

Although the story of Cassie, Ben, Grace and the Sinclairs is fictional, Josephine's courageous battle against cancer mirrors what my mom graciously endured.

Thank you, Mom. Your spirit was the ultimate ghost writer for this book.

Thank You

Thanks for reading my book—I hope you enjoyed it and will consider sharing it with friends and family and leaving a review online. I'm an independent author and consider myself a small business owner through publishing. Your support and feedback allow me to continue writing books and sharing them with readers, and I'm grateful to each of you.

Check out the latest news on books by Christina Edgar Olds:

christinaedgarolds.com

Facebook: Christina Edgar Olds, Author

Instagram: @christinaedgarolds

E-mail: info@christinaedgarolds.com

Want to read more from this author? Here's a sneak peek at her novel, *The First Summer*—available exclusively on Amazon.

The First Summer
A Novel
By
Christina Edgar Olds

Chapter One
October

Jason always left for work before 7:00 a.m., but he hung around on the day I moved out as if giving me five more minutes of his time would change my mind. He was staying in Muskegon and would keep the house for himself, along with our friends and livelihood. He didn't want the divorce but wasn't interested in having the kind of relationship I needed either, and I was done trying to make things work.

Moving day was dark and gloomy and matched how I felt about leaving the custom-built home we'd shared for ten years. I put my heart and soul into that house, spending hours agonizing over every detail. I'd gone back and forth about paint colors, deciding on Roman Column instead of Dover White, a difference so subtle it could barely be seen by the naked eye.

That was back when there was still an *us*, and our future seemed secure and predictable. Maybe I could sense trouble brewing, and my efforts to create the deep roots of the perfect home were an attempt to keep our happiness from slipping away. I'd envisioned living out a charmed existence at that address; my naivete allowing complacency in a marriage destined for failure.

"Are you really leaving me over something that never happened?" Jason always tried to make me second-guess myself, and most of the time, I'd allowed him to succeed in doing so.

"I don't trust you anymore," I said. "It's obvious we want different things, and working together all day and spending the evening trying to avoid you is more than I can take. It was ridiculous to think living together until everything was finalized would work."

Years earlier, we'd graduated from college, married, and moved back to Jason's hometown in Michigan—all in the span of a month. We ran his parents' print shop, which had been in the family for more than three decades, buying them out as soon as we could afford the payments. Neither of us had been aware of how destructive the pressure of working together would be or the personal price we'd pay to achieve *his* lifelong dream.

We'd invested all of our time and passion into the struggling enterprise, at first working alongside each other in every way. With my marketing knowledge and Jason's entrepreneurial spirit, we'd turned Parson's Printing into a profitable endeavor within a few years. We tried new things and spent money on advertising and promotions the elder Parsons hadn't even considered. And it worked, allowing us more success than we could have dreamed of.

Thirteen years later, we were accustomed to passing in the hall like coworkers who hardly knew each other. I couldn't pinpoint when things began to change, but there was no going back.

It had been late summer when I walked into his office after having lunch with a friend, delivering the other half of a Margherita pizza as a peace offering for an argument we'd had the night before. I'd been wrong about insisting we hire another person for the marketing team, and I wanted to make it up to him.

I pulled out his desk chair and sat, grabbing a pen and sticky pad to write a cute note about my willingness to share my food. Jason's laptop was open, and as I began to write the message, I glanced at the screen and saw one of my favorite pictures of him staring back at me.

Online now!
* Fit 35-year-old male, tall, dark, handsome
* Seeking: Women 21-30 for dating and fun

"What are you doing?" Jason's sharp voice from the doorway startled me.

"What are *you* doing?" I answered back, louder than what felt appropriate. I couldn't breathe as a million thoughts raced through my mind. He moved forward and slammed the computer screen down, the quick slap of the lid making me jump.

"How dare you spy on me. What are you doing in my office?" he demanded.

I couldn't believe he acted like I didn't have a right to be anywhere in a building we owned together. I picked up the small pizza box and deposited it in the trash can.

"I was going to share my lunch, but now I'm leaving you

instead."

The surprising discovery of Jason's dating profile had been more shocking than it should have been. He'd always been a flirt, and I'd grown accustomed to being ignored while he made every other woman in the room feel special. Knowing he could give others the attention I craved made his lack of affection toward me more devastating.

Jason swore he never acted on the dating ad he'd made for himself, but it didn't make it any less hurtful. I couldn't see moving forward with a man who was thinking about romancing someone else, even if they didn't exist yet. His secret desires, acted upon or not, were proof his feelings for me had waned.

I'd clung to the illusion of our love for too long. Seeing in black and white that the mirage had vanished gave me the resolve to do what needed to be done.

The doorbell rang just as I heard the garage door close as Jason left for the office.

"Are you Meg Parsons?"

"Yes, come in," I said, opening the front door to the moving crew. I'd taken the day off, but in twenty-four hours, I'd be back at my desk running a business with a man who was becoming a stranger to me.

"You don't look ready to move—you were supposed to have everything boxed for us. I hope this isn't going to take longer than what we agreed to. We have another assignment at noon and were told this was a small job."

"Not everything is going. I've organized and marked what I'm taking. The rest is staying here, so if you follow me, I'll show you what needs to be loaded."

This wasn't a favor the guy was doing for me, and I was in

no mood to take his shit. I'd had my fill of a soon-to-be ex-husband, aggressive attorneys, and my well-intentioned parents trying to tell me what to do, and I wasn't going to be pushed around.

As we walked through the house, I could almost hear my belongings calling out, begging me not to go. It was difficult to pick the things that would join me in my new life, abandoning the rest like children not chosen for a team on the playground.

Two hours later, I pulled my car behind the moving van and followed in a caravan to a month-to-month rental across town. As the fall colors of the tree-lined streets in our upscale neighborhood disappeared in my rear-view mirror, I tried to let go of a life that no longer belonged to me.

February

I took the last drink from a cappuccino and tried to look at ease in an environment that had become insufferable to me. Four months had passed quickly in my dingy, one-bedroom apartment, but living separately hadn't changed the undercurrent of tension between Jason and me. Everyone was on edge at our monthly staff meeting, and employees I'd cared about for years no longer made eye contact or engaged in small talk with me when we gathered as a team. I was on my way out, and everyone knew it.

As the meeting ended, Jason made a parting comment about his plan to buy a larger commercial printer with the hope of taking on more work for Muskegon Community College

"I want this completed by the end of the year. I'd like to have an employee committee in place to help us reach out to the college about what they might need from us," he said as employees collected their notes before returning to their desks.

I hung back to talk with Jason while we were still in a public space. A discussion in our private offices usually led to a fight.

"Starting a major project when we're in the middle of a divorce isn't a good idea," I said.

"I don't think you have anything to say about a business I'll be running by myself very soon. So why would you care?"

"It's not the time to spend money on an expansion. I still own half of this place, and you can't do anything without my approval."

His glare held longer than was comfortable, as if we were playing a game of stare-down, and neither of us wanted to blink first.

"What do you want from me?" His face flushed red, and his jaw clenched.

"I want you to wait to spend any large amounts of money until we agree on a settlement."

"And I want *you* to stop coming into work. I'll pay your salary if you just get out of here and let me run the place."

I hesitated for a moment as I contemplated my response. I was used to considering my words carefully before addressing controversial subjects with Jason. Since I'd filed for divorce, there weren't many topics that didn't fit into that category.

"That's the problem. We *both* own this company, but you've never seen it that way. I'll go because this is no picnic for me either. But make no mistake; you don't pay my salary any more than I pay yours. It's called a partnership. And if you understood what that meant, we might still be together."

That was the last conversation I had with Jason before

loading a POD with everything I had moved in October and headed for my childhood home in Washington, Iowa. My attorney handled the details of my abrupt exit, and I left without saying any goodbyes.

***

I'd heard of the term "boomeranging," where adult children return to live with their parents for economic reasons, but I never thought I'd be a statistic in the growing trend.

Even a bad relationship is hard to get over, and during my divorce, I felt like an unlovable failure who needed to be taken care of. Although returning home wasn't my first choice, it did help me realize how much my parents loved me.

In the beginning, Mom made all my favorite foods, and Dad planned fun nights out for the three of us. Howard and Virginia Royce had never been the kind of parents who put their children on a pedestal, and their overabundance of attention was both comforting and off-putting. They'd never risen to an occasion so valiantly. Still, it wasn't long before we realized a double chocolate cake or an order of chicken fettuccine from DiBonito's wouldn't get me back on my feet again or help Dad's rising cholesterol.

I needed something to look forward to, and thinking about frozen drinks garnished with umbrellas and warm sand between my toes were my go-to fantasies whenever things got complicated. What started as a fluke after entering "Daytona Beach VRBO" into my search engine grew into a longing so strong I couldn't stop thinking about it.

After my move back to Iowa, it took three more months to finalize the divorce. When the bickering between our lawyers started to feel like *they* were the ones splitting up, everyone retreated to their corners, and a deal was signed. My attorney told me it was Jason who ended things, agreeing to give me what I wanted. It was the kindest thing he'd done for me in years.

I'd significantly impacted Parson's Printing's success, and my divorce settlement provided the immediate cash flow I'd been waiting for. Although I would need to invest the bulk of the money and find a job eventually, it gave me a financial cushion allowing me the luxury of being able to do whatever I wanted in the short term.

My parents weren't as thrilled about my plans or lack thereof. They were pragmatic baby boomers who didn't believe in employment hiatuses, which might look like a questionable gap on my resume. I followed my gut anyway and rented a beach house for the entire summer, taking time for a life reset they couldn't begin to understand.

May

I'd been driving for two days with an overnight stay in a sketchy motel on the way from my parents' house to the Atlantic coast. Mom had suggested a reservation, but I wanted to travel as far as possible with no plan for stopping. I should have heeded her advice. The bed was lumpy, and my neighbors were anything but quiet. I was on the road again before 6:00 a.m., which wasn't long after the people in the room next to me had stopped arguing.

"Hi, Mom. Just wanted to let you know I'm back in the car," I said, recognizing she'd appreciate a call even if it was early.

"I still can't understand why you're going to Florida for the summer. You know your dad could get you on at the insurance agency. Why do you need to take more time off instead of getting a job right away?"

"Let's not do this again, okay? I'll call you when I get there. I love you and Dad so much, but I'm a grown woman and know what I'm doing."

I spent the time traveling between Iowa and Daytona Beach listening to an eclectic mix of pop and country tunes I'd chosen for my trip. The Spotify playlist included all my top picks, plus a few breakup ballads, which had become my battle hymns. My mood volleyed between mellow reflection and excited enthusiasm as my favorite songs kept me company in the driver's seat of my Volkswagen Beetle.

The sporty little car had been a birthday present from Jason, and I'd adored that tiny black Bug from the moment I'd seen it parked in the driveway with a red bow attached to the antenna. I'd felt special that day, knowing the effort he'd put into trying to make me happy; it was an emotion I hadn't felt often in our life together.

The car's impractical sportiness had never been more evident than driving cross country with my belongings stuffed in every nook and cranny. Had I known it would be the car I'd end up with, I'd have begged for a midsize SUV giving me a more functional vehicle for the long term.

Traveling down the interstate, the wind from each passing semi attempted to blow me off course like the challenges I'd faced over the previous months. However, the heavy traffic and rain-soaked highway did nothing but inspire me to keep pushing through. As I got closer to my tropical destination, exhilaration began to replace the stiffness in my body caused by sitting for too long.

"Daytona Beach—twelve miles!" I exclaimed, reading a sign posted on I-95. Fist pumping to the beat of the music, I danced in my bucket seat, thinking about arriving at the place I'd been dreaming about for weeks.

The small cottage sat close to the road. A driveway led to a double garage tucked underneath, and the textured exterior was pale pink. Paned glass highlighted by white shutters had window boxes not yet filled with flowers.

The home was old but had been loved and cared for, looking more shabby chic than used and worn out. Many of the older houses along Atlantic Boulevard had been razed. There were a few, like this one, left with the charm of days gone by and personalized with a name as if they were a beloved member of the family. A pastel-colored house would have stuck out as an eyesore in the Midwest. On the sunny coast of Florida, a place named The Pink Shell was the perfect summer escape.

My temporary home materialized before my eyes as the old door creaked open. Vertical blinds covered the back windows, so I dropped my purse and phone on the kitchen counter and moved toward the sliding doors. As the wand moved the slats to one side with a whooshing sound, light poured in from the wall of glass along the back of the house.

It reminded me of when I was a little girl and was chosen for a small role in the Southeast Iowa Ballet's production of *The Nutcracker*. When the heavy velvet curtain opened, and we danced onto the stage, it was a thrill beyond anything I'd ever experienced at my young age. The ocean view from my beach rental made me feel like I was taking a theatrical cue to enter the second act of my life, and excitement swept over me.

The beach house was small, but with the open floor plan, it didn't seem cramped. The woodwork was white-washed, and the furniture was eclectic but looked comfortable. The wide baseboards and crown moldings gave the small cottage a calm and pleasant vibe. Patterned chairs in brown and slate blue brought the color palette of the sand and sea inside, with subtle touches of beach décor enhancing the home's ambiance. It didn't seem stuffy, and the air-conditioning had been set so it was already cool. The owners lived on Long Island, and I assumed a management company looked after the place to ensure things were taken care of.

I couldn't wait to make my morning coffee and sit on the screened lanai, which extended from the glass doors toward the water. I unlocked the slider and went onto the porch, where the waves pounded against the shoreline. The air was hot against my face, and the smell of the ocean wafted through the space as the early-evening sky began to cast shadows in every direction.

I'd been nervous the place wouldn't be as nice as it looked online. Beachfront property would be hard to beat no matter what the inside looked like, but it was better than I'd expected. The first summer of the rest of my life was about to begin, and I felt like something wonderful was going to happen.

Made in the USA
Monee, IL
05 October 2024

67227581R00157